ADVANCE PRAISE FOR
milktooth

"Delightful, devastating, and darkly funny, *milktooth* brought me up short multiple times as it dug into the taboo and oft-overlooked topic of domestic abuse within the queer community... Sorcha is loveable, complicated, and all too relatable—I couldn't stop rooting for her to find her way to the love, connection, and home she craved."

Rose Sutherland, author of
A Sweet Sting of Salt

"This novel has my heart. A tender, intimate, wry, and relatable ode to found family. I loved it."

Kirsty Logan, author of
The Unfamiliar: A Queer Motherhood Memoir

"With *milktooth*, Jaime Burnet cements her status as a unique and urgent voice in Atlantic Canada's literary scene. Burnet's prose crackles with expectant energy, tension simmering just beneath the surface like a kettle on the boil. There is pain in these pages, heartache too, but also a fiercely abiding love reflecting the power of queer and chosen family to carry us through our darkest days."

K. R. Byggdin, author of *Wonder World*

"*milktooth* is as delicately layered and expertly crafted as the finest, dairy-laden pastry. An eerily accurate depiction of abuse, all-consuming love, and the dangers of idealizing one's life. Burnet is a force, a razor-sharp truth-teller. *milktooth* broke my heart in the best possible way."

Katherine Alexandra Harvey, author of *Quiet Time*

"Powerful, gorgeous, and painful, *milktooth* is a harrowing tale of love curdling into poison. With her haunting, insistent prose, Burnet shines a much-needed light on queer domestic abuse and its shattering effect on survivors. A brutal and beautiful read."

Elliott Gish, author of *Grey Dog*

HOMOGENIZED MILK

3.8%

3.8%

MILK TOOTH

JAIME BURNET

Vagrant PRESS

Vagrant Press is an imprint of
Nimbus Publishing Limited
3660 Strawberry Hill St, Halifax, NS, B3K 5A9
(902) 455-4286 nimbus.ca

Nimbus Publishing is based in Kjipuktuk, Mi'kma'ki, the traditional territory of the Mi'kmaq People.

Printed and bound in Canada

Editor: Whitney Moran
Cover design: Megan Fildes
Typesetting & tooth illustration: Bee Stanton
NB1742

Library and Archives Canada Cataloguing in Publication
Title: Milktooth / Jaime Burnet.
Other titles: Milk tooth
Names: Burnet, Jaime, 1986- author
Identifiers: Canadiana (print) 20240499379 | Canadiana (ebook) 20240499506 | ISBN 9781774713648 (softcover) | ISBN 9781774713693 (EPUB) Subjects: LCGFT: Novels.
Classification: LCC PS8603.U73786 M55 2025 | DDC C813/.6—dc23

Nimbus Publishing acknowledges the financial support for its publishing activities from the Government of Canada, the Canada Council for the Arts, and from the Province of Nova Scotia. We are pleased to work in partnership with the Province of Nova Scotia to develop and promote our creative industries for the benefit of all Nova Scotians.

FOR MY FRIENDS.

If you or someone you know is experiencing intimate partner violence, including physical, sexual, or emotional abuse, or controlling behaviour, you can find crisis lines and supportive services in your province or territory at **www.canada.ca/en/public-health/services/health-promotion/stop-family-violence/services.html**

There's one hour of the morning that's perfect. *The island of time* between seven and eight when I'm the only thing breathing in the room. Mice run in the ceiling a few feet above my head, but they don't count because they don't care if I drink my tea with full fat milk. At home I'm only allowed soy and it makes the tea grey.

Chris wouldn't like me saying *allowed.* I should probably use another word. I guess I should say *we believe a plant-based diet is healthiest and we're committed to clean eating and healthy living.* But this is my island of time and I didn't even say the word out loud. Even when Chris isn't in the room, she is.

She says I should read the newspaper with my free hour so we'll have something interesting to talk about. She says I waste it. It's called my free hour because none of hers are. She has to get up early and drive fifteen minutes north to get me to the bookstore for seven so she can get herself to work on time at the paper mill, half an hour's drive back south, then work all day long and a lot harder than I do, pick me up at six, drive us home, and sit at her desk in the office beside the kitchen, sending important emails until dinner is served, by me.

I say bookstore because it sounds better than convenience store, even though that's more true. Saying I left my job as a researcher in the city to sling smokes and lotto at a rural Kwik-Way feels sort of shitty, but I guess that's classist. Bookstore sounds so charming though, like wouldn't you want to escape the Big Smoke to work at a bookstore by the ocean? Wear a wool sweater and drink tea, pet the shop cat and look up over your glasses when the bell rings above the door? I wish there was a shop cat, but then those poor ceiling mice.

Aside from smokes and lotto the bestsellers at this bookstore are newspapers, milk, buttermilk scones, and fireworks. The back wall used to be lined with videos for rent, but once the area got reliable internet and piracy killed the video stores, Marg devoted the wall to books she thought would appeal to tourists travelling the Ceilidh Trail. Also for tourists is the small table beside the bread shelf, crowded with local crafts: walnuts with googly eyes wearing tiny sou'westers, crocheted pot scrubbers, green tartan bookmarks, and wooden signs painted with ceud mìle fàilte—a hundred thousand welcomes.

There are newspapers for sale too, which I could read. This morning, like every other morning, I hauled them up from the concrete step, bound in a damp stack, split the plastic ribbon holding them together with my little knife, and arranged them in the wire stand. Yesterday's papers sit on the counter, waiting to be beheaded and sent back for credit. I could read the front page while I cut off the headers, but this is my free hour and I'd rather read a book. I've been burning through the back wall since I started working here almost a year ago, even though most of them are pretty boring.

I keep my current read between the till and the lotto machine. It's a history of the county. I like the parts of the book about simpler times. Like when everyone had sheep and no one had pedometers. You would just walk all over the hills calling for your flock and no one knew or cared how many steps it took you to find them. And then you sheared them, and you and all the women in town washed and carded the wool, spun it into yarn, wove it into cloth, and then came together around long, low tables in someone's dim kitchen and warmed it with your breath and the movement of all your arms in tandem, pulling and pushing the wet web, singing songs, wringing and pounding the mass against the table until it was thick with your effort and ready to keep you warm through the winter.

This place sounds poetic when I think about it like that, like some feminist separatist shepherdess commune and not the patriarchal colony it was. The book was written in the 1920s, when historians didn't bother pretending to be neutral. It hails the settlers for reclaiming the land from its wild bondage, like those fields were just dying to escape from all that terrible nature. It uses the term "white man's burden" like it's a perfectly noble thing for one to take up.

I close the book and tap my phone. Fuck, I missed a text from Chris. How long ago? Six minutes. Maybe I can say I was in the bathroom.

> *Sorry baby was just in the bathroom*
> *Going to read the paper for a bit before I flip the sign*
> *How was your drive?*

You don't bring your phone to the bathroom?

How does she know?
> *I guess I forgot*

Well have a good morning anyway.

Chris sends this retort within seconds. With a period. And I write *you too love xoxo* as if I can't tell how mad she is by her punctuation. Like I don't already know the drive home will be almost completely silent and dinner will be a slow-motion fencing match and we will sleep back-to-back again with no touching and definitely no sex.

I take my mug to the back room and rinse it in the low sink. It seems like everyone on this island is shorter than me, including Chris. At first she said she liked it but now I think it threatens her masculinity.

I open the fridge and look at my tofu wrap that I can't eat until noon and my depressing plastic containers, one filled with green grapes and the other with carrot sticks. Otherwise it's just an old box of Arm & Hammer and a carton of whole milk. Forbidden milk. Chris says it's unhealthy. Won't allow it in her home. *Disgusting*, she calls it. But I love it. I grab the carton and chug. It coats my tongue, fills my cheeks, sluices down my throat thick and sweet. My head falls back and I drink and drink until it's gone. I come up for air gasping like I just surfaced from the bottom of the ocean, teeth aching from the cold.

I'm allowed to write off milk to use in tea, but Marg is going to start to wonder why I go through so much so fast.

I walk to the front door to unlock the deadbolt and flip the sign, and before I've made it back behind the counter the bell above the door rings. I know who it is without turning around, from the drugstore lilac perfume and the military snare of toenails on the wood floor. And also because these two come in at the same time every day.

Bon matin, Madame Comeau, I say. Bon matin, Sophie.

Mme Comeau is from Chéticamp where all you hear in the Robin's Donuts on a Sunday before church is French. She moved to Judique for an English fisherman when she was young. But, she told me, she will not pronounce it like the locals do, those hard Anglo consonants an offence to her tongue. I prefer the way Mme Comeau says it anyway, and I like the chance to talk to her using the few words I still remember from high school French, and from watching *Amélie* at least fifty times.

Sophie pulls on her leash, straining around the counter and choking from the collar pulled tight around her skinny neck. She sniffs the box of treats I keep back here but it's empty. I let her put her whole head inside to confirm.

I can get her a carrot stick if you think she'd eat it, I offer. Une petite carotte?

Mme Comeau waves away the offer. She's fine, she says. Sophie, assis.

She picks up a newspaper from the stack and flashes a peace sign, which means she wants two LOTTO MAX Quick Picks with

Tag. I key the request into the machine and it spits out the slips. Mme Comeau pays in exact change. À bientôt, she says, and Sophie's toenails drum them out the door.

I pick the book up again and then put it back down. Reading it makes me feel evil. Simpler times weren't actually simple, of course. I mean, yes, I would love to sing Gaelic songs in a warm wooden cabin with no men in it and drink mead or whatever, and yes I do appreciate a well-woven shawl and a bountiful garden and the absence of industrial pollution. That's part of why I moved here in the first place: the dream of leaving the modern city for an anachronistic rural life. But many of the bad parts of the city are still here, and the best parts, my friends, are now three hours away.

Here's what I do like to read: cookbooks. Sometimes I read them while I eat my depressing lunch. I can imagine the flavours almost well enough to taste them. Almost. I move my tongue around in my mouth like I'm feeling the textures of the dishes, like that scene in *Hook*: if I believe hard enough, if I really try, the bite I'm pretending to chew will materialize in my mouth. But I'm too old to play the game properly, so it never does.

It's all for the best, because if the food did magically materialize I would have to enter it into the app. It tracks all my calories and is also a pedometer, so I actually do take my phone to the bathroom and everywhere I go because I want full credit for every step I take. I should log the litre of milk but then I'd have to answer for it later. When Chris first installed the app on my phone and synced it with her own, it seemed like a reasonable thing a health-conscious couple might do together. Now it feels like something else.

Why did I drink a litre of milk? I can't really say, but it's not the first time. Something about the thickness and the weight of it and the shock of so much cold liquid filling my stomach so fast is reassuring, like dropping an anchor to hold me in place. And if I were to be really honest, I'd have to say it's also a secret rebellion.

It feels better to think about as a secret rather than a lie, though I'm not quite sure of the difference. Cookbooks are safer. If I only read about food then I don't need to enter it into the app and there's no need to parse the morality. Though even reading about food feels like an indiscretion, especially when I read about dairy and even more so when I read about meat. Like the recipes tourists laugh at when they stop in for a bag of Ruffles and flip through a traditional cookbook. Pot-en-pot, rabbit stew, seal-fat cookies, eel chowder. It's not that I actually want to eat a rabbit. I would never. I was vegetarian for years before I met Chris. But when something is forbidden, just thinking about it can give you a real thrill.

When Chris and I first met she wouldn't kiss me after I ate eggs or dairy. Brush your tongue, she would call as I scrubbed my mouth out in the bathroom of her apartment. This after I'd come over with an empty travel mug in hand, the inside walls thick with milk foam. At the time it felt like it would just be easier to cut it out. The dairy, I mean. Not my tongue.

Or pretend to cut it out.

I'm supposed to enter everything I eat and drink into the app and I omit milk every single day. And sometimes cheese, or a buttermilk scone. How could I give up real scones? On Saturdays I bake vegan scones for breakfast and Chris says you can't tell the difference, but that's because the last time she tasted milk or butter was fifteen years ago. I can tell because the last time I had milk and butter in my mouth is always only hours before.

The bell over the door sounds and in strolls Lorraine. I tell her that her hair looks great. She just re-dyed it. Every couple of months she picks up a new box from the Shoppers in Port Hawkesbury to touch it up. Her shade is called "Dublin," a very particular copper. She's so dedicated to it that when the store is out, she just waits. Once she had to wait three whole months and the usual thin strip of silver that parts the middle of her scalp spread like a river overrunning its banks. When it's freshly dyed and she wears her teal windbreaker, like today, the high contrast makes it look like she's vibrating and I have to give my eyes a break from looking at her. Lorraine has some kind of internal slot machine of phrases that she offers to me in different combinations each morning, like workin' hard or hardly workin'; another day, another dollar; and the early bird gets the worm—or sometimes, another day, another worm, ha ha ha. She buys the paper and Player's Light and Lotto 649 with the same numbers each time. I have them memorized. You have a nice day, Lorraine says as she heads back out the door. Don't work too hard!

Never, I say, and pick up the bad book one last time. I think I'll read a few more pages and then hide it in the back room so no one can buy it. It mentions food, though only briefly. Grain grown by men, ground by women in a hand-cranked stone quern. They must have made a kind of scone, some dense puck of bread softened by butter to make it easier to chew, the coarse grain grinding their teeth down in turn. The book says they called it a brà, the quern. What would they have called a scone? Or maybe that is their word. It's too bad I speak no Gaelic aside from my own name, Sorcha, and I probably don't even pronounce that right.

The bell again. Sometimes it rings in my dreams and wakes me up, and my movement wakes up Chris, and then she's mad and neither of us can get back to sleep for at least an hour. This time it's Glen, on schedule for a newspaper and smokes. I turn to the shelf behind me for his brand and punch it into the register before he gets to the counter, but he shakes his head.

Thanks my dear, he says, but I'm trying to cut back. Half a pack a day, that's my agreement with Joanne.

Good plan, I say. They're so expensive. Plus, you know, your lungs. How's Joanne?

Good good, he says. Dropping her off in Port Hawkesbury this afternoon so she can get the bus to see her cousin in Paqtnkek. They'll knit all weekend, drink gallons of tea. A regular party.

Glen brings a Ziploc bag of extra cookies to me whenever Joanne bakes them to mail to their grandkids. I don't enter those into the app either. Chris doesn't understand how I can't lose these stubborn last five pounds, but secretly I want to keep them. I need them to get me through the winter. When I'm too thin I'm always cold and my sit bones grind against wooden chair seats and my tits deflate. Even now at the beginning of September the air is starting to cool, and Marg says I can't turn the heat on for another month because it's too dear. So I eat secret snacks and drink secret milk and keep my hands tucked up inside my sweater sleeves. I wish Glen had cookies for me now.

Just the paper then? I say.

He nods and picks one up from the stack.

I ring it in, say goodbye to Glen until tomorrow, and return to the fridge. I take the plastic container of grapes back to the counter and open it up, pull them out by the stem and spin them around, examining. I like to hold them in my mouth for a minute to warm them up before breaking the skin. A weird preference maybe, for warm grapes. I enter them into the app. Chris will receive the update.

We've been getting lots of exercise up here on the Island, eating healthy. Chris loves her job, the mill really values her. The community here is so friendly and it's good to be closer to the ocean. This is what I tell Ruth via text, and Linh, and Dana. The three people I miss most. The part of me that knows things have become a bit fucked doesn't seem to have direct access to my mouth, or thumbs. Or maybe I'm too proud to admit that Ruth was right. Maybe I'm too stubborn. It's possible the right word is ashamed.

But I'm pretty sure all relationships are hard and people just don't talk about it. My parents' marriage is just Bible verses and a loud television and dinners made exclusively by my mother and chest-deep resentment sealed in a bungalow that smells like Febreze. I don't think I've ever heard either of them say anything truly nice to the other. I once saw my dad try to hold my mum's hand while we were walking back to the car after church, but she wouldn't let him.

Dana and Liam are sweet as hell in public, they hold hands all the time, but I'm sure they have their private shit too. When Linh and I dated we nearly annoyed each other to death, though we did have the nicest breakup I've ever heard of and were back to being friends within a week. I can say for a fact that Ruth and George's relationship is perfect, since we all lived together in an old house with very thin walls for three years and I never once heard them fight. Respectful political debate was the height of it, like whether the internet can be used to help overthrow capitalism or is an irredeemable tool of the oppressor. Ruth once told George he was being obtuse and felt so bad later that she bought him flowers. On the other end of the spectrum, my last serious girlfriend used to shove me into walls when she was mad. I'd say Chris and I fall somewhere in the middle, which seems like a reasonable place to be.

The main thing is, I want to have a baby. And I'm thirty-one so I'd better do it soon. If I have to find and woo and settle down with another dyke who wants kids, save up for sperm, and chart my cycle,

I'll probably be forty and infertile. Or maybe I'll never find another partner who wants kids. What then? I could adopt, I suppose. Or pick up some guy in a bar and fuck him without a condom and never speak to him again. Guys love that kind of thing, right? But I think Chris could be a good mom. She can be the serious one and I can be the fun one.

So though this is not the best relationship, and though I am jealous of Ruth and George and their perfect love, it's also not the worst. Chris hasn't shoved me into any walls. But I do sometimes feel like there's a little worker sitting in some back cubicle in the office of my brain, writing memos that I never read, applying for promotions and being denied, stealing small things out of spite: highlighters, a stapler, bits of my self-control. Maybe I need therapy. Maybe we should go together. Unfortunately rural Cape Breton isn't the easiest place to find a couples' counsellor for dykes.

My phone pings. *I have a headache*, Chris says. Period. She doesn't say who caused it but we both know. I shouldn't have kept her waiting for a reply all those minutes. Too much stress makes her ill. *Sorry love*, I write, *thinking of you. I'll give you a neck rub at the house xo.* But without the period.

The house could be home but it doesn't feel like it yet. And if it's home, then what's Halifax? Still the place I want to go home to. Dana's baby is already almost six months old and I've only seen him through the tiny window of my phone. I want to feel his sharp little tooth with my thumb and smell his head before the newness wears off. Some days my arms feel so empty. I haven't had a good hug in months.

On Friday nights Chris and I sit on the couch after dinner and watch action movies. She loves when things explode. I imagine myself back with my pack, on Linh's deep red couch with Linh and Dana and Ruth, a bottle of amber bourbon on the table beside an orange and a knife and a jar of cherries in thick glowing syrup. Ruth easing strips of peel from the orange with the knife, pulling a lighter from her pocket and squeezing oil from the peel into the flame before dropping the singed rind into a glass, followed by a couple of cherries and a good pour of liquor. Repeating this ritual through the evening, never letting our glasses empty. On our last night together, just the four of us, Linh lounged beside me, telling Ruth that if she were a proper bartender she'd muddle the drinks. Ruth flipped Linh the bird and used that to give the bourbon a stir. Linh took a sip and said tastes *fucking* great and we laughed so hard because we were drunk and we loved each other.

My pack is only three hours away but Chris says she doesn't have time to drive down for the weekend, and she doesn't trust me to take her car alone. Once in our early days she threw the car keys at me without warning as a test of my reflexes, but I didn't catch them, so I'm not allowed to drive. I asked for a do-over but she said the test doesn't work a second time.

God I miss them. I haven't seen them since last December. And I need to hold that baby. I ache for my own and gravitate toward all others. Dana's baby pulls on my womb like the moon.

If only Chris were like sweet Glen, driving Joanne to knit with her cousin. Though he isn't driving her the whole way, just to the bus.

Wait, I almost shout into the empty store, reeling from the idea. The bus!

I could get the bus to Halifax. Tomorrow! Catch it in Port Hawkesbury like Joanne does. Surely Chris could be convinced to drive me the half hour to the stop. Maybe she would even welcome the idea of a weekend to herself. There must be a Saturday morning bus. I could get to the city by the afternoon, pick up a milky latte from my favourite café, walk along the harbour and uphill toward the Citadel, breathing in the salt air and the exhaust I'd been so keen to escape. You'll miss the city, Ruth had warned. You yes, the city no, I said. But as usual, Ruth was right.

I text her first. My thumbs trip over each other, typing so fast.

> *Are you in town?*
> *I'm thinking of coming down this weekend*
> *Can I see you??*

Linh is next, then Dana.

> *Are you free?*
> *Do you want to hang out??*
> *I miss you!*

I lay my phone face up on the counter and stare at it, willing my friends to answer. And they do, minutes later, because they're the best. Even Dana, who probably has her arms full of baby. They would love to see me, they say, of course! *Come back to us*, Ruth writes, *my dairy queen.*

I cradle the phone in my hands, magic portal to friends. I search the bus schedule and find one that leaves on Saturday morning. Then I flick back, back, back through my photos until I find all our faces fitted inside the frame, the muscles of our mouths loose with booze and eyelids heavy, hair and limbs tangled as we crowded together on Linh's couch for a final picture on my last night in the city.

Though it's up there on the list, the farmers' market is not the gayest place Chris and I could have met. First is Pride, second is the gay bar, and third would probably be a gender studies class. Actually, first might be meeting her as the girlfriend of a close friend. I've done that one. In fact, I've done them all. Our farmers' market meet-cute is the most wholesome start to a courtship I've ever had. It's almost embarrassing.

But I am getting older, so maybe wholesomeness is to be expected. It kind of creeps up on you. Pride was only fun when I'd just come out, kissing in public felt like a revolution, and I hadn't yet begun to see the parade as a moving commercial. The gay bar was my haunt in my early twenties when I was happy to spend the final few dollars in my bank account on shots for myself and my friends and whatever cute queer with an undercut and lip ring I was trying to pick up. That was my type. I guess it started with Linh, though they took their lip ring out after their gums started to recede. See? Old.

I think part of my turn to wholesomeness was spurred by the fact that I wanted to have a baby. That I want to have a baby.

Before I met Chris, I briefly considered trolling local pubs for men to take home, men too drunk to remember my name but not too drunk to fuck. Men who would be thrilled to finally encounter a gal they didn't have to pressure not to use a condom. Are you fucking nuts? Ruth had said when I told her my great idea. You want a side of chlamydia with that baby? She said that if I wanted to get pregnant so bad she could help me find a donor. Or I could just pay for sperm, she said. Tested sperm. But I didn't have the money for fancy tested sperm, and a not-terrible, not-creepy guy who was willing to donate his sperm and have nothing to do with the baby it would help create proved very, very hard to find.

So there I was, yearning for a baby and wholesomely smelling a bundle of fresh basil when I noticed Chris looking at me from the next stand over. Goddamn, I thought. A dyke in buttoned-up plaid, hair like a young Leo, face like a young Demi, shorter than me but who wasn't?

I smiled. Do you want to smell it, I asked her, a bit of a weird first line.

Chris smiled and stepped forward, bending her head toward the basil. She smelled. So fresh, she said. What are you going to make with it?

Pesto pizza, I told her, with pears and pecans. The alliteration makes it extra good.

She laughed. She said it sounded delicious, that she was always trying to think of new vegan dishes. I told her I usually made it with goat cheese but if she wanted to come over and try my recipe, I could make it without. Where did that come from, I wondered. Some mysterious burst of confidence propelled the words out of my mouth before I had a chance to stop them. Chris smiled and handed her phone to me. Put your address in here, she said. I'll be over tomorrow at seven.

The next evening, in the few hours that remained before Chris came over, I cleaned. I collected the many dirty cups around my room. I hauled my musty clothes and sheets to the basement washing machine. I heaved my window open to air out the smell of sleep. I swept and swept and swept.

Is this your delayed reaction to the hundreds of times I've asked you to stop hoarding all the cups in your cave of a bedroom? asked Ruth.

Yes? I ventured.

Liar, Ruth said. I bet your date would like if you finally cleaned the bathroom too.

It's next on my list, I said, calling love yooou as Ruth returned to her room.

Love you too, dirtbag, Ruth called through the wall.

By the time I'd finished cleaning, my fingers were prunes. I'd done all the dishes and even mopped the kitchen floor. The rest of the house wasn't as bad as my room because Ruth always did her chore wheel chores, and so did George, her feminist communist boyfriend. I was the bad roommate, the slacker.

I had half an hour left. I showered fast and peered at my face through the porthole I'd cleared in the fogged mirror. Wiped the black smudges from under my eyes and applied fresh lines to my lids, dabbed concealer on my under-eye circles, dark as a bruise from staying up late for the past week, writing a grant for a new research project on glyphosate and amphibians, my mind swimming with shiny salamanders and their tiny jewel eyes, their permeable skin. I hung my towel neatly in the bathroom and dashed naked to my room to look for clothes, but they were all in the wash.

I knocked on the wall.

Yes? Ruth answered.

Is George home? I asked.

No, she said.

I pulled on my last pair of clean underwear and scooted to her room.

Not to be a bad feminist, but that's a bit of a slutty first-date outfit, she said.

Ha. Can I borrow something cute?

Ruth dressed me in a short flower-print dress and a jean vest. She pinned part of my hair back over my ear with a silver clip.

You're good at this, I said.

I know, said Ruth. So am I supposed to hide during your date or what?

No, no. Come say hello so you can give me your take later. But if things sound like they're going well please don't come out to ask me where I put the laxatives or something.

If you stopped eating so much cheese you wouldn't need the laxatives.

Jesus, I said.

I won't embarrass you, said Ruth, spritzing my collarbone with a warm scent. I promise.

Chris arrived while I was blending the pesto. I'd texted her earlier to let herself in the front door when she arrived so I could avoid the awkwardness of doing it myself. She said hey and I turned to face her. She was wearing a thin denim shirt, buttoned up to the throat. Unsurprising, I thought, that we'd both worn denim. Loose black jeans, hair perfect. She ran her hand back through it so it flipped to one side, a move that reminded me of my nineties celebrity boy crushes who, in retrospect, all looked like lesbians.

Chris had brought white wine in an insulated bag. She pulled out the bottle and held it up to me with both hands like she was my waiter. It's a sauvignon blanc, she said. I imagined her showing up to a high school party with the same, plus some banana chocolate chip muffins in a Tupperware. Probably with a thick, slicked-back ponytail, probably in khakis. Though it was hard to imagine her drinking underage. My heart swelled for her.

Awesome, I said.

People try to pair pesto with chardonnay but it doesn't align with the herbaceousness of the dish. Sauvignon blancs pair better, especially this one. Its top notes are grapefruit and grass.

Cool! I said, and told my brain that the third thing to come out of my mouth had better be smart. I was really glad I'd mopped the floor. I took two wineglasses from the cupboard and invited Chris to pour.

These are technically red wine glasses, she said.

It's all we've got, I shrugged. I usually drink from a jar.

Chris looked surprised and then maybe a bit charmed, I hoped. They'll work, she said, and offered a glass of wine to me. I wrapped my hand around the bowl and Chris told me to hold it by the stem instead so the heat from my hand didn't transfer and mess with the flavours. I smiled and held it properly and took a sip.

Grassy, I confirmed.

Ruth came into the kitchen. Hey kids, she said. I'm just looking for…oh what was it I was looking for? Starts with an L… She winked at my wide-open eyes. Lemonade, she smiled. I almost punched her in the arm. I'm Ruth, she said, and offered Chris her hand.

Chris, said Chris.

Ruth opened the fridge and grabbed the jug.

So what keeps you busy, Chris? she asked, pouring lemonade into a jar.

Mostly work, Chris said. I'm a mechanical engineer.

Oh wowww, Ruth said, and I hoped only I could hear the sarcasm. Chris smiled proudly. Poor oblivious Chris. I wanted to protect her.

Ruth asked where she worked.

At the shipyard, Chris said.

On navy ships?

Yep.

Keeping the state war machine going?

Uhh, said Chris.

Ruth, I said, would you like to try this wine?

Ruth smiled. Sure! she said, knocked back the last of the lemonade in her jar and held it out to me. I just *love* chardonnay.

I rolled my eyes at her. I knew she'd heard us talking through the wall.

It's actually a sauv blanc, said Chris. To align with the herbaceousness of the pesto.

You know a lot about wine, huh? Ruth asked.

I took a course, said Chris.

Cool, Ruth said, I'm sure it'll be an *interesting pairing*. She raised her eyebrows at me and took the jar of wine to her room.

Chris put her hands in her pockets and studied her shoes.

She thinks she's funny, I said and shrugged in apology.

She's not, like, your ex or something?

No, I said. I did used to date one of my other best friends, but haven't we all?

Chris did not confirm that we had all. She pressed her lips together in an approximation of a smile. From looking at her I guessed she'd had maybe one girlfriend in her entire life, who had crushed her heart like an overripe strawberry. I wanted to pop her collar and give her a hickey and make her feel cool. If there was one thing I held on to from countless Sundays in church and thousands of Bible verses recited at me by my parents, it was the unquenchable desire to save.

I just have to give the pesto one last buzz in the blender, I said. Do you want to roll out the dough?

Chris stared at me for a second and then recovered. I can do you one better, she said. I took a pizza class.

She washed her hands at the sink beside me and lifted the dough from the stainless steel bowl where it had been rising, took a handful of flour from the bag beside it and sprinkled it onto the counter. She formed the lump into a small round pat and pressed her floury fingers gently into its centre and out toward the edges, forming a rim. She flipped it over and did the same on the other side.

This dough is perfect, she said, looking up at me through her nineties heartthrob hair.

I blushed.

She put one hand on top of the dough and held up the fingertips of her other hand to me.

You want to use your fingers to lift the edge of the dough and gently stretch it open, she said.

Jesus Christ, I hoped that innuendo was on purpose. I watched while she slid her fingers under the rim of the dough and curled them, stretching it gently toward herself, flipping it over onto her open palm and back onto the counter, working her way around its circumference until it was a thin round sheet.

· Done, she smiled.

I'm so impressed, I said, and took a big gulp of wine.

I spooned pesto onto the dough's smooth surface, spreading it out to the rim. I asked Chris if she lived close to the market and she told me she did, in an apartment building around the corner. I knew the one, sleek and new. Ruth and I had bitched about it before—ugly, gentrification, yuppies, etc. But sexy heart-bruised socially awkward lesbian engineers had to live somewhere, right?

It's a good spot, she said. It has a great view.

I bet, I said. I wanted to see it. Specifically I wanted to see it while drinking coffee and wearing one of her old T-shirts. I tried to imagine what old T-shirts she would have. Dalhousie Engineering maybe, or, like, Nickelback? She seemed like she probably had bad taste in music but I could deal.

One day I'd like to buy a house outside the city though, she said. Somewhere quiet, by the ocean.

That sounds dreamy, I said, imagining us living together in a charming seaside cottage. Fuck, my brain. It is a master projectionist. I caught Chris's eye for a silent moment and she swallowed audibly.

We assembled the pizza and finished the bottle of wine on empty stomachs while it cooked. The pizza tasted even better than it would have if we were sober. Chris ate two slices and I demolished the rest. Half-drunk Chris smiled easily, made a joke that was actually pretty funny, or at least funny to half-drunk me. Too bad the wine didn't get the chance to bring out the herbash…herbaceous…ness of the pesto, I said, and she laughed.

We talked for an hour after we ate. We kissed for twenty minutes at the front door. I know because Ruth timed it. I ran my fingers through Chris's perfect hair and she surprised me with some pretty bold tongue. I'd expected more austere kissing from an engineer who drank sauvignon blanc. She told me she would text me soon. I was so flushed from the wine and the makeout that after we said goodbye I went to the bathroom and splashed my cheeks with cold water.

Ruth came and stood in the doorway. Nice date? she asked.

I dried my face on the fresh towel I'd hung up just for Chris. Yeah, no thanks to you, I said. Ruth rolled her eyes. She's really nice, I said. And she's a great kisser.

Ruth said she could tell from the stupid look on my face. She told me to please remember that being good at kissing doesn't mean someone will be a good partner. Do you have anything in common? she asked, looking at me seriously.

We both want to live outside the city one day, I said.

Oh my god, Sorcha, if you're talking about moving in with her on your first date I'm actually going to have to ground you.

Okay, Mom, I said. How are you going to enforce that?

I'll tie you to your bed, Ruth said. I have the skills.

I told her she didn't have to tie me to my bed, I wasn't going to do anything stupid.

Okay, Ruth said. But you know you fall kind of fast. And I got a bit of a weird vibe from her. She seems so…particular.

I think she's interesting, I said.

You mean hot, said Ruth.

I cut my eyes at her. I mean *interesting*, I said.

Ruth's eyebrows remained up.

It was just a first date, I said. I'll take it slow, I promise. As if that was something I definitely knew how to do.

he tea bag sits in a spoon, resting on the edge of the sink. I sit on the toilet as a chair, the locked bathroom my private office for as long as seems reasonable. Ten minutes or so. Long enough for the bag of tea to cool so I can press it into my eyes, an old trick to bring down the swelling.

The lock on the door is a hook-and-eye that I screwed into the hardwood. It was difficult to do because we don't have a drill, so I had to dig a little hole in the wood with the tip of a knife to give the screw something to grab onto, and I bruised my thumb twisting it in. I found the latch in a jar of nails the former owners had left in the basement. When I found it I was crying down there again as if that was the basement's purpose, an underground crying shrine.

That was about a week after we'd moved in. I'd been in the bathroom changing my menstrual cup, something one typically likes to do alone, when Chris opened the door without knocking. Again.

That was her new thing. She hadn't done it at the apartment but she seemed to feel, now that we had moved together to a faraway land, that our relationship had reached the next level, and this level did not involve doors. We shouldn't feel ashamed around each other, she said after the first couple of times she walked in on me. I didn't consider being in the same room as your pooping partner an important relationship milestone. But this time I was in the middle of pulling a cup full of blood out of my body and she opened the door and looked at me like she was just checking in, and I said I'm changing my fucking menstrual cup, and her face dropped and she said god you're a bitch and slammed the door.

I rinsed the blood off my fingers. I looked at myself in the mirror and I was crying. I need a lock, I thought, and I went to the basement and found the hook-and-eye and screwed it into the door without saying anything to Chris, and she saw it but didn't say anything to me. So now I can be sure of ten private minutes to poop or bleed or cry as needed.

The bus will leave in half an hour and I won't be on it. I should have been more strategic, picked a time when Chris didn't have a headache to ask.

Don't you want to spend the weekend with me, she said. She told me it hurts her when I say I miss my friends. Am I not enough for you? She's asked me this many times. You think I'm not cool enough, not fun enough. We were going to have scones, she said, and go for a run.

That's our Saturday routine, scones and a run.

Of course you're cool, baby, I said. I wondered how many times I'd told her that over the past year. I'd lost count. We have so much fun, I said.

What is fun? the disgruntled worker in my brain wrote on a Post-it, which it stuck to the closed glass door of the office of my frontal lobe. I waved the thought away.

Maybe we could miss our run this one weekend? I asked. It might be nice for you to have some time to yourself. I suggested I bake scones that night so we could eat them together early the next morning before she drove me to the bus. Wouldn't that be fun, I asked, scones and a tiny road trip to the bus stop? Road trip, woohoo!

They say absence makes the heart grow fonder. I could send you a postcard from Halifax!

Fuck you, Chris said.

I somehow hadn't realized until that moment that we had once again rolled into those deep ruts from which there are no turnoffs, the ones that lead down the steep hill where the brakes are useless and then to the cliff from which we fall and smash. In that weightless moment just after we rolled off the edge, Chris said, not for the first time, that my friends hate her, that I still have a thing for Linh, and that I can't be trusted to go to Halifax alone. That I'm fucking immature, that I just want to get loaded and party like I'm twenty-one but I'm not twenty-one and when am I going to realize that? And do I really think I can ever be a mother when I don't know what it means to settle down?

That last one stung. I couldn't help but cry about it.

I am settled down, I said, my voice shaking, I'm very settled, we've been here for a year, I love you, we've only been back to Halifax once. I just want to see my friends.

Your friends, your friends, she said. I'm supposed to be your friend, your best friend. What about me?

On our last night in the city before we moved to Cape Breton I remember, vaguely, my slow fingers fumbling with the key in the lock of the door to Chris's apartment, and Chris opening the door before I managed to. The bourbon glow and lingering warmth of my friends' arms abandoned me under her stare. Why was I so drunk, she asked. I'd been wearing lipstick when I left the house and only traces of it were left, why was that? I kissed it off on the rims of all my bourbon glasses, I joked, words slurred. Chris didn't find that funny. We rolled off the same cliff and smashed on the same rocks, and I leaked salty drunk tears into the couch cushions until I fell asleep, Chris silent behind the slammed bedroom door.

My ten minutes are up. I flush the empty toilet, wipe tea from under my eyes, brush my teeth and tongue, and tie back my hair.

From the window above the kitchen sink I can see the glowing edge of the sun crowning the trees, their leaves just beginning to bronze. I turn on the oven and lift a steel bowl from the stack on the shelf beside the sink, and a bag of flour from the low cupboard.

Like every Saturday morning, Chris's cat, Della, comes padding over, the pouch of her old belly swinging, thinking the bag is her food. It's flour, dummy, remember? I whisper, crouching to let her nudge me with her cheeks, scratching the fur over her smooth little skull. The affection makes my eyes sting and I stand up quickly and blow out my breath. I lift the ring of measuring cups from their hook and sink the largest one into the flour. It falls into the bowl with a puff but holds the curve of the cup at its centre. I stare at it like it means something. I grind in salt, tip in a teaspoon of baking powder, and drag my fingers through the mix, breaking up the soft shape.

Baking as proof of love is a file stored in a cabinet in my brain, though if I open it up and review its contents I see it's not surefire. There are plenty of successful birthday cakes and cookies in my archives but also several fuck-ups. Like the time I baked a sponge cake for Linh's birthday with lemon buttercream between the layers, but was so stoned that when I took one swipe of icing from the finished cake, it was like I entered a twilight zone in which there was nothing in the universe but me and the cake, and by the time I realized what I was doing I'd scooped all the buttercream filling out with my finger and sucked it off. I had to buy Linh a shitty pound cake from Sobeys instead.

One of the oldest memories in this brain file is a movie I watched when I was seven, where these kids make a cake for their mom on her birthday. It looked so fun that I wanted to do it too. In the movie the kids get up early while their mother is still asleep, and when she comes downstairs and into the messy kitchen and sees the cake, she's so happy, and her kids run over to her with their flour-dusted faces and she wraps them up in her arms and kisses the tops of their heads. She wore a pink bathrobe and matching fuzzy slippers, I remember that.

That year, on the eve of Mother's Day, I set the alarm on my clock radio for 5 a.m. I put the whole thing under my pillow, which was uncomfortable to sleep on but meant my mother wouldn't hear it when it went off. I told my sister the plan. Being five, Aileen would generally do my bidding. She was excited to make a secret cake. She had seen the movie too.

When the alarm sounded I scrambled to shut it off, crossed the carpeted aisle between our beds, and whispered in Aileen's ear that it was time. My sister, sleepy but obedient, rubbed her eyes and put on her slippers. We padded down the hall, past our parents' closed bedroom door and into the dark kitchen. I whispered for her to get a big metal bowl out of the cupboard and to be quiet about it, while I slowly slid a chair over to the counter. I stood on it like I knew my mother would never allow, and climbed onto the countertop, also very much forbidden.

The flour was on the top shelf in a mustard-coloured Tupperware container shaped like a drum and bigger than my head. I wrapped my small hands around it and pulled it toward me but, unprepared for its weight, my hands lost their grip and it dropped onto the counter and rolled onto the floor, where its lid blew off like the end of a confetti cannon and sent up a thick powder cloud.

I froze with my teeth clenched and Aileen froze with her mouth open, and our father came running down the hall with the baseball bat he kept under his side of the bed, hit the light switch, and saw his two daughters: one on the floor holding a large steel bowl and one on the counter, eyes wide and hands up like a criminal.

Sorcha! he shouted. Get down from there!

My mother strode past him in her flannel nightgown and bare feet across the floor thick with flour, yanked me off the countertop by the arm, and slapped me across the face.

What do you think you're doing? she shouted.

Making a—

Scaring the living daylights out of your father and I, getting your sister into—

Making a c-cake for—

Sneaking food? You know you're not allowed to—

No, it's for you, I—

Enough backtalk, she barked, and shook me so hard my teeth clattered together and the rest of my words fell down my throat.

I WAS ALLOWED TO COME out of my room for church, but not breakfast. Aileen was given a time-out on the stairs and a piece of toast, being the younger one and therefore only partly at fault. At church I sat on the pew between my mother and sister. The sermon was about mothers, in honour of the day. Children, obey your parents in the Lord, the reverend read, for this is right. Honour your father and mother, that it may go well with you and that you may live a long life on the Earth.

My face was wet with tears at the injustice that I hadn't been saved by my intentions like the kids in the movie, but I closed my eyes and prayed, nevertheless, that God would make me good. And I vowed that one day, I would kiss my kids' heads and eat the cake, no matter the mess.

The day after my first date with Chris I had to give my phone to my coworker Yusra so I could get some goddamn work done. I'd tried turning it off, putting it in the bottom drawer of my desk, zipping it up in my backpack and throwing it into the furthest corner of my work space, stuffing it under the stack of journal articles I was supposed to review and organize before my meeting with the director the next day. But my will was weak and no matter where I put the phone, every few minutes I would be cradling it in my hands again, waking it up, waiting for it to please tell me that Chris was thinking about me too.

This is stupid, I told myself. Why don't you just text her first if you like her so much? It wasn't a butch/femme thing, it was a pride thing. It was too scary, and probably too soon. And also, Ruth was right—I fall fast. Maybe I lack some kind of brain-regulating switch or emotional modulator. I want the instant gratification. I want the intensity and attention. Like how I can't not finish a pint of ice cream in one sitting. I just can't. So, because I lack some essential internal function, I outsourced it. A one-day buffer was my new rule and I told Yusra I would pay her in coffee to enforce it.

This led to only minimal improvement. My productivity was still shit. My mind was a telescope, my fingers spatulas on the keyboard, my lips doing their best to kiss themselves.

Ahem, Yusra said from behind me, an hour or so later. I didn't turn.

Yusra, I said, don't give me that phone back. I can't be trusted.

Actually, she said, it seems that whoever isn't texting you has opted for another method.

I turned to see her all but obscured by a massive orchid in a brass pot. Not one of those grocery-store orchids, but what appeared to be the mother of them all, roots curling over the pot's edge and dozens of crisp flower faces staring at me.

This is heavy, Yusra said. And your desk is a mess. Are you going to clear a spot or should I put it on the floor?

Uh, I said, surveying my desk. The floor please.

She deposited the orchid and returned to her cubicle. This was worse than the phone. I couldn't face any direction without catching the flowers looking at me, and when I closed my eyes I was back in my dark front hallway, drunk on wine and kissing kissing kissing.

I opened my eyes to see Yusra's face peering over our shared wall.

You got a few texts, she said. Do you want your phone? I'll forego the coffee if I don't have to do this anymore.

I held out my hand sheepishly.

> *I hope you like the flowers.*
> *I had a great time with you last night.*
> *Can I see you again soon?*

Heat crept up my neck and into my cheeks. I closed my eyes and pressed my lips together, smiling. Yes yes yes yes yes, I whispered to myself. Then I set a timer for ten minutes and when it went off, texted back, *Yes!*

At the end of the day I had to get a cab so I could bring the enormous orchid home. My room was still startlingly clean from the night before and I hoisted the pot onto my dresser. The thump roused Ruth, and she came to stare at the blooms hovering over their obviously expensive pot.

I suppose, she said, this is what you call taking it slow?

She started keeping a list of things Chris bought for me. She stuck it to the fridge, but I made her take it down. It read: *obscenely large orchid, "proper" wineglasses, pizza stone, Matt Good tickets, vegan coffee cream, running shoes???, most basic birthstone necklace, vibrator.* Ruth said it all felt a bit too *Pretty Woman*. She would not drink from the pretentious wineglasses and said the vegan cream was gross. She did admire the vibrator, which was fancy and blessedly quiet. But running shoes and a delicate gold birthstone necklace? She asked whether Chris knew me at all. And besides, Ruth said, Chris and I weren't even compatible signs. She said she could tell right away without even having to ask that Chris was the worst sort of Taurus. She had counselled me after my last breakup about seeking an easier match, a nice Libra, or maybe an Aquarius. Even a Leo. She'd done George's full chart on their third date as a precautionary measure. This is real shit, she said, it's important. I agreed, but said it wasn't everything.

I did feel like a bit of a traitor to the cause though, accepting bougie things from an engineer. But it wasn't fair to define Chris by her job, was it? And who wouldn't like a pizza stone? I definitely liked the vibrator, though I only used it on nights I was alone, which had become few. Matthew Good was the only overlap between my and Chris's musical tastes. She seemed to have inherited hers from her older brothers: all white man rock. But for me, Matt Good is gay teen malaise, smoking with my secret high school girlfriend, Angie, feeling there was no future for us beyond the RadioShack in Hanover, worried we'd rupture from boredom. But look at me now, I said to myself. Look at my handsome girlfriend. Look at my running shoes. And look at my willpower! I could drink the vegan cream. I could give up dairy! People give up lots of things, smoking, gambling—

Sorcha! Ruth yelled through the wall, overhearing me reasoning with myself. Dairy is not a vice!

Well, I said, silently this time, I could give it up all the same. For love. I hadn't told Ruth about that part. She would say it was too soon. But when the sex is this good it speeds up the process, especially for me. A direct line runs between my heart and my cunt like a tin-can phone. You just hum into one end and the other end sings.

he last time I spoke to my mother, Bonnie, was three years before Chris and I met, so she didn't have a chance to weigh in. But she wouldn't have recommended I take it slow. She would have recommended conversion therapy.

It must have been summertime because my dad was mowing the lawn and couldn't come to the phone to say hello. Usually just that one word, though sometimes hi Sorcha, how's the weather? Possibly how's school or work, depending on the stage of my life at the time. Then yep, yep, okay well here's your mother. Bonnie would call at least once a month and give me the report from Chesley. Mostly just about our small family: herself, Dad, Aileen. Her parents died within a year of each other when I was ten. They had lived around the bend from us on 4th Ave, with the Saugeen River running through both our backyards. Ours was fenced, but at Gran and Grandad's we could walk right to the bank before Bonnie noticed we were missing—and when she found us she would lose it. Oh, Bonnie, I heard my gran say, you never fell in. That's not the point, said my mother.

Chesley was called Sconeville until the 1860s, and when I learned that in school I thought it must have been the reason my Scottish grandparents picked it as their new home after the war. But that was because I was in grade two and didn't know when the war was or how to conceptualize a past beyond the lives of people I could touch. Chesley's town slogan is "The Nicest Town Around" and I think it sounds kind of sinister, like the town is on a hellmouth but is trying to keep it quiet. The real reason my grandparents moved there is because my grandad lost his job at the gasworks in Inverness. He'd been exchanging letters with a former neighbour who had moved to Chesley a few years before, to work at the furniture factory, and wrote to my grandad that they were hiring. Plus, Chesley had a Free Presbyterian Church of Scotland, so it was plainly God's will.

My grandparents came over on a boat with Bonnie, who was a baby at the time, but not with my aunt Agnes, who was fifteen. Agnes still lives in Scotland, probably. Though she may be dead. My mother has never spoken to her sister, as far as I know. Bonnie says she's crazy, even though that's not a very Christian thing to say. Apparently Agnes renounced God and ran away from home, so I guess she deserves it? I'm sure Bonnie says the same about me.

As a teenager I thought of Agnes as my patron saint, like she could hear my prayers from my bedroom, to which I was often banished for smoking cigarettes or being sullen in church. I thought she must know what it was like, that she wouldn't put up with that shit. I mean obviously she didn't, since she ran away. In the years leading up to fifteen it felt inevitable that I would one day run too. Like the 27 Club but for disaffected small-town youth.

So Bonnie never talked about her sister because she would have nothing to say. She talked about my dad and Aileen and her quilting friends. My dad didn't have friends, I think because he felt that normal adult men shouldn't. His parents both died before I was old enough to remember them, from lung cancer and a heart attack, respectively. I think that's partly why I was so regularly sent to my room when I came home smelling of smoke. He has an older brother in Sudbury and a younger sister in Pittsburgh, but they don't talk either. Not because of supercilious Christian shunning, though. I think they're just lazy.

On our last call, Bonnie was telling me about a quilt her group was making for a church fundraiser. She was complaining that the stitches on one of the quilter's squares were irregular because the woman hadn't bought the proper weight cotton thread. These were our best conversations, about nothing of consequence. In conversations like these we were not enemies, unlike the ones about, for example: my living too far from home, my decision at sixteen to stop attending church, my choice of study (biology, the natural enemy of divine creation), electoral politics, Michael and Janet Jackson (whom Bonnie maintains are the same person), women having short hair, men having long hair, and so on. It should not come as a surprise that I didn't come out until this phone call, when I was twenty-seven years old and nearly two thousand kilometres away.

Ruth had come out to my parents shortly before this, via me. It's a wonder my relationship with them didn't rupture then. Or when Ruth first became my roommate, before she changed her name to Ruth and started using she. What did I do wrong, my mother asked when we moved in together, that my eldest child would choose to live unwed with a man? We're friends, I said, Jesus. Then Ruth started going by Ruth and Bonnie refused to say it. Each time she would use Ruth's deadname, I would say I have no idea who you're referring to, I don't know anyone by that name, and Bonnie would say yes you do, Sorcha, your roommate who thinks he's a woman. And I would say please try harder next time, Bonnie, and hang up.

This time, after she'd told me about the quilt, about how Aileen's job at the RONA was going, and how she hoped her boyfriend would propose soon, that my dad's gout had subsided, and that they needed to re-tile the shower, she asked about Ruth, though she didn't use her name.

Call her Ruth, I said.

No, Sorcha. God doesn't condone it and neither do I.

Ruth is Jewish, I said. Your god's take is irrelevant. Her Jewish mom calls her by her name and so can you.

We pray for him at church, Sorcha. And we pray for you. God knows the influence he's having on your life.

And in that moment, I decided to pull the trigger.

I was queer long before I met Ruth, I said.

What? said Bonnie. What?

Remember Angie? I said. Angie was my girlfriend.

Angela? Bonnie shouted. Angela is not a homosexual! She's married! I've met her husband!

Angie is bi, I said.

I don't know what that means, Bonnie snapped. But I know you, and God knows you. He knows this isn't your true self, Sorcha. You've fallen in with a bad crowd but you can resist the pressure. Resist! You have to go back to church. I've talked to the reverend in Halifax, he's waiting for you to come. Repent and change your life. God hasn't given up on you yet and His forgiveness is the greatest—

I hung up the phone quietly like I was sneaking out of the house one last time. I pressed the tears back into my eyes with my palms and wiped my nose on my sweater sleeve. Did you hear that shit, Agnes? I whispered. What the fuck. I wondered if Agnes was gay too. That would explain the running away, though there are plenty of reasons to run from our family.

I shuffled down the hall and slumped against Ruth's doorframe. She was folding laundry on her bed and looked up at me from a pile of socks.

I heard some of that, she said. Are you okay?

I sighed and wiped my eyes. Yeah, I said. Though I don't think Bonnie will be.

You want to get ice cream? asked Ruth.

I need to get ice cream, I said. You're the best.

You know me, she said. She climbed off the bed and slipped on her flats. I'm always up for coming-out ice cream.

We linked arms on our walk to the store. I scream you scream, whispered Ruth. I scream you scream, I said back to her. I scream you scream, she shouted, then we shouted, like unruly kids rather than grown-ups with office jobs, joyfully disturbing the peace.

After that I got a couple voicemails from the reverend. He had pamphlets, he said. And he could connect me with someone who'd been through what I was going through, someone who had put their trust in God and overcome. I deleted them all. I did not receive any messages from Bonnie.

I still haven't.

I t's just over a year now that we've been in this house. I've learned to bake but not to play the autoharp, as planned. I picked cloudberries one August weekend, boiled them into jam, and arranged the three jars on the kitchen shelf like glowing trophies. I built the shelf, too, a rough slab of tree I bought from Glen, varnished and mounted on cast iron brackets, and draped with a fairy light string. It makes for a very charming photo. Fifty-eight of my followers agree.

Yesterday morning I opened the first jar of jam, hoping its sweetness would fix things. I set two warm scones on a wooden board beside the jam jar, a pat of margarine, and a dull knife. The scones had come out a bit stiff again. I need to troubleshoot my method. I filled Chris's enamel mug with coffee and a pour of almond cream. I took the scissors from their hook, snipped a sprig of rosemary from the potted plant on the counter, and laid it on the board in a way I thought looked sweet. This made for a charming photo too, and I took one to post, but couldn't think of a caption that didn't feel like a lie.

I crept up the creaking stairs with my offering. The bedroom door was closed but I could hear the patter of Chris's fingers on her laptop keys like moths bumping into a windowpane. Then I heard the typing stop and the low clearing of her throat, which I took as an invitation to come in and make amends. I balanced the wooden board on my upturned hand while I knocked. She said something I couldn't make out but that didn't sound like no, so I entered.

Good morning, I said quietly. I made you breakfast.

She ran her fingers through her hair so it flipped to one side, a move I still can't help but swoon for, even when anxious. I asked how she slept. She said okay, considering. I offered the scones, said I'd opened the first jar of cloudberry jam, which garnered a pressed smile. She put her laptop on the nightstand and folded her legs to make room for me. I laid my offering down and climbed gratefully onto the bed, but in my relief didn't pay proper attention to my weight so that when the mattress dipped under me, it swelled beneath the board like a wave under a boat and spilled hot coffee onto the white sheets.

Fuck, Sorcha, fuck, Chris said.

I'm sorry, I'm so sorry, I said, scrambling to get off, my retreat causing the cup to spill again. I tried to save the scones from the coffee but they were already soggy. I wanted her to eat them, I wanted her to like them and for us to have a good day.

The sheets, Chris said. Leave the fucking food and strip the sheets. She was off the bed and standing by the door. I pulled the sheets off while she grabbed her clothes from the dresser. I'm going for a run, she said, and stomped downstairs to the bathroom to change. Get the sheets in vinegar before the stains set, she shouted.

I descended to the basement, blotting my eyes on the mess of fabric in my arms. I pushed it into the steel drum, poured in soap and a glug of vinegar, and set the dial to soak. I slid down the side of the machine until I was sitting on the concrete floor, firm and certain. It wouldn't betray me like the mattress had.

I imagined an alternate morning on which I hadn't fucked up, on which I'd put the board on the nightstand or sat on the bed carefully, like an adult would, and Chris and I had eaten breakfast together and she'd looked at me like she loved me, or at least liked me. My nose ran and I wiped it with the inside of my sweater sleeve, still crusty from the last time.

God I'm gross. Maybe I really don't know how to be a grown-up.

I examined the crust. From last weekend, I remembered, after I'd left a hummus-coated spoon in the sink. What's this doing here, Chris had asked. Are you too busy to clean up after yourself? That was the beginning, and I remember crying by the end, but it's hard to remember the in-between. I must have given an excuse rather than an apology, or maybe I'd said I would do it in a minute. Chris cleaned the spoon herself and threw it in the drying rack. Slammed the door to her office. Did not sit at the table with me for dinner. I stared at the crusted snot and considered peeling off the sweater and dropping it in with the sheets to be renewed, but didn't.

I'm wearing it again today, but the crust is on the inside so you can't tell, and the sheets are clean and returned to the bed. Chris ate a scone with cloudberry jam for breakfast and told me the jam was good. We went for a run up the dirt road behind the house, puffing our breath out like ghosts into the blue morning air—in-in, out-out, in-in, out-out—and when we turned the bend in the road and saw a deer, Chris smiled at me, a real smile. I'm feeling much better.

As I slid into my jeans and tied up my Docs, Ruth appeared in the doorway of my room.

Matt Good tonight? she asked.

Yeah! I said.

Do you ever feel…Ruth began, then stopped. Hope it's fun, she said.

You want to come to dinner with me and Linh? I asked. Chris was going to come too, but she has to finish up some work before the show.

George and I are going to my mom's for Shabbat dinner, Ruth said. But eat an extra-large poutine for me.

I laughed. Oh my god, how did you know?

I know you, Ruth said with a smile.

Don't tell Chris, I said.

I would never, said Ruth.

Linh met me in the sidewalk lineup. Hey buddy, they puffed, and squeezed me a sweaty hello, their bike helmet knocking against my head. You stoked for the show?

So stoked, I said.

I thought we were going for sushi. Where's Chris?

She has to work late. And I need a dairy fix. These curds are the best.

I've heard there was a secret curd, Linh sang in their best gravelly baritone. That Sorcha ate and it pleased her buds, but you don't really care for dairy do ya?

I snickered and punched them softly in the shoulder.

We ate our poutine on the hill with starlings and pigeons milling around us, waiting to be tossed a limp fry.

You know starlings are an invasive species, I said, chewing.

I know, Linh said. You tell me all the time.

Yeah, I said, but their population is still growing. I read there are now over 200 million in North America.

Is that bad? Linh asked, spearing a giant melted curd.

Undecided, I said. They reproduce at a higher rate than most native birds—two nests per year with four to six eggs per clutch— and they take over nest sites from native species. So that's not good. But they've been here over one hundred years and are pretty much naturalized. And both mates care for the eggs and young. They're amazing parents.

No surprise you're a sucker for a good co-parent, no matter how invasive.

Oh shut up, I said.

Linh walked me to the arena, rolling their bike alongside, talking about how they couldn't wait for fall, how they drank four litres of water today just to stay alive. They missed flannel, they wanted to drink pumpkin beer. Why was this summer so bloody hot?

At the doors we looked around but couldn't see Chris. She must be inside, I said, and hugged Linh goodbye, getting gently clonked on the head again. I rapped my knuckles on their helmet. Bike safe, I said, and went in.

There Chris was, waiting just inside the doors.

Hey! I said. You should've come out to say hi to Linh. We didn't see you.

I gathered, she said flatly. I saw you.

Okay, I said. I felt like she'd poked me with a pin and my excitement was leaking from the hole.

How was work? I tried.

Fine, she said. You always hug your friends like that?

What do you mean, "like that"?

It looked a bit close to me. A bit long.

A bit close? I asked as people started streaming in behind me.

I wouldn't hug my ex like that, Chris said.

Oh, geez, I said. Linh and I dated so long ago, for the shortest time. We've been buddies for years. Plus, I do always hug my friends like that. I reached out and squeezed Chris's hand.

If you say so, she said.

I held her limp fingers as we entered the dark arena, which was usually a hockey rink. Where did the ice go? Was it under the flooring somehow, under our feet? I stopped and put my palm to the ground.

What are you doing? Chris hissed.

I want to feel if it's cold, I said. Do you think the ice is under the floor?

How should I know?

I dunno. You're smart, it seems like something you might know.

Well I don't, she said.

We stood side by side while people around us talked loudly and hugged hello and jumped up and down, waiting for the opener. I looked at Chris and Chris looked ahead at the empty stage. Surely she could see me looking at her, could feel it? I looked at her harder and squeezed her hand. Nothing. I let go and reached for my phone in my pocket, woke it up, and looked at its glowing face to see if anyone else wanted to pay attention to me. Ruth had texted me a heart and a cow and a little smiley face whispering shhh. I chuckled.

Is that Linh? Chris said, finally turned to face me.

No, I said.

Let me see.

Are you kidding?

No. If you want me to trust you, prove it.

Trust means believing me, not needing proof.

Prove it now and I'll believe you next time.

Fine, I said and rolled my eyes. It's from Ruth, see? Just some silly emojis. I flashed the phone in her face.

Don't roll your eyes at me, Chris shouted over the din.

Don't yell at me, I said.

I'm not yelling, Chris yelled. I could feel people watching us. I'm going outside for air, she said. Stay here so I can find you.

I wrapped my arms around myself as Chris disappeared behind me. I didn't turn to watch her go. I tried to wipe my eyes without being obvious. A girl I didn't know came over and touched my arm. Are you okay? she asked. I nodded. My ex-boyfriend was jealous too, said the girl, it sucks. I said thanks, it's okay, gave her a fake smile, shrugged.

The opener came on and all the bodies around me surged, carrying me along with them toward the sound. Yes, said all the workers in my brain, we want the sound! The sound would neutralize Chris's words, drown out her tone. Give us the sound, the loud sound! the workers shouted, loud sounds being a balm I'd administered throughout high school via headphones, knocking all other noises out of my head. I moved toward the stage, faced the noise and glowing lights. Resentment melted off me and my crossed arms fell to my sides and I started to dance, swaying and bouncing and shaking my head and jumping. Jumping! Jostled by all the jumpers around me shouting the words to all the songs. Songs, songs, how many songs? At least three, four. Where was Chris?

I turned to look and there she was, a few rows behind me. I threaded myself back through the crowd toward her.

Hey, I shouted.

She spoke through tight lips. I couldn't make it out.

What? I yelled over the music, bending my ear toward her.

I told you to stay where you were, she shouted into it.

The band came on, I yelled. No one stayed where they were.

I saw you. You didn't even try.

What do you mean you saw me? You didn't go outside?

I was giving you a chance to prove I could trust you.

What? That's crazy, I said.

Don't call me crazy, Chris yelled through clenched teeth. She pulled back and looked at me so fiercely I thought she might bite me. Enjoy the show, she said, in the tone you'd use to tell someone to go fuck themselves. She started to push her way back through the crush of bodies.

Was this another test? Was she waiting to see if I would follow? A part of me felt I should, but then the drums sped up and everyone around me was headbanging and dancing so hard, and when I threw my own head forward and forward and forward I felt so much better. And so I stayed. I stayed for the whole thing and it was fucking great, the height of my teen daydreams, a rock show in the city, lights and smoke, sweat and anonymity, drums kicking me in the sternum, guitars mining my inner ears, and all the words I'd sung since I was sixteen coming out of my mouth and hundreds of other mouths at once, about the shopping god and overpriced bubblegum and bodies in the water.

And at the end there was no Chris waiting by the exit or around a corner. I couldn't tell if I was disappointed or relieved. I walked home alone in the cool night air with the crescent moon hanging in the sky like a scythe, and thought to myself that maybe it was a sign I should cut this thing off. I would talk to Ruth, tell her what happened, see what she said. But then I remembered Ruth was at her mom's. They usually got mildly drunk on kosher wine and played rummy after dinner. Ruth and George would probably sleep over in her childhood room, where I'd slept over too, beneath her faded Sleater-Kinney poster. I'd see her in the morning. We could get coffee and walk along the harbour and I'd solicit her wisdom. I texted her and asked if we could talk the next day, so I couldn't double back on my intentions.

Then I turned the corner onto my street and there was Chris, sitting on my front stoop.

No, said a worker, as cold spread through my chest and my spine compressed. But oh, look, said another worker, look how sweet. Chris was holding grocery store flowers and a tub of Rice Dream.

It was the best I could find at this hour, she said. Can I come in?

I made myself wait ten seconds before answering to at least make it seem possible I'd say no. But as soon as I saw the flowers I knew I'd let her in. I took a slow breath.

Okay, I said.

She stepped to the side so I could unlock the door. She followed me down the dark hallway and into the glowing kitchen, where the bulb over the stove had been left on. I turned around and leaned back against the counter, arms crossed. Chris placed her gifts on the table.

Can we sit? she asked.

I'd like to stand, I said.

Please?

I uncrossed my arms and pulled out a chair.

I just want to talk, she said.

She ran a hand through her hair and looked up at me, head bent down like a bad dog and eyes wet. She told me her last girlfriend had slept with her ex while they were together. That she wanted to trust me but she'd been betrayed.

I feel like you don't think I'm cool, she said. That I'm not as cool as Linh and your other friends. I'm so scared you'll leave me. I love you so much.

My heart went soft. I knew what it was like to feel small and bad and banished. Chris sniffed and wiped her eyes.

I'm so sorry, she whispered. I hate that I acted that way. I...hate myself sometimes. She pressed her fingers into her eyes.

Her despair made me want to be her ride or die, to fix her with my love and make her feel cool and strong, make her forget all about her cheating ex.

I reached across the table for her hand. I didn't know that, I said. But there's no reason to be jealous. I think you're amazing.

She swallowed and looked up. You're not going to leave me?

I squeezed her fingers. I'm not going to leave you.

Can you just maybe not hug Linh? For now? she asked.

I considered. I loved hugging Linh. They were one of my best friends. But Chris had been so hurt, and she just needed this one small thing from me while she healed. I had the power to salve her fear. So I agreed.

I love you so much, said Chris.

I love you too, I said. And I did. I kissed each of her knuckles like I was casting a soothing spell, and got up to get a spoon for the Rice Dream.

When I checked my phone later in the bathroom while Chris lay sleeping in my bed, I saw Ruth's text: *Of course girl, hope everything's okay*, and a purple heart.

All's good, I texted back, *nevermind xo*.

I thought at first that Chris was from somewhere else. Something about her made her seem new in town. But she'd grown up in Dartmouth, just across the harbour. Her parents still lived there, though her brothers had moved away.

Have you met any of Chris's friends? Ruth asked me, about a month after our first date.

It was a fair question. I guess that's what made Chris seem new—I hadn't. As far as I knew, she wasn't attached to anyone, to any scene. She'd never mentioned a single friend.

I brought it up the next day. So when do I get to meet your friends? I asked, as if the thought had just happened to float through my brain. She'd already met all of mine, or my three best anyway. Plus my work friends, since she kept driving over in the middle of the day to drop off healthy lunches for me. They were all quite impressed. Even ostensibly straight Yusra admitted Chris was a babe.

Mm, Chris said, I don't really hang out with anyone these days. I guess I don't connect with people that easily. I mean, other than you. She looked at me and smiled, and I felt special. Amy was my best friend, she said, and then. She meant it to be the end of the sentence. The end of the conversation. Amy was her ex, the betrayer. I dropped the question. So what if she didn't have friends? She could be friends with my friends.

The summer was ending, it was almost September. After so many years as a student, this always feels to me like the true new year. But it was still so hot out. People were wearing shorts and flip-flops and eating on patios. When we woke up in Chris's crisp bed in her air-conditioned apartment one Saturday morning, I suggested we go out for breakfast. She had this favourite vegan place—the perfect seitan, she said, the best beet smoothies—but we'd never been.

Let's go! I said.

Yeah, she said, yeah okay.

I pulled on shorts and a T-shirt and brushed my teeth. I had my own drawer in her dresser, my own fancy electric toothbrush in her bathroom that she'd bought for me to match her own.

We walked down the street holding hands in the sun. People rode by on bikes and jogged with their dogs. I wondered what Ruth and George were up to. I hadn't been home in a few days. Ruth had texted to say she missed me, but I figured she and George probably liked having the place to themselves.

I squeezed Chris's hand. What are you going to get? I asked. I love talking about food before I eat it. She said she usually got the breakfast bowl and a beet smoothie. I was very interested in this smoothie. I'd never considered drinking beets. And then we turned the corner and saw all the chairs set out on the sidewalk filled with people eating from beautiful plates of food and Chris said fuck and whipped around.

Oh yeah, I said, looks a bit busy.

She clapped a hand over her eyes. No, it's fucking Amy, she said.

Oh, I said. I looked over and saw a table of three women with their heads bent close, talking. One looked up at me.

Chris stalked away and I followed, back around the corner where Amy and her friends couldn't see us. She ran her hand through her hair, jaw clenched and nostrils flared, looking like she had at the show. Even though it wasn't about me this time I was wary, like she could incinerate me with her fiery breath if I said the wrong thing.

We could go somewhere else? I tried.

She snorted and rolled her eyes. We used to eat there together all the time, she said. I haven't been since we broke up and the one time I try to go of course she's there with her fucking friends. I wish you hadn't suggested it, she said, and looked at me like I had personally arranged for Amy's presence.

Sorry baby, I said. I took her hand. We could eat inside? You wouldn't have to see her at all. We need to drink beets. We must. I smiled and kissed her angry cheek, which softened a little. Just hold my hand, I said. Don't look at her and we'll walk right in.

Chris let out her breath and allowed me to lead her by the hand back around the corner. I kept her on the outside so I could buffer Amy's friends' stares. I tried not to look but caught one of their eyes. She looked concerned. I recognized her, though just barely, from a dance floor maybe, or Pride, or something else gay and apolitical. There are a few different scenes in the city that overlap ever so slightly, like a queer Venn diagram—queer punks, bisexual hippies, political queers, rural dykes, professional gays, Oakleys lesbians—so if you don't run in the same circle and you've never happened to drunkenly make out, there's a decent chance you don't know each other. Like me and Chris. I'd never even seen her until the farmers' market. I didn't think I recognized Amy either, though she was sort of hiding her face with her hand so it was hard to tell. Was she ashamed of cheating? Her friend's arm was wrapped around her shoulders, and as Chris and I walked through the door of the restaurant I could hear her friend telling her to breathe.

We waited for the server to come take our order, and I watched through the window as Amy and her friends got up, opened their wallets for cash, and left their breakfasts half eaten on the table.

They're gone, I told Chris, whose back was to the window.

Good, she said.

She ordered a breakfast bowl and a beet smoothie but was too worked up to eat or drink much. I got waffles with maple syrup and coconut whip and it was so good that, in spite of the tension, I wolfed it all. I said whatever I could think of to try to take Chris's mind off the run-in. I read her horoscope out loud from the arts weekly, but she said it didn't make sense. I told her what I'd been learning at work about the effects of glyphosate on amphibians, the rates of mortality and malformation. I'm trying to eat, she said, can you not talk about dead frogs? Someone walked past the window with a pug strapped to their chest like a baby and I told her to look, but she missed it.

She picked at the food in her bowl, tried to sip her smoothie through the paper straw, but she'd waited too long and the straw had gone soft. She took it out of the glass and dropped it on the table, pink foam oozing onto the wood. And I picked it up and put it on my plate and wiped up the mess with my napkin.

still think of them often, even though I don't have to. I would look for them on our Saturday morning runs but Chris runs too fast. She never wants to detour with me to the marshy spot through the woods behind the house to lift rotten logs and look beneath. She doesn't like to get her hands dirty, or her feet wet.

Amphibians are a keystone species, central in the food web—they eat many things, and many things eat them. This means that if they're in trouble, we all are. Nova Scotia has eight species of frog and five species of salamander. And though I love frogs, salamanders have my heart. It's their tiny jewel eyes, their gentle smiles, their dainty toes, their secret lives. They make no sound and can't hear. They feel vibrations through the earth.

My research sometimes made me cry, reading for hours about damage and death to such sensitive creatures. I was preparing a paper on glyphosate before I left, to back the centre's position that the province should ban it. Glyphosate-based herbicides help softwood trees grow in clearcuts by killing off the competition—maple, birch, pine, poplar, alder, cedar, hemlock, willow, heath, fern. And they're toxic to amphibians. Eroding their mouths and intestines, altering their behaviour, mutating their bodies, killing them in devastating numbers.

My coworkers understood. Yusra loved little brown bats the same way I love salamanders. When the bat population started to recover a few years back after being nearly wiped out a decade before from white-nose syndrome, a fungal disease, Yusra baked bat cupcakes and brought them into the office to celebrate. I hugged her. I'm so happy for you, I said, as if the bats were her family, and she said thank you, thank you, and blinked her weepy eyes. You have to be kind of weird to get into this work. Weird and zealous and sensitive, to care enough to do it.

I'd dreamed of working at the centre while I was in school, but never thought they'd hire me. I did a placement in my final year and Yusra was my mentor. I thought she was cool as hell. She biked to work even in the frequent rain. She brought her fair-trade coffee in a travel mug with a sticker on it of the Very Hungry Caterpillar that said *EAT THE RICH*. She had a tattoo on her hand that said *unless*—a Lorax reference. I crushed on her even though she was straight and married. I worked so hard, wanting her to like me. And she did. She gave me an amazing report. And against the odds, despite the centre's meagre funding, they gave me a job.

When I gave my notice, Yusra came to my cubicle and said what are you doing. With no inflection. I told her the plan, how excited I was to grow my own vegetables and live outside the city. I'll do my own fieldwork, I joked, go rogue. But what will you do for a job, she asked, staring at me. I said I wasn't sure. You're not going to find another position like this, she said. Not in this economy.

I know, I said.

But I didn't really know, at the time. Not the way I know now.

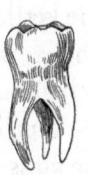

When we were kids it was Aileen's job to set the table and mine to wash the dishes. Every evening after supper I squeezed lemon soap into the sink and turned the hot water on full blast, brought the step stool out of the pantry, put on my very own pair of yellow rubber gloves, size small, and stepped up. From that height I felt older than ten. And alone in the kitchen, I could look out the window and think about whatever I wanted with no interruptions. My dad in front of the television with a can of beer and my mum at the dining room table with a cup of tea, reading or scrapbooking. Aileen quietly doing homework or playing in our room. For half an hour at least, I was alone and five-and-a-half feet tall, tall enough to see out.

I took my job seriously. I was very careful. I made sure nothing clinked loudly enough to be heard from the dining room. I did not misjudge anything's weight, nothing slipped from my rubbery grip. When the dish rack was full, I pulled the gloves off finger by finger and hung them up, then dried the dishes gingerly with a tea towel and stacked them on the counter, as instructed, since I was still too short to put them away in the cupboards. Then I did my homework at the kitchen table.

This night I was doing my four times tables. My teacher had taught us a song for fours so it was easy, I just sang it softly to myself and filled in the blanks. I was humming and multiplying on my fingers and tapping my socked foot on the linoleum. Bonnie came into the kitchen and picked the kettle up from the stove to refill for tea. Just as she did, the telephone, which was attached to the wall beside her, rang. I pushed my chair back to get it, but she twisted the tap off, lifted the kettle from the sink, and reached for the phone. The kettle swung wide and into the glasses I'd arranged on the counter, like a bowling ball into huddled pins, which smashed into shards and flew in all directions, across the counter and into the sink and onto the floor. I gasped so hard I choked.

Jesus, Sorcha! my mother shouted, which she really wasn't supposed to say. Why didn't you put these away? Look what you made me do!

As I ran over to help I stepped on a thick splinter of glass, the feeling of it slicing into my foot as shrill as the sound of the phone still ringing on the wall. Blood bloomed through my white sock.

What's wrong with you? my mother yelled over the ringing. Use your head. I started to cry. Get out, she shouted, just get out.

I crawled down the hall on my knees to keep the blood off the carpet. In the bathroom I closed the door but didn't lock it because we weren't allowed to. I found the tweezers, sat down on the toilet, and peeled off my sock. I wiped my eyes with the back of my hand so I could see. The glass was sunk deep in the thick skin of my heel, and the tweezers couldn't grab the end of the shard. They made this sound like tick, tick, tick each time they failed. I hunched over and squeezed my heel as hard as I could while snot and tears dripped from my face and blood dripped from my foot onto the floor. Through the seeping blood I could see a clear stem, like an icicle fallen from the roof and sunk into snow. I pinched it with the tweezers and drew it slowly out. I held it up to the light—two centimetres long, glazed red and shaped like a sail. I washed the blood off my heel and covered it with a thick Band-Aid. I wiped the blood off the floor. I wrapped the glass sail in toilet paper and threw it in the garbage.

In our room, Aileen was reading a book to her bear. She asked if I was okay. I said yes, and got into bed.

In the morning I pulled the glass out of the garbage can and put it in the old egg carton I kept under my bed, along with my carefully collected specimens of moss and rocks.

You *know this is the biggest dyke stereotype, Ruth said, sitting at the* kitchen table.

Shush, I said, as I wrapped my fancy wineglasses in newspaper. It's not a dyke thing. It's a love thing. Weren't you and George only together a few months before he moved in here?

It was a year, George called from the bedroom. And she still thought it was too soon.

That's right, Ruth said, even a year is pushing it. Two years is better. Two months is... Ruth paused and looked at me. I looked back at her. I felt like her teen daughter getting married without her blessing. But Ruth didn't know Chris, not really. Chris was just awkward, she didn't translate well in a crowd. When we were alone she could be so sweet, and sometimes even funny. If only my pack could see her like I did, could see the way she shone when you loved her right.

When we got back to her apartment last week, carrying a compostable box of her uneaten breakfast, Chris turned to me and took both of my hands in hers and said thank you for your support, I'm so lucky I found you, you're so wonderful, I just want to move to a little house by the ocean with you, away from this city. I want to leave all these shitty memories and start something new. And she kissed my hands and kissed my arms and led me to the couch where she got me off three times in a row. We lay there together with her cat and watched TV, and she stroked my hair until I fell asleep. It could be like this every day, she said to me when I woke up. Della wants you to move in too, and you could just pay utilities.

It sounded pretty idyllic to me, and also practical. I loved Chris, I loved Della, I liked the idea of not paying rent. But I said maybe we should wait a bit longer, a tiny Ruth sitting on my shoulder, whispering in my ear.

But I want to be with you forever, Chris said. What would we be waiting for?

I thought that was a good point. In the context of forever what was too soon, really? Plus I was at her apartment nearly every day anyway. I'd tried to have her over to my house more often, but no matter how many endearing things I told Ruth about her—she can juggle! she took a woodworking class and built Della a cat tree! she sings Matchbox Twenty in the shower!—I couldn't convince Ruth to like her, and on principle she refused to pretend.

We got in a fight about it.

Can't you be around Chris without grilling her? It's exhausting for her to have to defend herself every time she sleeps over, I said, using Chris's words.

But her politics are bad, said Ruth. I know this city is small but it doesn't mean you have to settle.

I told her that was rude.

Seriously, Sorch, Ruth said, what boxes does she tick for you other than hot dyke over thirty?

She's smart, I said, she's a great cook, and she loves me. Just because you date men and have a bigger pool to choose from and found the perfect feminist boyfriend doesn't mean you get to police my relationships.

That was a low blow, invoking the cops. I knew I shouldn't have said it.

Ruth shook her head at me. I'm not *policing* anything, she said. I'm trying to look out for you. And you really think there's a huge pool of men in this city who date trans women? She told me she was going for a walk before she said something she'd regret.

She was right, of course. The things I'd said were stupid. And though I wouldn't admit it to her, what she'd said was true. I considered whether, if I were straight, I'd date a mechanical engineer who was a runner, wore a smartwatch with a pedometer, and read *The National Post*. Probably not. But the queer dating pool in Halifax was very small, and I was thirty. So I could either move to a big city and make a Tinder account and do my best to find a queer Libra environmentalist/therapist/gender studies prof who played the mandolin and listened to *Democracy Now!* and ate real ice cream by the tubful and wanted to have a baby, or I could stay here and date Chris, who was an amazing lover and a great cook and who seemed like she would make a dependable co-parent. Actually, when I reasoned it out like that, I felt sort of noble about being with Chris. I didn't have to find someone just like me. Since when was that a virtue? Maybe Ruth was being elitist.

I didn't say that to her, though. I apologized. And I called Chris to tell her I was going to spend a night at home, that I wanted to hang out with Ruth and watch a movie like old times before I uprooted myself.

Why don't you watch a movie and come back here after? she asked. I'll miss you.

That's so sweet, I said, but I don't want to wake you if I come in late. Plus, it's good for us to spend a night apart once in a while. Right?

She was silent for so long that I wondered if she'd hung up on me. Chris?

What about our morning run?

I'm sorry baby, I'll have to skip it just this once.

I had secretly been looking forward to a weekend off. It was romantic how much Chris loved being together. But I missed my friends. I also sort of missed myself.

She sounded sad. I love you, she said, bye I guess.

Bye, I said. I love you too.

George found something to do out of the house and Ruth and I watched *A League of Their Own* on my bed in our pajamas, surrounded by a buffet of snacks: a bowl of salt and vinegar chips, a bowl of Cherry Blasters, a bar of salted dark chocolate, a bowl of soy mint chip and another of chocolate peanut butter Häagen-Dazs, my hands-down favourite. I usually snack straight out of bags and tubs because I'm lazy and unrefined but Virgo Ruth had set out a proper spread.

We'd gone together to the Sobeys down the street to get the goods, and Ruth had picked up the Häagen-Dazs. Want some, my dairy queen? she asked. I told her I was trying to be good. Dairy is not evil, she replied. She told me that strict diets were more about control than health, that technically they're eating disorders.

What about your mom? I asked. She keeps kosher.

Yeah, because it makes her feel closer to my bubbe, plus the animals die better deaths. You're just doing this to appease your despotic girlfriend.

I sighed. Can we not, please?

Ruth said fine, she would just buy the ice cream for herself. I bought the tub of soy mint chip like an alcoholic ordering a soda and felt proud of myself, but after smoking a joint on the walk home, five minutes into the movie I'd easily eaten more than half the bowl of Häagen-Dazs. Ruth acted like she hadn't noticed, but it clearly put her in a good mood.

We painted our nails blue and read our horoscopes. Ruth is a total Virgo. You can tell from her snack bowls and chore wheel and reasonably paced relationships. And her judgyness. But other than her judgments re: my relationship with Chris, I'm usually onside, I pass the test, I'm in the club. Maybe I ate the ice cream with Ruth because I knew it would please her, that she'd see I was still my own woman. The dairy queen.

Yet I continued to maintain to Chris that I'd been vegan since July. And though I pretended to go to sleep in my own bed after Ruth and I yawned and hugged and said goodnight, I quietly got dressed and snuck out after Chris texted me that she was lonely and begged me to come over.

I MOVED MY STUFF INTO Chris's apartment over the next month. First a box of kitchen things, then a suitcase of books. The autoharp that had lived in my closet since my early twenties was relocated to Chris's closet. The giant orchid moved onto her credenza, a word I'd never heard until Chris said it to me. And I packed two milk crates full of ivy and jade and kalanchoe, all outgrowing their jars and handleless cups.

Linh offered to strap the plants to the back of their bike and zip them over. They'd stopped by on their way home from work for a swig of juice from the fridge and were standing in my bedroom doorway, holding the carton.

Oh, I said, picturing Chris's face if Linh, who I was not allowed to hug, were to show up at the apartment. Thanks so much, I said, they're just, uh, so delicate. I don't think they'd do well over bumps. And Chris said she can pick them up tomorrow with her car.

I'm literally a professional, said Linh, who runs their own bike courier business. I can handle your babies.

I just, I think Chris is probably working from home tonight, and she gets, like, really distracted if people show up out of the blue.

Yeah that's fine, said Linh. I'll just drop them off. I'm hanging with the pack soon anyway.

Oh, yeah? I said, trying to act like I hadn't just been knifed in the heart. For the first time I knew of, I had not been invited.

You're welcome to come, buddy, Linh said. You just haven't made it out the last few times so we figured you had plans.

Oh thanks, no it's fine. I do have plans, I guess.

Cool. Pass me your plants.

I couldn't think of how to divert Linh's offer without seeming weird. What would be worse? If they showed up at the apartment by themselves, or with me? What would Chris say to Linh if I wasn't there? What would Linh say to Chris? The possibilities made me sweat. Better to be there, I thought, as a conversational chaperone. I still hadn't told Linh I'd agreed not to hug them anymore and had been hugging them in the meantime like a philanderer. Secret ice cream and forbidden hugs. Was I the worst girlfriend in the world?

Want to walk over together? I asked.

If you're ready to go now, sure, said Linh, and finished the juice. I'll get you back, they said, shaking the empty carton.

It's Ruth's, I said.

I'll buy her a drink at the bar then.

I wanted to go to the bar. I felt like a kid who had to practice piano instead of getting to play outside with my friends. I zipped a load of clothes into my backpack and lifted my antique mirror from its hook on the wall.

Where are you all going tonight, I asked, trying to sound whatever about it.

Liam's band is playing at the Seahorse. You and Chris should come, if you want.

Liam is Dana's partner. Dana was the only one of my pack about whom Chris hadn't expressed reservations. Maybe I could convince her to come if I said Dana's name the loudest and Linh's and Ruth's in a cough.

Maybe, I said, hoisting the overstuffed pack onto my back.

On the walk to Chris's apartment I half-listened to Linh talk about the hot legal-aid lawyer they'd been couriering documents for, about whether I knew her from around, whether maybe she was queer. Emma. I said I didn't recognize the name. She looked like she could be, said Linh. They got a vibe. She always smiled at them and brought the documents right out and handed them over personally instead of leaving them with the receptionist, and once she touched their hand. Didn't I think that sounded a bit crushy? A bit gay?

I was scanning my brain, trying to sort out how to tell Linh about the no-hugging rule without making Chris sound like my jealous boyfriend. Should I blame it on myself, I wondered. Say that after years of hugging, all of a sudden and for some reason I can't explain, I just don't want to hug them anymore? But that would be awful, and Linh would never buy it.

Out loud I said it did sound like the hot lawyer had a crush on them. And speaking of, um, touching, I tried, in weird segue, uh, Chris is feeling a bit...I mean, I mentioned to her that we dated forever ago, and she, like, well, her last girlfriend cheated on her with her ex, and Chris is feeling, I dunno, insecure? About you and me? So I think it would feel better for her if we didn't…if we didn't hug, or touch each other. For a bit.

I looked over at Linh.

Sorch, they said, stopping their bike in the middle of the sidewalk and peering back at me. That's stupid. Did you tell her it was literally years ago?

Yeah, I said.

I hug you like I hug my little brother.

I know.

You're one of the last people I'd want to fuck.

Thank you, I said in mock gratitude.

I mean, we don't have to hug if you don't want to, they said, looking ahead.

It's not that I don't want to hug you, I said. You're one of my best friends. It's just…Chris has been through a lot with her ex and she's just kind of sensitive, you know? I don't want her to feel insecure. I think she'll probably be okay once she gets to know you better. Maybe I can get her to come out tonight?

Linh smiled flatly. Sure, they said.

We got to Chris's building and Linh wheeled their bike into the elevator. I pressed the button for the ninth floor and asked if they were okay.

I'm okay, Linh said, looking at me closely. Are you okay?

Of course, I said. I glanced back at myself in the elevator mirror. I was okay, wasn't I?

At the door to the apartment, Linh unhooked the bungee cords from around the milk crates and lifted the crates to the floor. Safe and sound, they said. Text me if you're going to come out later. I nodded. See you, they said and paused, then waved with an uncertain hand.

I waved back. Bye, I said, thanks.

I unlocked the door. Chris was sitting on the couch with her laptop and a glass of wine. I leaned the mirror against the wall by her running shoes.

That can't go there, she said.

I know, I said, just putting it there for now. I brought some more stuff over.

Sounds like you had help.

I felt caught but tried to act casual. Oh yeah, I said, Linh helped me with my plants.

I opened the door to bring the milk crates inside and Chris said oh, Linh.

We didn't hug, I said. We talked about it and they understand.

You told them what I said?

No, not what you said. Just a bit about what happened with your ex, and how, you know, it'll take some time before you're comfortable around them.

I can't believe you told them that, Chris said. You make me sound like a jealous fucking boyfriend.

I didn't say out loud that I'd actually tried my very best to not make her sound like a jealous fucking boyfriend. What I said was baby, what should I have told them?

Chris shut her laptop and stalked to the kitchen, poured herself another glass of wine and drank from it deeply, staring out the window like at least the view was loyal to her.

Linh invited us out to see Liam's band tonight. Want to go?

I need to work, said Chris. You go.

This is a test, yelled a voice from the back office of my brain. If being told to stay in one place was a test, being told I could go was likely one too. But I did want to go. When was the last time my pack and I had all hung out? Too long ago. Weeks, maybe even months. Liam's band was a bit poppy for my taste but they were loud, and loud was what I needed, a balm for my brain.

I walked over to Chris and wrapped myself around her back, murmured how nice it would be to go out together, a chance for her and my friends to get to know each other, low-key, fun band, dancing, and I'll buy you a drink, I crooned, kissing her ear and jaw. I could feel her slowly relenting, muscle by muscle. I put on some music, a band she liked, and I jumped around her and held her hands until she was laughing. I'd broken through her brooding! I felt so triumphant, like my love was a panacea. We did shots and got dressed to go out, and I scattered compliments like petals at her feet all the way to the front door, where we finished the last swig of wine and kissed as we stumbled to put on our boots. I texted Linh to say we'd see them at the bar.

We walked down Gottingen Street holding hands, tipsy and laughing. We'd never been this drunk together and it was fun to see Chris being stupid in public, singing, nearly walking into a tree. Inside the door of the bar we took our wallets out to pay cover. ID, said the bouncer, and I showed him mine, smiling under his scrutiny. My hair was longer in the photo, and red, but I'd since dyed it brown and chopped it into a bob with bangs. I wondered if, to strangers, I looked like a completely different person. Okay, the bouncer said, and I exhaled.

He turned to Chris, who was looking through the folds of her wallet. Shit, she said, I must've left it at home. Can you just let me in? I'm thirty-five, I'm an engineer. Here's my business card. She held it out to him like a badge. He glanced at it but wouldn't take it.

We don't accept business cards, he said.

So I have to walk all the way home, Chris said, in a tone I had only previously heard directed at me. The look the bouncer gave her made me think he was about to ban her for life.

I'll walk back with you, I said, squeezing her hand. It's only ten minutes.

Chris turned and looked at me like I'd spat in her face.

Next, the bouncer said, looking at the person behind us, and Chris's hand tightened around mine. She marched back out through the door, pulling me behind her like a bad kid made to leave the party. Outside, people were smoking and laughing, a dense cloud hanging over their heads. Chris pushed through them, towing me along. Around the corner of the building she dropped my hand and turned, teeth clenched behind tight lips.

Hey, I said, trying to soothe her. I've forgotten my ID lots of times, and the apartment's really close—we'll be back before Liam's band even starts.

I don't care about the fucking band, she said. You embarrassed me in front of that bouncer.

Baby, I said, my pulse throbbing in my neck like my blood was trying to escape. I was just worried he might kick us out. He wasn't going to let you in.

She looked at me like I was so stupid. You don't think I deal with power-tripping assholes all the time at work? she said. You don't think I can handle myself?

Of course I think you can handle yourself, I said. I could feel people listening all around us. Hey, I said quietly, moving closer. Can we please not fight about this here? I'm sorry, okay?

You're so fucking patronizing. You try to handle me in there and then you try to handle me now? You think I'm making a scene?

I closed my eyes against the pricking tears but they leaked out anyway, like traitors. Can we please talk about this somewhere else?

You started this, Chris said, louder. You made me come out tonight even though you knew I had work to do, made me drink too much before we left, rushed me out the fucking door so I forgot my ID, and then made me look like an idiot in front of the goddamn bouncer.

Without even having told my feet to do it, I started to walk backward, away from Chris. Like they just said oh we'd really rather not, if we could just be over in this direction instead, that would be good, that would be best. Or maybe it was the disgruntled worker whose memos I never read. Maybe they saw their chance and decided to take the wheel.

Are you walking away from me? Chris yelled.

No, I said, my voice cracking as my feet carried me backward across the sidewalk. Please don't let my friends see this, I thought. What was happening to our fun night out? It seemed so certain, a minute ago, the fun. We were supposed to be dancing and doing shots and making out in the bathroom. I turned and stepped off the curb and Chris grabbed my arm hard as a car honked.

She yanked me back toward her.

You're acting like a child, she spat, walking into traffic for fuck's sake.

I wiped my streaming eyes with the back of my free hand.

Let's go, she said through gritted teeth, still holding my arm, and started to march me up the sidewalk.

Hoping to pass invisibly through the crowd, counting on its collectively short attention span, I said nothing and let myself be led up the hill. A block past the bar, still crying, I stopped walking and Chris let go.

I don't, don't understand why you're so mad at me, I said, hiccupping against the dark doorway of a closed store. I didn't mean to, I, I'm sorry. I just, just don't know why you're so mad.

I wished the doorway were a cave into which I could disappear and sleep for months.

You don't understand why I'm so mad at you? Chris said incredulously. You made this into a way bigger deal than it had to be.

I guessed she was right because I couldn't stop crying. I was too drunk, too ashamed, too sad about the fun we would now definitely not have. I sobbed in the amber and red of the changing traffic lights that shone on my face, the black of the alcove into which I'd backed draping my body but failing to swallow me whole as I'd hoped it would.

Chris stepped toward me and wiped my wet cheek. Listen, she said softly, let's go home, you can get cleaned up, I'll find my ID, and we'll come back in time for the show, okay? Would that be nice?

The relative sweetness, like the taste of water after you've thrown up, flipped some switch in me and my tears stopped. But I continued to hiccup. I let Chris hug me. I said okay. But by the time we got home I was so tired. My eyelids were thick from crying, the skin shiny and stretched. Makeup would not fool my friends. Staying in would be easier. Chris was in a much better mood at her apartment, but if that switched again, at least no one would be around to see.

I changed into pajamas. Chris made me tea and sat with me on the couch, lifted my feet up and put them in her lap.

I forgive you, she said. I love you.

I felt like a bawling baby who'd finally been picked up, sleepy from the effort and heavy with endorphins. Chris kissed the tops of my feet and my ankles and knees. I watched it like a movie until I found myself lifting my hips so she could take off my pajama pants. She worked her way up until her warm mouth was on me, such a different mouth than the one she'd spoken with outside the bar.

Before I fell asleep I drank a tall glass of water to make up for fluid lost to tears and sex. And when I woke in the morning, I drank my tea in the bathroom while the bag cooled in a spoon on the edge of the sink, and when it had I pressed it into my eyelids.

Let's go, Chris called cheerfully from the hall. I squeezed my legs into the thick shiny spandex she'd bought for me and pulled an old hoodie over the shirt I'd slept in. Wiped tannin from under my eyes and scrubbed my teeth. When I opened the door she was stretching in the hall, ready to run. C'mon lazy bones, she said jovially, like she was trying to overwrite the night. My bones would have liked nothing more than to rest alone on the couch for the next hour, but they moved to the door and the small ones in my fingers laced the small ones in my feet into my new running shoes.

All relationships have their ups and downs, read the memo on top of the inbox in the office of my brain. And a peppy worker brought it to the lunchroom and tacked it up over the coffee machine.

The body as a map. It's not a perfect metaphor because there's so much that would be missed if you only considered the surface: organs, bones, neural pathways. Though maybe a felt map, of the whole body and not just the skin. That way it would show the seam on my radius where it broke and knit itself back together when I was six, after I rolled off my bed on purpose just to see what would happen. And my stomach, from the time I was nine and Bonnie caught me straining the pulp out of my orange juice and hit me so hard I lost my breath—what a waste of food, did I think we were made of money? And the small tear I can still see if I look with a hand mirror from the too-thick fingers of my nineteen-year-old weed dealer, fingers I didn't want inside me but which I also didn't protest because I was fifteen and felt, I don't know, flattered. And the feeling I got when I stood up in front of my tenth-grade English class to read a poem I wrote about moths, and my beautiful teacher with the daisy tattoo on her wrist said how lovely, and my heart was a marching band. And all the secret gentle touches from my secret high-school girlfriend, Angie, under tables and in dark movie theatres and inside our zipped-together sleeping bags.

It would show the scar from when my first not-completely-secret girlfriend and I cut our palms and pressed them together, as a pagan kind of promise or maybe a sort of wedding, and kissed under the full moon and held each other's bloody hands all along the Halifax Harbour, provinces away from my parents. Jen and I would get stoned on Citadel Hill and in the alleyway beside our student res. We watched every episode of *The L Word* and *Buffy* like it was our religion. We got drunk in the night and went dancing downtown. We got drunk in the day and stumbled into a tattoo shop and dared each other: a bottle of holy water for Jen, a stake through the heart for me. The map would show that too. And it would show the imprint of Jen's hands on my chest from when she started shoving me into walls, and the crescent moons in my arms from where she'd dig her fingernails in.

It would show the worker in my brain who, on the day after I broke up with Jen, observed all the other workers fucking up, falling down, crashing out, but was somehow able to stay alert enough to navigate me to the hospital, where I told the woman at the desk that I seemed to be having some kind of mental breakdown, did that mean I'd made the wrong choice in leaving my girlfriend? I told her that Jen had been surprisingly understanding when I ended things, did she think I should ask her to take me back? Or maybe God was finally punishing me for being gay, though it seemed like a strange time for him to mete it out, you'd think he would have been pleased. Also I was so thirsty, did she know if there was a water fountain around here somewhere?

The woman asked for my health card and took my pulse and called a nurse to take me through the sliding doors to a room with a bed. The nurse clipped something on my finger and looked into my eyes with a tiny light. She asked me to pee into a cup. After a while she came back and asked if I had consumed cannabis. Like, ever? I asked. No, she said, recently. I said I didn't think so. She asked if I could have eaten some by accident.

That one coherent worker, like a captain steering through the roughest sea while the rest of the crew passed out or vomited over the side of the boat, remembered the flower and the cookie and the note that Jen had left outside my dorm room that morning. I hope we can still be friends, the note read, and I'd cried and held it to my heart and smelled the flower and eaten the cookie. And then had a mental break.

Ohhh, I said to the nurse, the cookie! I'm fucking stoned!

It appears so, said the nurse. She asked if I could call someone to take me home.

I texted Jen. *Did that cookie have weed in it?*

No, why? she wrote back a few seconds later. *Are you okay?*

No, I wrote.

Omg what's wrong? Can I come over?

I called Ruth. I knew her from the café we both worked at, but not well. It was before she changed her name. She was funny and nice and smart and had her own apartment. I told her I was accidentally very high at the hospital and asked if I could please come over. I couldn't go back to campus blitzed out of my mind. I couldn't go back to Jen. Ruth gave me her address. I took a cab and when it pulled up, she was sitting on the concrete steps outside her door, waiting for me.

She took me inside. Her place was tiny and immaculate. She tucked me in on her couch with a soft blue blanket and made me mint tea. I told her what had happened, what I thought must have happened. What the fuck, she said, that's so fucked up. You believe me? I asked. Ruth said of course she did. I told her the other things that had happened, the shoving and the fingernail marks. Fuck that bitch, she said, and made me say it back to her over and over again like a counter-curse, until I was laughing so hard I got the hiccups because I was still so very stoned.

A whole-body map would show where the glass shard sunk into my heel. How my sister's little hand used to fit in mine. Where I pierced my own bellybutton with a safety pin. The swell of my stomach full of ice cream. A whole-body map would show all of these things.

he name of the place is partly what convinced me. It felt meant to be. In pictures it was almost as beautiful as the original Inverness, where my mother was born but where I've never been. This was Inverness County, Creignish specifically. A little white house in a grassy clearing with overgrown garden beds, encircled by trees. From the second-floor bedroom window, you could see the ocean.

I daydreamed of Chris and me with a bottle of wine and homemade pizza, baked on the pizza stone, taking a break from home renos, wearing overalls covered in dust from chipping away old plaster to expose thick ceiling beams and chimney brick, unveiling hardwood beneath the musty carpet. Della, a purring grey orb on a chair by the wood stove, copper pots hanging from hooks, fairy lights and ivy climbing the bookshelves, the orchid in a bay window, stretching out its tendrils. I'd have to leave my job but surely, I thought, I'd find one on the Island in my field. Eventually. Yusra was doubtful but, as

Chris said, there was plenty of nature to conserve up there. And in the meantime I could do all the wholesome DIY anti-capitalist shit I'd always wished I had time for: grow a vegetable garden, make my own soap and candles, can jam, bake bread, finally teach myself to play that autoharp.

It had been a month since I moved into Chris's apartment. After the night she forgot her ID, there had only been three, maybe four, other times. Times when things happened and I cried about them. Was that reasonable? I would like to be able to view some sort of graph generated by some kind of formula, like where x for Times Things Happen is divided by y for Span of Time and the result, z, is plotted on a spectrum of normal, okay, maybe not okay, maybe bad, and bad. Otherwise how am I supposed to know? What am I supposed to compare myself to? If these Times happen mostly in private, how are you supposed to know what the average z value is or how much crying is standard? I know we fall somewhere between Ruth and George, who are perfect therapized angels, and my parents, who only speak to each other when necessary and never sit beside each other by choice. So does that mean we're fine? Average? I would appreciate a more specific measurement.

You would also need to factor into the equation the Times Good Things Happen, and the degree of their good. After that first month of living together, I felt that when all was accounted for, the scale tipped well toward the positive. Chris made me breakfast, and lunch, and dinner. I used to just eat half a box of crackers with half a block of cheese for lunch at work, but every day, *every day*, Chris would bring me something fancy and delicious, like a panini or tempeh wrap or mushroom burger or quinoa salad, stuck with an *xo*'d Post-it declaring how smart or cute or tall I was, and I would eat it at my desk like a professional grown-up woman. And even though I kind of hated it (and still do), she made me run, which I understand is good for me. No one else had ever called me a goddess, and though it felt a bit nineties, I loved it. No one before had sexed me up so perfectly and so often, soft and warm when I was sleepy and rough when I needed it. Each day after she brought me lunch at work I'd walk her out to her car, and we'd kiss in the alley beside the building like we were fifteen years old and secretly gay at summer camp. She spooned me all night while we slept. She rubbed my feet while we watched TV. She traced her fingers across my back and kissed each link of my spine.

So if things were mostly intensely good and sometimes intensely bad, that was still better than mostly fine and sometimes not fine, right? In the equation? Since math isn't my strong suit I just had to assume my theory was correct. It didn't accord with Linh's relationship philosophy, which they had summarized to me thus: if it's chill, chill; if it's not chill, don't chill. Things with Chris were never really "chill," but Linh's a Sagittarius so, you know.

It was hard to say exactly what the things were that happened between me and Chris, or how they happened. It felt like walking in a neighbourhood you think you know, and then after a while you're lost but you can't remember where you took a wrong turn. Like when Chris burned her finger making breakfast and then I dripped tears onto my desk all morning at work, or when we ran out of laundry soap the night before she had an important meeting and I cried myself to sleep on the couch. I guess she's right that I make a big deal out of things. I seem to cry about everything. I really shouldn't have insisted on keeping my old copper pan with the brass handle that gets too hot, and I really should have stopped at the store on my way home and remembered we were low on detergent.

I promised to be more thoughtful. I supposed I hadn't had to think about my shortcomings in the recent past because Ruth was so patient. But now it was time to grow up and be a good partner and not just a subpar roommate. I wrote myself lists of things to remember, like *wash and put away your mug immediately after use*, and *don't make plans with friends without checking in first*, and *call before you come home from work in case we need anything*, and *don't drink water before bed because when you wake up in the night to pee Chris can't get back to sleep so neither will you.*

Chris is very thoughtful. I'm always thinking of you, she said, I wish you were always thinking of me too. I do think of you, I said, but she said I don't show it. I texted her an article I was reviewing about the impact of glyphosate-based herbicides on the embryonic development of Japanese quails, but she didn't even read the abstract.

I wrote her a poem about lichens—a symbiosis of two partners: one a photosynthetic organism, one a fungus. It was meant to be romantic but she said she didn't get it. I gave her a moonsnail shell I'd found on the beach with my pack the previous summer, but I later found it under the bathroom sink behind the toilet paper.

Her job was pretty stressful. Her boss was an asshole. And she wanted to run somewhere other than on the sidewalk or up and down the one green hill in the centre of the city. She needed a change. She hated always worrying about crossing paths with Amy and her horrible friends. She saw a post for a position at the paper mill in Port Hawkesbury, and applied. What did I think, she asked. Would I come?

I thought that a paper mill was probably better than warships, not for amphibians but in the larger scheme of things. And a change always sounds good when your life feels bad because the change should transform the bad, or at least distract you from it. Lose your job and cut bangs. Get a tattoo when the snow refuses to melt. Get dumped and move to Montréal. I supposed I could use a change, too. I'd lived in this city for twelve years, and we could always come back. I pictured a Chris who breathed clean ocean air, who ran through the woods, who was caring and kind and calm. If my love wasn't enough by itself to save her, maybe my love plus oceanside rural life could do it.

Of course she got the job, she's smart as hell. And then she found the old farmhouse in Creignish with a wood stove and clawfoot tub for sixty thousand. She could buy it outright, she told me. It would be all ours.

It was perfect, a back-to-the-land lesbian dream come true.

I had coffee with Ruth on Citadel Hill and showed her the pictures. She said the clawfoot tub was cute but couldn't I have a bath in Halifax?

Chris's apartment only has a shower, I replied.

Then have a bath at my house, she said.

But Chris got the job in Cape Breton.

Then move back in with me and George and visit her on the weekends. We haven't filled your room yet.

Ruth, I said.

Sorch, said Ruth. You'll be so far away. Not just from me. From everything. Is there even a store you could walk to?

I hadn't thought about that. But Chris has a car, I said, and wouldn't it be peaceful, away from everything?

Yes, from everything, Ruth said. Away from your job that you love, your friends, music—

I believe there are cèilidhs on the Island.

Ruth rolled her eyes. Oh yes, just your cup of tea. Just, please, take a little time before you decide.

FOR A WEEK, I THOUGHT. Inverness County, the little house, the wood stove, the tub. No store, okay, but canning jam and playing the autoharp. I could learn to knit. I could conduct an informal study of the local amphibian population. And wouldn't it just be the loveliest place to raise a baby?

On the weekend, Ruth invited our pack over to the house and kicked George out for the evening. I thought Chris might be sad I was doing something without her, but she smiled and said of course, sounds fun, tell them I say hi, as if the mere idea of moving to Cape Breton had already soothed her.

When I got to the house it felt like I'd never left. Maybe Ruth hadn't found someone to fill my room because she was waiting for me to return, like parents who keep their kid's room the way they left it, ready anytime they need, just in case. Like Ruth's own room at her mom's house, with her Sleater-Kinney poster and her rollerblades and her chronologized collection of *Adbusters*. My bedroom became Bonnie's quilting room a month after I left, so when I went back to visit I'd had to sleep on an air mattress under the sewing table.

On my way over I picked up two growlers of pumpkin beer to share. Ruth and I drank it and ate Fuzzy Peaches at the kitchen table while we waited for Linh and Dana to show up. The pumpkin and peach go quite well together, a very good pairing yes, we said in our fake posh accents and cheersed. Dana arrived, pulled a bottle of Grolsch out of her bag, and sat down. She popped the ceramic top and took a swig. Ruth asked for a sip to see how it would pair with the candy but Dana said she thought she was getting a cold.

Then Linh banged through the door with their bike helmet clipped to their messenger bag, knocking along the wall of the hallway and into the kitchen. They pushed their sweaty bangs off their forehead and said how can it still be so fucking hot in October, I'm dying for a beer. Dana passed them the bottle of Grolsch and Ruth said I thought you were getting a cold as Linh swigged, and Dana smiled and shrugged, and Linh said yuck this isn't beer, and Dana said it's ginger beer, the closest I'll get to the real thing for a while. We all looked at her for a second before we figured it out and then we clapped for her and cheered. She and Liam had been trying for over a year. The night became a celebration of tiny new life, a cluster so small that Dana said it still felt hypothetical. She'd only just found out a few days before but couldn't keep it to herself.

Can we hug you? we asked. Is it safe?

Yes, she laughed.

I hugged her and wondered if there was a pregnancy equivalent of a wedding bouquet toss. I wanted Dana to pass her good fortune on to me. I wanted it to be my turn to create something precious and new.

How can you leave us, Sorch? Ruth asked when we were nearing the bottom of our growlers. Who's going to teach Dana's baby about frogs and salamanders and the right wineglass to use for sauvignon blanc? I asked her to please stop trying to break my heart. She said the same back to me. Then Dana said it's okay, we know you'll come back to visit us all the time, and Linh put on the Yeah Yeah Yeahs and we danced until Dana was nauseous.

The next morning I woke up mildly hungover, found the water glass Chris had left on the nightstand for me, and took a sip. Dana's golden kernel of news reformed itself in my filmy brain and I smiled, slid an arm around Chris's waist, and kissed her neck.

I had such a good night, I whispered. Dana's pregnant!

Chris squeezed my hand and murmured that that was great.

The words climbed up my throat and I held them in my mouth for a minute before resolving to let them out in the form of a test. Before now there had never felt like a right time to ask. But if I could have this one thing, if I could be next, then all the things I'd have to leave behind would be worth it.

Do you want to have kids? I tried to ask as if the question wasn't a net holding up my heart.

Chris turned over to face me. I used to think I didn't, she said. But with you I do.

The room glowed.

I kissed her. I'll come to Cape Breton, I said.

She rolled on top of me, her soft weight, and held my face in her hands. We'll be so happy, she said, I promise. And she made love to me so sweetly and sincerely, as if we could make a baby right then by our sheer will.

We drove. *Chris rented a trailer to tow behind her car, packed with* all of our stuff. The best time to drive to Cape Breton would have been two weeks earlier, on Thanksgiving weekend when all the leaves were still on the trees. That's what we were told by the guy at the gas station in Sheet Harbour. But some leaves still glowed at us from low branches.

Della meowed for two hours from her crate in the back seat before throwing up wetly and beginning again. We opened the windows to blow the smell out of the car and pulled into the overgrown driveway of a massive splintering barn so Chris could clean out the crate. I held Della in the back seat. I told her she just needed to calm down and take a nap and that we'd be there in another hour. I asked Chris through the open window if you could give cats Gravol. She said she didn't think so. She finished wiping out the crate and we tried to entice Della back in by throwing treats inside, but after a while we gave up and she rode the rest of the way to Creignish on my lap.

We drove along the eastern shore, past huge rusting boats heaved up onto the land like dying whales, salt-bleached sheds, a flat raccoon. I fed Chris carrot sticks and pita dipped in hummus. I offered to drive and she looked at me like I was joking. It was fine. I liked looking out the window with Della anyway.

We crossed the causeway, a built-up land bridge to the Island. It felt like Cape Breton had lost some of its essential islandness, being tethered like that. We drove north. After we passed a green highway sign that read *Creignish / Creiginnis*, the English and the Gaelic, and a few minutes later, the Creignish church, Chris pulled into a grassy driveway and drove between two rows of birch trees until our house emerged in front of us. She shut the car off and we sat for a minute, looking at it through the windshield. White clapboard on the bottom half, white shakes on top. Deep red ivy snaked along the first-floor window and then splayed like a many-fingered hand, reaching up to the roof, which was a bit mossy, as the realtor had warned. But for sixty thousand we weren't complaining. A covered porch shaded the front door and I could faintly see my future self, sitting in a chair just to the left of it, reading a book, Della birdwatching at my feet.

Welcome home, Chris said with the sweetest smile, and kissed me. I got out of the car with Della in my arms and Chris found the right key after a couple of tries and I carried the cat over the threshold.

Inside it was smaller than it had looked in the pictures, but the old wooden floors glowed in the afternoon sun. Faded wallpaper with twists of pale flowers, easily twice as old as me, was pasted to the walls and curling up at the seams. I put Della down and crept around the house like we didn't own it, like maybe the real owners were still there, reading the paper in the next room. The kitchen was small but beside it was another room, the dining room I guessed. We could probably knock that wall down. And there was a bright sitting room, or I thought perhaps I should call it a parlour.

Chris went down to the basement alone to inspect the fuse box, because she's braver than me, and I went upstairs. The red runner was worn and I could smell the dust rising under my feet as

I climbed. At the top I switched on the light because the doors to all the rooms were shut and the hallway was dark. Why would you close them, previous owners, unless you're hiding behind them? I couldn't think of any other reason. I counted to five and forced myself to open the first door.

No one was in the rooms of course, just bare wooden floors with darkened rectangles where the furniture used to be. A bed there, a dresser there. The window of the first room looked out over the driveway, the rows of birch trees, and across the highway to the ocean. This room would be ours. I imagined watching the sun go down over the water before bed and Chris coming up behind me and wrapping her arms around my waist. It was perfect. It would be perfect.

I heard the front door and saw Chris walk out toward the car. I heaved the swollen window open. This is our room! I called.

Are you going to help me unpack or what? she asked.

Of course! I said, and ran down the stairs so fast that I fell down the last four and broke my finger when I put out a hand to save myself.

THE NURSES AT THE HOSPITAL in Sydney were very nice. They x-rayed my finger and showed me the image, pointing out the break. I asked if I could keep the x-ray. They said no but let me take a picture of my skeleton hand. I thought I would just get a little splint, but they plastered a cast around my broken pinky and its neighbour and all the way up my arm to the elbow. They said it was the best way to immobilize the finger so it could heal straight. They asked what colour cast wrap I wanted and I said orange, because I heard it was hunting season around here and orange was probably the safest choice.

Chris ran errands while I was x-rayed and plastered. She went grocery shopping and to the hardware store and liquor store and dollar store. So efficient. She seemed put out when I first stumbled out of the house, bawling and cradling my hand like it was a dead bird, but then she softened and gave me a hug and said we could stand to make a trip to Sydney. It seemed the Island really was chilling her out. When I was done being doctored she picked me up out front of the hospital and took us for Lebanese. Then we drove home in the dark and I fell asleep, waking only when she parked the car in the driveway and kissed me on the cheek.

I like taking care of you, she said.

We went inside and fed Della, and I sat on the kitchen counter drinking water from my cupped left hand while Chris tried to find her sleeping bag and camping mat in the trailer. She came in with both plus a bottle of local whisky she'd picked up in town, and two tumblers with $1 stickers on the bottoms. She'd also bought, for the same price, a wooden sign with fake leaves and berries glued to it that said *Home Sweet Home* in a rustic font. That's so tacky, I laughed, who are you? I like it, she said, and not ironically. She hung it on a nail in the wall beside the front door, above a hook for our keys.

We went upstairs and she set up the camping mat inside the dark rectangle where a bed had been. Della padded into the room and I laid out my sweater for her on the floor. We drank the whisky and Chris got me off twice, and I only hit her in the back of the head with my cast once, and she wasn't even mad.

I TEXTED MY PACK ABOUT the drive up and our first night. Dana said she thought breaking a bone in a new house was unlucky and suggested a cleansing spell that involved sweeping and salt. Ruth told me not to drink whisky on painkillers. Linh said they and their new lawyer girlfriend, Emma, were training to bike up for a visit next summer. I missed them already.

Chris and I managed to get all of our stuff out of the U-Haul and into the house in time for her to drop it off and get the deposit back, but unpacking took forever. I couldn't lift my end of the mattress with one hand and we didn't have any friends in Creignish to help carry it upstairs, so we set it up in the parlour. After that, my top priority was getting my plants into optimal light and Chris's was hanging up her dress shirts and pants so they wouldn't be wrinkled for her first day of work on Monday. The rest of our things emerged from their boxes in the order we used them. My autoharp was last but instead of putting it in the closet, I sat it in a chair in the parlour so I would see it every day and be guilted into learning to play it.

EVERYTHING WAS SO GOOD, until Sunday night. I was baking squash and sweet potatoes and unpacking photos from back when they were still a physical thing: me and Ruth, me and Linh, me and Dana, and all of us together set in thrifted golden frames. I had my little hammer, one of two tools I brought to this relationship, and a jar of picture hooks I'd pulled out of the wall of my old bedroom. Chris was setting up the dining room as her office, expertly assembling her desk.

Which wall can I put these on, I asked, standing in the doorway and holding up the stack to her in my un-casted hand. Beside the big window in the parlour maybe?

Do you have to put them up? Chris asked.

I held the pictures in front of my heart like a shield. I'd like to, I said.

Well I don't want them in the living room. It'll look cluttered.

Okay, I said carefully, the bedroom?

I don't want to look at your friends in our bedroom.

The kitchen? I tried.

No, said Chris.

The bathroom, I said, aiming for levity.

You're being ridiculous.

Yes, I said.

This is our house, said Chris, her voice hard. We should put up pictures of us.

My spine contracted. I could feel myself getting smaller.

But you put a picture of your parents on the mantel, I said, quiet.

That's different, she said.

How? I asked, my eyes starting to sting.

Don't say *how* to me like that, said Chris.

Like what? I asked. I could see the cliff in the distance.

Like a fucking bitch, she said.

I'm not a bitch, I said, feeling like I was already falling from it.

I'm done, said Chris. She leaned forward and swung the heavy wooden door to shut me out. But it banged against my hand full of photographs and they hit the floor in a crash of metal and glass. I stared at Chris through the still-open door. Get a broom, she said, like I was from another planet and didn't understand the effects of gravity on breakable objects. I turned around and tried to remember where the broom was, took a step and felt a shard of glass slide into my foot, deep and shrill. My vision blurred. I hobbled to the kitchen, knowing somehow that I deserved it, the pain.

I couldn't see the broom but smelled the squash burning in the oven. I grabbed a mitt, pulled the smoking pan out and set it on the stove, limped over to the window above the sink and wrenched open the sash with my weak left hand. The smoke detector Chris bought at the hardware store in Sydney went off, but I had glass in my foot and only one working arm. I called her name.

She came stomping around the corner in her shoes, crunching over bits of glass, and emerged in the kitchen as if onto a smoking battlefield.

Can you shut the alarm off? I yelled over the piercing sound. She surveyed the room—our burnt dinner, the open window, my bleeding foot—grabbed a chair to stand on, twisted the alarm out of the ceiling, and pushed the button to silence it.

You're useless, she said. Tossed the alarm on the table, grabbed the broom from beside the fridge, and left the room.

I sat on the chair she'd stood on and lifted my foot up, took off my sock with a bloom of blood near the toe. I'd done this self-surgery before. But I couldn't see a glint amid my seeping blood or feel the shard with my fingertips. I squeezed, but nothing came out.

Chris stomped back into the kitchen with a dustpan of glass and dumped it into the garbage can. She seized the pan of blackened vegetables and dumped them in too. She threw the pan in the steel sink and it rang like a bell. What are we going to eat now? she demanded. What am I going to bring for lunch? Tomorrow's my first fucking day and you do this. She held her arms out to the room and the havoc I had wreaked.

I hadn't realized until that moment that I was already crying, but passively, just sort of leaking. And then my body heaved and shook and I cried like I was trying to exorcise something through the holes in my face. God! Chris said. Why are you *always* crying? That made me cry harder. She was digging through the cupboards and freezer and grabbing pots and filling them with water and slamming them down on the stove, pouring in rice and frozen vegetables, stray grains and peas skittering over the countertop, and I put my bloody sock back on my bleeding foot and a worker in my brain drove my body to the door, and my un-casted hand opened it to leave, to go I didn't know where, just out, outside, and Chris's hand shot over my shoulder and slammed it shut.

Where the fuck are you going, she said. It wasn't a question. The answer was nowhere. I looked at the *Home Sweet Home* sign hanging on the nail beside the slammed door and it did look ironic after all.

WE MADE UP LATER. Chris brought a bowl of dinner to me on the couch and put on a movie. She kissed my hands and my orange cast and asked if my foot was okay. I said yes, but I never was able to get that bit of glass out. I still feel it, every now and then.

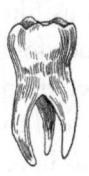

It took a few months before I found the job at the bookstore. I was surprised Marg hired me as such a recent come-from-away. But she said she was tired of running it by herself and no one else had applied, so I shouldn't be flattered.

The months before I was hired were strange for me. I'd never been unemployed or out of school for so long a stretch. I didn't know anyone in Creignish. It was too cold to plant anything other than garlic, which only took me a couple of hours. I didn't have lye to make soap and was too scared of it anyway after *Fight Club*. There were no berries on the branches to pick for jam. The autoharp looked at me out of its one judgmental eye like it knew I'd never learn to play it, like it was ready for me to give up the pretense and pass it on to someone who could love it right.

I did teach myself to bake scones, though they were rather dense. I did tramp back through the woods behind the house to a marshy spot, gently lift up logs and rocks, and note what I found beneath: two yellow-spotted salamanders, three red-backed salamanders, and in a puddle to my left, one frog that hopped away too fast for me to classify it as a leopard or a pickerel.

Here's what I mostly did while Chris was at work all day: obsess. Over various things—celebrity marriages, my softening jawline, first and middle names for our future children, whether I should get a perm, whether Avril Lavigne died and was replaced by a body double, and my friends' lives as filtered through internet feeds. I would sit with Della on the couch for hours, scrolling my phone until I got a headache and had to get up to drink water.

I left the house every now and then. Like when Chris dropped me off in Sydney for the day to have my cast cut off while she was at work. Afterward I ambled to the harbour and went into every single store along the way, killing time. A gift store, a bookstore, drug stores, a café. I got a secret fancy coffee with real milk for the first time since September. I felt that my bones needed the calcium. I wondered if my finger wouldn't have snapped had I not given it up.

I wandered until I reached the statue of a giant fiddle, where I took a selfie, holding up my un-casted hand, triumphant. I found a baby store and browsed and browsed, imagining all the bougie things I would buy for our future kid. The hand-painted wooden blocks, the felted bunnies, the organic cotton sleepers, the knitted hats. I looked at the price tags and thought it was a good thing my partner had a Real Job. For Dana's future baby I bought a moss green sleeper with red berries printed on the toes, and a balm for Dana's belly made of calendula and seaweed. I thought about buying another sleeper to match, but I didn't want to jinx it. Because what if, like the pictures of my friends, Chris had decided I couldn't have this other thing that I loved. That I wanted so badly to love.

I made myself get off the couch and go outside at least twice a week to walk along the highway. I stared at the ocean and at other people's houses because that's all there was to look at. I worried the neighbours would think I was weird, or lost. I wished I had some company. A tiny, sleepy companion bundled in a carrier, warm against my chest. All the neighbours would want to talk to me then, to ask how old my baby was, touch their tiny feet in tiny knitted boots, tell me they had my eyes. I imagined them turning from blue to green, as mine did.

I walked to the community hall across from the church and found a dirt trail behind it, which I followed for an hour until I came to an arm of beach reaching out from the land. It was early November and no one was around. I took off my sweater and jeans in the cold white light of the sun and waded into the numbing ocean until my legs felt like stilts. I could see the mainland across the water.

You can come back whenever you want, you know, Ruth had texted me after I wrote to her one afternoon that I was lonely. She and George still hadn't found a roommate. *I love it here*, I replied, *but I'll visit soon*. Halifax was less than a three-hour drive away but it felt farther, especially because Chris wouldn't let me drive. I wondered how long it would take me to swim across the Strait of Canso and walk the rest of the way. I'm sure someone would stop to pick up a soaking wet woman on the side of the road. Was that a good idea? The Ruth on my shoulder said no. I would give it a couple more months, I decided, and then ask Chris if we could make the trip down for a long weekend. Anyway, I was sure she'd want to visit her parents for Christmas.

This thought buoyed me and I dove. The cold closed my throat and silenced my brain. I opened my mouth and let the salt in. I saw my hands and strands of my hair in front of me, suspended in dark water and felt, for the few seconds before my legs forced me back to the surface, not lonely, but perfectly alone.

Glen's back to a pack a day. *Joanne's not happy about it but he's just* not ready. He says he needs to get through the holidays and then come January first he'll quit cold turkey. I told him I understood. Almost no one gets quitting right the first time.

Mme Comeau and Sophie were in earlier for the paper, lotto, and dog treats, and Lorraine for the paper, lotto, and smokes. Her hair is growing out again and the silver strip down the centre of her brilliant head makes her look mystical. Creignish could use a witch. I'd like to consult one. I should have taken Dana's advice and done that house cleansing spell. Maybe I can still do it before December.

Because in December we're flying to Ontario. Not on vacation. And not to visit my parents, of course. We're going to make a baby. I haven't told Ruth. I haven't told anyone.

Last December we drove back to the mainland for Christmas, as I'd hoped. I was dying to see my pack, but the idea of a week in

Chris's parents' too-hot house in Dartmouth stressed me right out. They keep the thermostat at twenty-seven degrees. Whenever we were there I would flush a deep burgundy and sweat through my shirt and chug glass after glass of ice water.

Chris's brothers didn't come. One lived in Alberta and one in Nebraska, each with a wife and a handful of kids. Chris listed all their names off to me once or twice, but since I'd never met them I couldn't keep them straight. I would have appreciated the natural buffer offered by a herd of children. But I supposed that since the TV was always on, I wouldn't be expected to talk much.

Dana had been sending me pictures of her belly. She was just starting to show. When I told her we were coming to town, she and Liam invited the pack and our plus-ones over for snacks and wine, and Chris surprised me by agreeing to come. She even signed the card I made to go with the gifts for Dana and her future baby.

I suggested we take the bus so we could get into the holiday spirit, i.e. wine, but Chris said she wanted to drive. Upstairs in her childhood bedroom I dressed in my party duds: a leopard skirt, black leggings, and a royal blue sweater. I brushed my teeth and daubed on dark lipstick. Downstairs, Chris was sitting in the living room with her dad, computer open on her lap while Nick watched football, each of them in an armchair. Della had come with us because we still didn't have any friends in Creignish to look after her, and she was sitting with Nick, eating a Dorito. I could hear Janet cooking in the kitchen.

I'm ready, I said, sweating in my sweater. Chris glanced up and said she just had to finish sending an email. I went to the kitchen and poured myself a glass of ice water. I asked Janet if I could help with anything but she said no, so I sat on the couch and watched football with Nick while Chris typed. At the commercial break I asked Chris if she was ready. Almost, she said, without looking up. Nick called to Janet for another beer.

Baby, I said quietly, can we please go soon? We're already late.

It's not a movie, Chris said. It's a party. We can be late.

Janet delivered the beer and Nick pointed to his empty Dorito bowl.

Ten minutes later Chris finished the email and went upstairs to get dressed. Fifteen minutes after that she came down in a button-up shirt and sweater, dark jeans, hair greased and combed. Nick had ordered two more beers from the kitchen in the meantime and passed one over to me, and I was chugging it on the couch to lower my core temperature, hating football a little less and Chris a little more as I neared the bottom of the can. I worried that I'd betrayed Janet and women in general by accepting it, ordered thusly by Nick, but my cheeks were throbbing. I held the can against them.

Let's go, Chris said, shaking her keys.

I downed the rest of the beer and ran to the kitchen to toss it in the recycling bin, scooted back to the front door, put on my shoes, and grabbed the present.

Chris was already in the car. You look handsome, I said as I got in, trying to lay the foundation for a pleasant evening. I directed her to Dana and Liam's. The sky was grey but it wasn't cold enough for snow. I flipped down the visor and looked at myself in the mirror. I'd left most of my lipstick on the beer can and had forgotten to bring the tube, so I wiped the rest off on the back of my hand.

Classy, Chris said.

You know me, I said.

When we arrived at the house it had just started to rain. I opened the front door without knocking, calling hello hello! But everyone was in the kitchen, laughing and talking loudly. Chris and I took off our wet shoes by the door and I led us down the hall to the kitchen doorway, blasted by the sound of Dana and Liam and Dana's sister Kendra, and Ruth and George, and Linh and Emma, all but Dana half drunk on mulled wine. Ruth saw me and slid from her perch on the counter to wrap me in a tight hug. She smelled like I remembered, amber perfume and rosemary shampoo. Linh yelled my name and ran over from their chair at the table, wrapping themselves around Ruth and I both, which I hoped would get a pass from Chris, being a group hug on a special occasion. Dana got up from her seat by the open window, ducking under our arms and popping up in the middle of the hug like a seal. We smiled at each other and swayed in a huddle like best friends at a middle school dance.

I heard Liam introduce himself to Chris and ask her if he could get her some wine.

Sounds like I need to catch up, she said.

Me too! I called.

I ran over to hug George hello while Liam ladled mugs of mulled wine. Linh grabbed my hand and pulled me over to the kitchen table to introduce me to Emma. She was so sweet, and I thought Chris would appreciate seeing that Linh had a girlfriend, that it might shake up her theory about Linh and me. Liam brought me a mug of wine and I hugged him in thanks. I introduced Emma to Chris. She's a lawyer, I said, thinking Chris would be impressed.

Oh, a liar? said Chris, a joke her dad would have made.

No, I said after no one laughed, the good kind. Emma works at Legal Aid.

To keeping criminals on the streets, Chris said, and raised her mug in toast. I smiled an apology at Emma and Linh. Emma asked Chris what she did, and Chris began to tell her about her job at the mill.

How are you, buddy? Linh asked me. Still jumping in the ocean?

No, I said, it's too cold now. You still biking?

Oh yeah, Linh said, gotta keep the biz going. I have studded tires.

Chris kept looking over at us while she talked to Emma about how paper is made, how the debarker and thermomechanical pulper work, blah blah. I could feel her listening to everything I said.

Chris and I are planning some home renos, I told Linh. I think we'll start ripping the old carpet off the stairs. The house is so old and interesting, you and Emma should come visit.

Cool, said Linh, for sure, we want to.

So, Chris said loudly. How did you two meet?

Emma smiled, flushed with wine and attention, and told the story of her mega crush on the babely bike courier. How after couriering everything she could think of, she eventually had her assistant call Linh and ask them to pick up two coffees from the café down the street and deliver them. And how, when Linh got to the office, Emma said one's for you if you like, and they sat on the stoop out back and drank their coffees in the autumn sun, and Emma said I have a crush on you, obviously, and Linh said oh me too, and that was that.

I had both my hands over my heart. I loved the story, loved hearing Emma tell it after already having heard the other side of it from Linh. You guysss, I said, that's beautiful! I picked up my mug and reached across the table to where Emma was sitting, and cheersed her.

Nice, said Chris, and then, like someone's weird aunt, asked, are you two exclusive?

Um, yep, said Emma.

Can I get anyone more wine? I asked. We brought a bottle to add to the pot.

Sure, said Linh.

I'll help you, said Chris.

I went to the counter where our bottle sat beside the stove and began to pick at the wrapper around the neck.

There's a proper way to do that, Chris said, picking up a corkscrew from the counter and taking the bottle out of my hands. She levered the knife open and cut the foil.

What's wrong? she asked me as she cut.

Nothing, I said. Though it was maybe a bit weird to ask if they're exclusive.

Why is that weird? Chris said. I don't know what dykes are doing these days.

Right well, Linh's not a dyke. I just mean, why do you need to know?

Chris looked at me as she twisted the screw. You know why, she said.

Dana appeared at the counter beside Chris and said she would cut another orange for the wine. Chris filled her own mug before pouring the rest into the pot. I remembered Dana's present, said I'd be right back, and went to find the bag in the hall by our shoes. I turned back for the kitchen, and there was Chris.

Oh, she said, looking at the gift in my hands. I didn't know where you were going.

Okay, I said, feeling like a leashed pet.

She led us back to the kitchen where Dana was dropping chunks of fruit into the hot wine and told her we had something for her. I held out the gift and Chris took it from me and passed it into her hands. Dana called Liam over and they opened it together. She twisted off the lid of the belly balm to smell it, and Liam held up the moss green sleeper and everyone aww'd at the tiny size of it and the berries printed on the toes, especially George, who adores babies.

Oh my gosh, he said. I can't wait to see your little one in that. Ruth smiled at him and squeezed his hand.

I guess you two won't be able to have kids, hey? Chris said, and took a mouthful from her mug.

All sounds stopped but the hiss of the simmering pot. Blood rushed to my face so fast it felt swollen. I looked at Chris and her wine-purple teeth, her half-focused eyes.

Excuse me? Ruth said.

What? said Chris. I just mean like, neither of you can get pregnant.

This was the time for me to say, Chris, that wasn't appropriate. To apologize to my friends and take Chris aside. I looked at Ruth, at her hurt and disgust. She looked at me and held up her empty hands.

Sorcha, she said.

My mouth was open in my swollen face, my eyes rattling around the room, knocking up against the staring eyes of all my friends.

Chris, I said, and turned to her.

What, she said again, like the sound of her name was a deep offense, like I should know better than to say it. I knew this was a bad idea, she said, downed her wine and set the mug on the counter with a hard clack. You're welcome for the gift, she told Dana and Liam, and turned to leave.

Linh and Emma stepped out of her way. I looked at Linh like they were a magic door that could reseal the circle and keep me here forever. Could I stay? Move into my old house with Ruth and George if Ruth would still have me, beg back my job, hope Chris would ship my stuff to me and not burn it? I heard the jingle of her keys in the hall, the shuffle of her shoes. She was drunk. And about to drive. I ran past Linh, out of the kitchen and into the hall just as Chris slammed the door behind her. I grabbed my shoes and ran in my socks out onto the wet stoop.

Chris! I called as she got into her car. I stumbled down the slick steps, across the seeping concrete, and knocked on the window in a panic. Chris, I shouted, crouched down and staring through the blur into the dark car at her furious slouch, my knuckles rapping against the streaming glass. She started the engine. Let me in, I yelled, please! She unlocked the door and I clambered into the car.

Baby, I pleaded, don't drive.

I'm fine, she said with her hands on the wheel, staring ahead into the rain.

Can't we call a cab? I beseeched her, my hands arranging themselves in prayer, thumbs pressed to my breastbone and fingertips jammed under my chin.

And come back *here* to pick up my car? Chris sneered, like *here* was a trap. No, she ruled, and threw the car into gear.

Can I drive, please, I tried. I didn't drink much, please?

Sorcha, she said, like my name was a knife she meant to cut me with. Shut. Up.

I felt my jaw lock and my mouth seal itself. I sat back in my seat and fumbled for the belt, clicked it into its holster and cradled my shoes on my lap like they were creatures I had sworn to protect.

We drove home in a barrage of rain beating down on the shell of the car, with the air at max blasting fog from the glass. Chris drifted across the lines and back again as we drove over the bridge, high above the dark harbour, and I squeezed my shoes in my hands and held my breath. I was sure she was going to scrape the car along the toll booth, she was so close, but somehow she didn't. She threw her coins in smoothly and floated on under the lifting barricade. Part of me hoped she would hit something, a curb or a sign or something small and non-sentient, to snap her out of it before we died, but a few minutes later we pulled into her parents' driveway, unscathed.

She was out of the car a second after she parked. I jammed my fingers into the seat belt button to release myself and sogged after her in my socks up the wet asphalt and across the stepping stones sunk into the dead December grass. I was afraid she was going to lock me out but she had only shut the door in my face and I was grateful.

Nick was still watching football with Della, his empty dinner plate on the table beside his armchair. Janet was cleaning in the kitchen. Hey, Nick said without turning from the screen. Hi Nick, I said shakily through my tight jaw, and placed my shoes safely on the mat by the door. I took off my sopping socks and cupped them in my hands, carrying them up the carpeted stairs. I wanted to wring them out in the bathroom sink but when I reached the top, I saw a line of light beneath the closed door. I went to Chris's room and sat on the edge of the bed holding my socks, drops of water slipping through my fingers onto my slick leggings and dripping from the ends of my hair, head bent, gazing into my cupped hands like I was holding the body of Christ, awaiting the cup of salvation.

I heard the lock pop on the knob of the bathroom door, the suck of the wood from the frame, and Chris's footsteps down the carpeted hall, at a pace that sounded calm.

Hey, she said. You look cold. Do you want to have a shower with me?

I wasn't cold but I was shaking. Okay, I said through closed teeth, all the muscles of my neck and shoulders and face winched tight. I followed her to the bathroom. She took the socks from my hands and threw them in the sink. She peeled my sweater off and slid my leggings and my clinging skirt down and dropped them onto the floor. My damp skin tightened and I shivered despite the house's oppressive heat. I held my arms over my breasts, my hands clasped under my jittering chin, while Chris ran the water. She stripped off her own damp clothes and led me into the steaming shower.

The water was almost too hot to touch. I held my hands open against it to protect my body from the shock and then slowly leaned in, letting it drum into my skull, hoping it would blast everything that had just happened out of my head and limbs and down the drain.

Chris wrapped her arms around me from behind and kissed my neck.

I didn't mean for us to leave the party like that, she said into my ear. I tried to talk to your friends but I feel like they're always waiting for me to fuck up.

That's not true, I said, water beating into my chest.

You wish Emma was your girlfriend, with her cool job. I know you're embarrassed of what I do.

That's not true, I said again.

I try to fit in with your friends. I try so hard. But you all make me so fucking self-conscious and then I say something wrong and everyone looks at me like I'm the enemy.

Chris, they don't.

Maybe you should just break up with me, she said, holding me so tight my lungs hurt.

I struggled to turn around inside the slippery circle of her arms. Her face was wet from the spray but I could see that she was crying. It scared me, as if all of a sudden our house was streaming water from the ceiling and the wooden beams had gone soft and were buckling under the weight. I'd never seen her do more than wipe away a few stoic tears. I didn't know this face, pinched and grimacing, lips drawn back, shrinking down like she was being crushed from above. She sat on the shower floor and I sat down with her, holding her arms as she sobbed, saying baby baby into her broken face, hot water raining down on our heads.

You'll leave me, she said, her voice wet and cracking. Like Amy did.

I won't, I said, holding her arms tight, pressing them in toward her body like I was afraid they'd fall off.

Aren't I good to you? Don't we have a good life? A nice house? She looked up at me through her dripping hair, cheeks red and eyes swollen. I held her face in my hands, trying to smooth it back into its usual shape. I wrapped my arms and legs around her, lifting myself into her lap.

Of course you're good to me, I said into her neck. I had done this to her, let her get so hurt. I should have worked harder to make a space where she felt safe enough to be herself, the sweet parts only I got to see.

But do you love me?

Of course I do, I said.

Chris pulled back from my clasping limbs and looked at me like she was about to drown.

You can't leave me, she said. I'll die.

I could see my own tiny face reflected in her wet eyes.

Sorcha, she said. I need you. Promise me.

I nodded my head and kissed her, water streaming into my eyes and ears and mouth. I promise, I said, and felt holy, like I had saved her.

Dana and Linh *texted me that night to ask if I was okay. Ruth did not.* In the morning I wrote her a long apology while Chris was in the bathroom. I said Chris was sorry too, that she had been drunk and anxious and wasn't thinking. Hours later Ruth wrote back *Yeah, okay Sorch, I'd rather hear it from Chris if I thought she was actually sorry. I love you but I'm hurt. And I'm worried about you.*

Of course Chris was sorry, I thought, but she would feel too vulnerable to say it. If only I hadn't let this happen. I couldn't think of how to reverse it, how to mend it. So I said nothing.

When we got back to Cape Breton I sent Ruth a picture of the winter ocean, and of a pie I baked, and a video of Della hunting a moth. Over the next month we slowly got back to talking, but I could feel she was far away, farther than the three-hour drive. Like she knew I wasn't telling her my whole truth and didn't trust me anymore with hers.

On the couch in the parlour with Della in my lap, I looked Ruth up on my phone and scrolled through her grid of photos like a jealous lover. She and Dana and Linh lacing up their skates at the Oval the night before, cheeks bright with cold. I loved skating and none of them had texted me to say they wished I was there. Maybe they didn't wish I was there, anymore.

Loneliness squeezed my throat and I cried shakily onto the cat. She jumped off my legs and padded over to the wood stove, sat down, and stared at me. What? I said to her, sniffing thickly. She curled up on the floor in the glow of heat and closed her eyes.

Fuck, compose yourself, I commanded.

I shuffled to the kitchen in my slippers and turned on the tap, filled my hands with icy water, and baptized my face. I leaned under the faucet and filled my mouth, swallowing and swallowing and swallowing like I was trying to flush myself clean. I pressed my face dry with the dishcloth and looked out the window, down the empty driveway lined with birch trees, bare of leaves.

You should go outside, I whispered.

I slid my arms into my coat sleeves, hauled on my boots, and pulled a hat over my greasy hair, wet at the ends from the sink. I couldn't find my mitts so I pulled down my sweater sleeves and balled the fabric in my fists. See you, I said to Della, and went out the door.

The icy air slowed the swelling of my eyelids and froze the ends of my hair to points. It hurt to let it in through my nose so I breathed through my mouth instead, surrounding my face in fog. The deep trenches of the driveway from a hundred years of wheels were filled with ice and crusted with salt, which I had shaken down its length before Chris left for work that morning. I crunched along one of the ruts, waiting to see the ocean rise up across the highway. I felt I needed to be colder, more than my face in the sink and the wind biting my cheeks. Ocean cold. Dark and underwater, alone on purpose.

I walked past the houses of neighbours I still hadn't met. A small dog barked at me from a picture window. In the cemetery beside the church, Jesus hung on his cross at the top of the hill, frozen in sacrifice. I stared at his nakedness in the frigid air and considered that maybe I didn't need to be colder, after all. Maybe I didn't need to be underwater.

I crossed the road and walked down the gravel driveway of the community hall, a squat box with vinyl siding, a brick chimney, three windows, a blue door. The clouds hung low and leaden over the water, the gulls seeming to glide just beneath, their voices cracking over the roll and hush of the waves.

On the wall beside the door of the hall was a plastic sheet in a frame with pieces of paper beneath it, a bulletin board of sorts. Maybe it would tell me how to make friends here. I sidled over to it, glad no one was around to see me care. Through the condensation on the inside of the plastic I could see pages printed from a printer low on ink: one for a free square dance workshop next Friday, one for a fishcake and bean supper on Saturday, and one for Chase the Ace every Sunday.

Could I square dance? It seemed like the thing to do around here, but Chris would never let me go alone. I wondered whether I could convince her to come. I wondered how the other square dancers would take to two queer come-from-aways. We'd talked about it a bit before we moved. It would be fine, Chris said, but she grew up in Dartmouth so what does she know. I grew up in a town with eight churches in a one-kilometre radius and under two thousand people, and didn't come out until nearly a decade after I left. Creignish was even smaller than Chesley.

In the corner of the bulletin board was one more page, written by hand in slanty half-calligraphy. *Wanted,* it said, *friendly man or woman (woman preferred) to work at Marg's Convenience & Curiosities in Judique. Full-time. Call and ask for Marg.*

I appreciated the unabashed gender preference. And actually, I'd been to the store. On a weekend in November Chris and I had driven up the western shore to hike the Skyline Trail, and I'd forgotten our water bottles because that's the kind of thing I do, unfortunately. We were only ten minutes from home, driving past the church in Judique, when I realized I'd left them on the kitchen counter. Before Chris could work up a fury I pointed out the hand-painted sign for Marg's on the roadside. In seafoam paint against the dark wood it read: *Pop, smokes, lotto, books, crafts, maps*

& FIREWORKS, in bold all-caps as if to say LAST, BUT NOT LEAST.

We pulled in five minutes later and there was Marg. I knew because I said so are you Marg? as I placed two water bottles on the counter, also seafoam green. Marg inhaled her yes the way Islanders do. It was still early morning and her tea steamed beside the till in a clay mug. She wore a pilled oatmeal sweater and purple-rimmed glasses. I asked if the oatcakes on the stand beside the counter were made with butter. No dear, said Marg, shortening. I put those on the counter too, and looked at the other baked goods: molasses cookies, brown bread, buttermilk scones. My mouth welled. Buttermilk. If only. I glanced at the little round table beside the bread shelf, jumbled with crafts, and the wall of books at the back. I paid for the water and oatcakes, took my change, said my thanks, and hustled back to the car.

I didn't have a pen to take down Marg's handwritten number, so I dug my phone out of my coat pocket. The cold had sucked away its battery, but just before it died I took a picture of the ad and another of the heavy grey sky, hanging like a stone hammock over the churning ocean.

I did not walk to the arm of beach and wade into the freezing water. I went home, plugged in my dead phone, put on the kettle, and dropped a split log into the stove. When I was warm and composed, my stomach full of tea and Della back on my lap, I called Marg's store and she answered. I told her I'd been there in the fall, and that I'd seen her ad. I said I'd like to apply for the job, could I bring in my resume? She told me to drop in anytime for a chat. No one had applied yet and she was sixty-seven this year, she said, and needed to spend less time behind the till and more with her grandkids.

When Chris got home from work, I told her about the job. The store was only a fifteen-minute drive north, I said, and it would be nice for me to have something to do during the day.

Can't you look for a job between here and Port Hastings, Chris asked as she poured herself a glass of wine at the counter, so I can drop you off on my way to work? I'm sure some other convenience store is hiring.

It's not just a convenience store, I said. It sells books too. We stopped there on the way to the Skyline Trail, remember?

Chris relented. She admitted a job would do me good. She helped me print off my resume in her office beside the kitchen, and left work at five the next day so she could drive me to the store before it closed at six. You're the best, I crooned, kissing her cheeks and hands and thanking her over and over until she said okay that's enough.

GOOD EVENING DEAR, MARG SAID when I came through the door, the bell ringing over my head. She was reading a book behind the counter, a mug of tea beside her, her purple glasses low on her nose. It was nearly February and the sun had already set. I'd washed and brushed my hair and curled my eyelashes, wanting to look wholesome and dependable. I offered her my hand to shake and gave her my resume. I told her we'd had the oatcakes when we stopped in last and that they were perfect. I said I'd love to work here, that it was just what I needed. She looked at the stapled pages I'd handed her through her low-set lenses.

Well, she said, looks like you're probably smart enough to work the till. A degree in environmental studies. And you were a researcher?

Yes, I said, back in Halifax.

Did you come here with your man, then? she asked.

No, I said, and drew a long breath before I told her I came with my partner. She's working at the paper mill, I said, watching Marg's face to see how the pronoun landed.

Marg sort of tilted her head to one side and looked at me for a second. Well you know, she said, my granddaughter tells me she's a bisexual so it's nothing to me. When could you start?

Tomorrow, I said with a smile.

Let's do Monday, said Marg. Come at seven so I can show you the ropes before we open at eight. And bring your own mug.

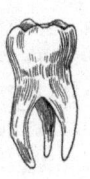

picked up on the workings of the store quickly enough, but the local accent took me longer. Like what the heck was a boonabraid? I heard it first from a twentysomething blond dude who drove to the store on his ATV in a Realtree coat and matching hat. He said he was looking for a boonabraid but seen we was out. I said sorry, what were you looking for? And pardon? when he said it again. He laughed at me and said don't worry about it, just a pap and smokes.

Everyone who came in asked where's Marg and who might you be and where're you from, until all the regulars knew I was Sorcha from the mainland, that I lived in Creignish near to the church, that my folks were in Ontario, and that I didn't have a man. Now that I've been working here nearly a year, I know Realtree wants a bun of bread, that is, a loaf, with his pop and smokes. And word's gotten out that though I don't have a man, I have a woman. The possessive localism doesn't sound particularly feminist, but it goes both ways and to be honest, I don't really care. Mme Comeau and some of the grey-haired Catholic crowd were weird about it at first, my woman, but Mme Comeau seems to have come around.

On Sundays the store is closed. Marg still works Saturdays and covers my vacations. Since our trip back to the mainland last Christmas, Chris and I have only vacationed on the Island. Three days in the Highlands in the fall, hiking through the park and driving up to Meat Cove just to say we'd been, and a week in Ingonish in the summer.

Ingonish was like a honeymoon. After I'd chosen Chris over my friends and promised myself to her on the shower floor, and we survived our first winter in our old cold house, spring and summer were a breeze. Once the leaves started to bud on the trees, the Times Things Happen became fewer. I know because I started marking them on the calendar in my journal. The journal is just for sketches and house plans, ideas for the garden. I don't actually journal in it because I know Chris reads it. And because of that, the way I mark Times is discreet: a dot in the upper right corner of the calendar cell to show that, on this day, I did something Chris did not like and I cried.

I started marking Times after we returned to Creignish from Chris's parents' house. We were sitting on the couch on New Year's Eve by the blazing wood stove, a glass each into our second bottle of sparkling wine. I was loose enough that I said baby, for our resolution this year I would really love if we could fight less. And Chris said what do you mean, fight.

I froze. Say it, said the one worker in my brain who is always trying to get me to say stuff, while the other workers furiously fired off messages to various parts of my body to abort abort abort.

I feel like, I said, looking into my glass like it was full of tea leaves and I knew how to read them. I feel, I said again. Bubbles released themselves from the sides of the glass and expired on the surface. The log in the stove popped so loudly that Della was startled off the couch. I closed my eyes. I feel like you get upset with me a lot, I said. I opened my eyes and turned to look at Chris. Her face looked like I'd thought it might but hoped it wouldn't. I'd hoped that her raw need and my salvational love on the shower floor a week earlier had changed something, had formed a new alliance between us, but the look on her face said it was not enough.

I won't recite the play-by-play as it's a bit fuzzy now, but by midnight I was crying in the freezing basement beside the washing machine, after having agreed with Chris that it was only me who needed to make a resolution, and that resolution was to stop being so goddamn self-involved. If I could make good on this, there would be no need for her to get upset. I had blown things up in my mind, she explained, imagined we had some big problem when we barely ever fought. Did I really think it happened a few times a week? It was more like a couple times a month at most. My negativity had amplified things, as usual.

I wondered if that was true. The days when I was jobless were like a knotless rope, frayed and unravelling. I couldn't trust myself to remember what had happened further back than the day before. So in defense of my sanity, the worker who made me say the thing told me to draw the dots. And it turned out I was right. Each month I did the math: the median and the mean. The January mean was four times per week; the median was three. February and March were the same. The consistency was almost reassuring. But when the crocuses pushed through the crust of dead leaves that covered our yard, the weekly mean dropped to three, and in May to two. By summer it was one, and I felt like maybe I was our saviour after all, that Chris had heard me even though she'd said out loud that I was wrong. And I stuck to the resolution I'd agreed to, or at least I did my best, which may have helped. I read vegan blogs and cooked us interesting new dinners. I wrote sweet notes and left them in Chris's lunch bag. I returned all of her texts within the minute. I kept the house so clean that if Ruth were to come for a visit (in an alternate reality in which I hadn't betrayed her), she would have been very impressed.

I was in a healthy relationship. Not a secret high-school relationship with a girlfriend who had a boyfriend. Not a relationship in which I was pushed into walls. A healthy adult relationship in which my dashing partner with a stable job got me up on Saturday mornings to go for runs in the woods behind our house, in which we discussed whether to paint the parlour dove or biscuit white, in which we brought our cat to the vet for regular checkups and gave her worm pills because she'd killed all of our mice. In which I only cried an average of once per week. It was in this oasis of health that we started to plan for a baby.

We were in Ingonish in July and the lupins were out. I had booked us a suite above a café off the Cabot Trail. The cedar shakes of the old house were painted pale yellow and the lupins in all shades of purple swayed thickly around it like a garden of fingers. When we pulled up, Chris rolled her eyes and said you would, this is a hipster paradise. I said if you're too cool for the adorable B&B, I believe that makes you the hipster. You think it's easy to find a place in Cape Breton that serves almond milk lattes and tofu scramble?

Chris smiled and leaned over to kiss me. Thanks for booking it, Sorch, she said.

I was so in love with her. Every morning that week we came down from our airy bedroom to the café, drank our almond-milk lattes, which were delicious in spite of their milklessness, ate our breakfasts, and walked to the beach. Compared to the mainland beaches, where my pack and I used to go for summer swims, the water at Ingonish was like a bath. We stroked back and forth parallel to the shore, and Chris held me in her arms in the water like I was her new wife and she wanted to carry me everywhere. We read books on our beach blankets and ate strawberries. We drank wine from our water bottles and took pictures of ourselves kissing. I thanked whoever— the universe, maybe fate, or even God—for bringing Chris to me and making her kind.

Chris looked at me like I was a babe. She said damn you look good in that bathing suit, and wow you're beautiful, and when did you get so hot? I felt like over the winter she had forgotten what I looked like. To be fair, I did mostly wear sweatpants and wool sweaters, and from January to March we'd had sex an average of once per month, under the covers in our frigid house. I know because I marked it with a dot in the top left corner of the calendar cell each time it happened. But in the salty summer air, on our crisp white bed at the B&B, against its driftwood headboard, Chris fucked me perfectly every night and sometimes in the mornings. It was like our sex at the very beginning. In the fresh bed in which we'd never slept back to back, on the plump pillows onto which I'd never wept, I could forget everything and come with abandon.

We were falling asleep on our last night in Ingonish, lightly sunburnt and radiating heat, the salt air floating in through the open window and kissing our shoulders. My lips buzzed from the scrape of Chris's teeth. My thighs were slippery from our sex. I love you, I said to her, meaning it with my whole body, trying to distill it into my breath so she could inhale it. I smoothed the hair from her forehead and looked into her eyes. I thought, this is the real Chris, I've saved her from whatever had its hold on her, whatever curse that plagued her, whatever demons or trauma that made her mean. I wanted to lock her in this form, fix her in this state. Braid an invisible tether between our eyes so the next time she was angry, I could tug on it by looking at her and she would come back to me.

I want to have a baby with you, I said.

She took my face in her hands. I need to have a baby with you, she said. Let's do it this winter and have her by next fall.

My eyes welled and tears slid sideways across my face. Really? I asked, beaming at her in the twilight.

Yeah, she said. I already found a clinic.

THE BEST CLINIC, CHRIS SAID, was in Toronto. I looked it up: it was a two-and-a-half hour drive from my parents' house in Chesley, the closest I will have been to them since I went home for my dad's sixtieth birthday five years ago. Chris and I made our baby plans on the drive home from Ingonish. By winter we could save up some money, but Jesus Christ not nearly enough. Chris had worked it out: econo return flights for $1,000, a $500 clinic registration fee, $1,400 for the sperm plus shipping from the States, where the good stuff comes from—clinics in Canada aren't allowed to pay for it and why would you jerk off into a cup for free, I guess—plus $1,200 to feed it into my uterus through a teeny tiny straw. Plus tax. So about $5,000, all told. And then because it usually takes three to six tries before you're knocked up, possibly $30,000 by the end, more than the cost of my still-outstanding student loans.

I couldn't believe what it cost to make a baby when straight people were just making them willy-nilly for free. I asked Chris if we could try to find someone who would just give us their sperm, or if we could pay them illegally. It wasn't any worse than buying weed from your neighbourhood dealer, right? Like, you're not really supposed to do it but don't we all?

Chris said no. I would always be the baby's mother, she told me, but her tie would be more tenuous, and she didn't want a known donor to call it into question. To Chris, a known donor was a potential dad just waiting in the wings to collect his rightful child through some dramatic lawsuit. Did I want to put her and our kid through that? Did I?

What about one of your brothers, I asked, then we'd both be related to the baby. I felt like a genius for suggesting it, but Chris said it was gross. And anyway, she said, their wives would never agree.

Adoption? I asked, betraying my body. I could feel it waiting, working to build the softest, richest home. Maybe this was why it wouldn't drop those last five pounds. I felt, with a creepy certainty, that I would get pregnant on the first try, despite the odds. That because I wanted it so badly and my body had been waiting so patiently, it couldn't help but take.

Listen, Chris said, I know it's a lot of money, but I have a good job. The clinic in Toronto has great reviews. We can have a baby that's just ours, that will make us a family forever.

A family forever.

Those two words were little pins in my heart. It was a nice idea, truly, and what I'd always wanted. But also it terrified me. Because what if you don't want to be a family forever after all? There's nothing like a child to stitch you to someone for life.

Chris reached over and grabbed my hand, and I squeezed back and smiled at her. I felt like we were about to leap through a portal to the future, but what if we'd picked the wrong door?

ON THE MONDAY AFTER WE got home from Ingonish, Chris made an appointment at the clinic and booked our flights, and I called Marg to ask for two days off, the second Thursday and Friday in December. That's a ways away, she said. I know, I said, it's a special trip.

And then we browsed donor profiles like we were trolling the apps for a threesome. *Ezra's green eyes pop against his smooth, tan skin, he is 6'0" and fit, he plays basketball and speaks fluent Russian. Jacob has a Roman nose and dimples and enjoys swimming and mountain biking, he is in graduate school studying music. Aaron has sparkling brown eyes and a bubbly personality and is working toward a PhD in math.*

Who wrote these profiles, I wondered. And also, how many other couples were going to end up with a dimpled musical baby who likes to swim? How would we make sure our kid didn't accidentally fall in love with their half-sibling? Would we have to make all their dates take a DNA test?

After a week, we found the one. Andrew—probably a fake name. Of all the donors we perused, he sounded the most like Chris. Brown eyes, brown hair, slim build. A runner, great. He liked to cook Italian food. And he was an engineering student. Chris selected one unit of sperm to be shipped to the clinic. I was sitting beside her on the couch while she typed her credit card number into her laptop, and I asked if we could pay the extra $20 for a picture of Andrew as a baby. She looked at me like I had asked if I could just have sex with him and get pregnant that way.

No, she said.

That's fine, I smiled, not wanting to ruin the moment like I somehow always managed to. It's better if we don't see it, right?

Chris placed the order and didn't talk to me for the rest of the day. But I didn't cry about it so I only marked a very small dot in the upper right corner of the calendar cell.

Maybe my magic wanes with the sun. Maybe the cold draws something sinister from Chris's core. Or maybe she has seasonal affective disorder, I don't know. Fall is usually my favourite time of year, but the leaves turned amber and burnt orange and brick and by the time they dropped, the weekly mean had risen to three.

We haven't had sex in over a month. And Chris reminded me last week that I was not adhering to my resolution. I forgot to clean Della's litter box two mornings in a row. I left that hummus-coated spoon in the sink. And I wanted to abandon her to visit my friends, who hate her. So I guess I only have myself to blame for her moods. Maybe the cold weather makes me selfish. Maybe that's it.

But you know who's really selfish, says a worker in my brain. Babies. Children. If one dirty sink spoon set Chris off, how would she react to a bin full of soiled diapers, a needy mouth attached to my tit? Squash puree on the floor and jammy fingerprints on the walls? How would Chris send pre-dinner emails amid the sounds of a fussing baby, or the clanging exuberance of a toddler? And for that matter, how would she sleep? Hush, I say to the worker, people adapt. Yes, the worker says, but sometimes they don't.

AFTERNOONS AT THE BOOKSTORE ARE slow once tourist season ends. My morning regulars have been and gone. I've restocked the pop fridge and dusted the shelves. I've eaten my boring wrap. And a secret buttermilk scone. And a Caramel Log. I'm a terrible person. The wind is so strong today. It blows through the cracks between the windows and the jambs and whistles and moans all around me, like I'm inside a giant bottle played by an enormous mouth.

For something to do I type Dana's handle into my phone and it produces a collage of her life. I scroll back in time. Dana and Liam and baby Oscar, now five months old. Oscar in a pile of leaves. Oscar in a pumpkin patch. Oscar petting a cat. Oscar in the bath. Oscar asleep. A hundred perfect Oscars, none of whom I've held. A brand-new Oscar against Liam's bare chest. The bouquet of tulips I sent when he was born in early summer. Dana's swollen belly when he was still inside it, and another and another, her belly smaller and smaller as I scroll back. A waiting bassinet. A well-poured decaf cappuccino. Dana and Liam at the lake. Me, Linh, Dana, and Ruth tangled on the couch on my last night. Dana and her sister on a hike. Dana and her parents eating lunch.

That would be nice. To have a sister with whom I would hike, parents with whom I would lunch. I would like, from time to time, to be able to peer in on my family as I do my friends. To see what Bonnie cooked for dinner, how much hair my father has left, whether Aileen is married yet. Sometimes I creep her Facebook but she mostly uses it for evangelism so I can't glean much.

After my final call with Bonnie, Aileen sent me an email. They'd clearly spoken, and Aileen said many of the same things our mother had: that this wasn't the real me, that I could resist sin, that God would forgive me but only if I repented right now, a time-limited offer that I personally did not recall reading about in the Good Book, though I hadn't read it recently so I supposed Aileen was the authority.

The bell above the door sounds and a woman wrapped in rust and ochre plaid comes in. She wears faded jeans and scuffed boots, her silver hair loosely plaited.

Good morning, I say, and she smiles.

Mateen va, she says.

A tourist I guess, though it's late in the season for them. Is that Russian? I guess aloud.

Gaelic, the woman says with a smile. For good morning.

Oh, of course, I say, feeling foolish, though I haven't heard much Gaelic since we moved here. Will you say it again, I ask her. I feel that I should know at least this. She says it again and I ask if she would mind writing it down so I can remember.

The woman comes over to the counter and I give her a pen and tear a page from the notepad we use for recording low stock. Madainn mhath, she writes.

I never would have guessed it was spelled that way, I say. I tell her I'd like to learn Gaelic but don't know any more than my own name.

And what's that, asks the woman.

Sorcha, I reply.

Interesting that you say it Sor*sha*, she says. Traditionally it would be an *r* like this, tapped on the roof of your mouth with the tip of your tongue, and then a short *ah*, a soft *ch* in the throat, as in *loch*, then *ah* again. Sorcha, Sorcha, she says to me slowly.

I try to say my name the way it's meant to be said, but it sounds spitty and harsh. It might be too late for me, I tell her.

Keep practicing, says the woman. Though Sorsha is very pretty. I'm Linda. She holds out her hand and I shake it. She asks if my family is Scottish, and I tell her my mother was born there but moved to Canada with my grandparents as a baby.

And how did your grandparents say your name?

I try to think back. I can't remember, I say. But I have an aunt who still lives in Scotland, I think. Maybe she would say it right.

Lovely, Linda says. She asks if I've ever been and I tell her I haven't. Neither has she, but she's always watching for seat sales to Glasgow. Her Gaelic comes from her parents, her family among the first to come to Cape Breton in the late 1700s from the Isle of Skye. For six months of each year she works at the living history museum in

Iona, making her home in a grass-roofed stone cottage. The tourists love to hear her speak.

I'm the village spinster, she says wryly.

No pretend husband? I ask.

No time for a husband, real or pretend, she says. I comb, card, spin, and weave wool all day. A spinster in the truest sense.

Right on, I say, down with husbands. I think of the book I've been reading about Inverness County, now hidden under the microwave in the back room. Do you have fulling frolics? I ask.

Every afternoon at three, she smiles. They're popular with visitors.

And did you make this? I nod at her wrap.

I did, she says. Dyed the wool with roots and flowers and wove it on a loom in my little cottage.

Wow, I say. I'm jealous of this woman, living the anachronistic rural life of my dreams while I track the number of carrot sticks I've eaten in my healthy living app.

Then my phone pings like a recess bell, signalling that social time is over. Sorry, I say, and pick up the phone to reply to Chris. Linda waves it off and walks to the humming fridge, dislodges a Coke, and picks up a box of scones.

I don't usually drink this stuff, she says when she returns to the counter, as if she owes me an explanation. But I like to mark my return to the twenty-first century with something modern and unhealthy. She winks and passes me a ten. I hand her the change. I wish she would stay and talk to me for the whole afternoon.

Bayanach lat, Sorcha, she says as she walks toward the door, her silver braid slipping back over her shoulder as she turns with a wave.

That was the best conversation I've had in months. I would search for a translation of what she last said but don't have a sweet clue how to spell it. Then I remember the little book I haven't yet read on the back wall, a beginner's guide to Scots Gaelic. I find it beside an illustrated history of kitchen cèilidhs. I flip to basic phrases. Ceud mìle fàilte, the only one I know because it's almost a cliché around here. Ciamar a tha thu for how are you, and madainn mhath for good morning, which Linda wrote down for me. Feasgar math for good afternoon and good evening, oidhche mhath for good night, and there, her parting words: beannachd leat, blessings with you.

I hope she'll be back. I'm in bad need of a friend.

My phone pings again and I drop the book like a caught thief. Chris is having a shitty day at work. I try to think of what I could make for supper to soothe her. Butternut squash soup would be comforting, and a squash has been waiting on our kitchen counter for something to happen to it. I send heart emojis and suggest soup.

I pick the book up off the floor. The pronunciations are spelled phonetically beside the phrases and I sound them out slowly into the empty store. By six I've had only four other customers and have made it halfway through the thin book. I decide to buy it, because I want to read it at home and also because I dropped vegan mayo from my lunch onto a page of questions that felt like a call out: Are you hungry? A bheil an t-acras ort? Are you thirsty? A bheil am pathadh ort? Are you happy? A bheil thu toilichte? I ask the questions out loud to no one. Or maybe to myself.

Chris pulls up as I turn the key to lock the shop door. I open the door to the car and get in. Feasgar math, I say, feeling clever.

Pardon, says Chris, throwing the car into reverse.

I repeat the phrase. It's Gaelic, I say, for good evening.

Why, says Chris.

I hold up the little book. A customer came in today and taught me how to pronounce my name right. Sorcha, Sorcha, I say, trying to make the new sounds with my throat and tongue. She works at the history museum in Iona, and speaks Gaelic to the tourists. She spins wool and wove her own shawl on a loom. Isn't that cool?

So what, Chris says, you want to learn Gaelic so you can talk to this woman? How old is she?

Uh, I say, a bit surprised, though I really should have seen it coming. Chris's jealousy hangs over us like a long shadow. She's old, I say reassuringly. I don't know, sixty or something.

Huh, Chris says, eyes on the road.

There are other people on Cape Breton who speak Gaelic. And my mum was born in Scotland, remember?

I thought you hated your mother, says Chris.

I wouldn't say hate. It's complicated. I might have an aunt in Scotland still, maybe she speaks it. Maybe I could teach our baby, I dunno. It's fun to learn something new. Keeps my brain fresh or whatever.

Okay, Chris says, in a way that is clearly meant to be the last word of this conversation. I sit back in my seat and look out the window into the dark.

I hadn't thought about having a crush on Linda, but after Chris's suggestion I consider it. Sixty isn't so old. Twice my age, but does that really matter? I imagine learning Gaelic and getting a job with Linda at the museum, playing two village spinsters, very close friends. The other villagers would whisper about us. Maybe they would stage a trial and burn us at the stake as a tourist spectacle. A crush on Linda wouldn't be hard to cultivate. She was kind to me and I'm hungry, thirsty for it.

*I*n the past week I've read through the little book twice. *I practice what I might say to Linda if she comes in again. Ciamar a tha thu?* And, *tha mi gu math, tapadh leat.* The snow that fell yesterday is still on the ground, instead of melting within a day like each time it snowed in November. *Tha i fuar an-diugh*, I say into the empty store in the direction of the door, imagining Linda has just walked through it. And over and over, I try to say my name.

Chris and I will fly to Ontario on Thursday. She put an app on my phone so I can chart my cycle. It says I'll pop an egg out on Friday. I wonder if it's right.

I keep thinking back to when we planned this, how the salt air felt on my sunburned shoulders, the taste of Chris's strawberry breath when we kissed. I miss kissing. I guess we're lucky we don't need to have sex to get pregnant.

When we planned it in Ingonish, I thought I could see us five months hence, curled up on the couch with Della, drinking a final glass of wine in front of the crackling wood stove and dreaming up names like spells, a garland of letters to wrap around our future kid. Maybe we'd even make a new last name that all three of us would share, and truly start fresh. I would teach myself to knit a blanket, Chris would build a crib. We would paint the little upstairs room beside ours yellow and lay a sheepskin rug on the floor, find an old rocking chair at some roadside antiques barn. Our house warm and waiting for new life.

But the more I think about how I thought it would be, the heavier my limbs feel, the emptier my stomach. I've been going through a lot of milk. I told Marg she should start deducting it from my pay.

On Saturday morning Chris said I hate you, you fucking bitch.

I remember the sentence exactly, because we parsed it. I was washing dishes from our breakfast and the previous night's dinner, setting the glasses upside down on a tea towel to dry. Chris put her phone down on the edge of the crowded countertop and poured herself a cup of coffee. She reached to grab the phone but knocked it onto the tile floor instead, where it landed with a crack.

Fuck, Sorcha! she said.

I stared at her, mouth wide. I was wearing rubber gloves and the kitchen smelled of lemon soap.

If you weren't taking up the whole goddamn counter my phone wouldn't be on the floor, she said. Why can't you do the dishes after dinner instead of leaving them till the fucking morning?

Chris, I said, unable to wipe my quick tears with the soapy gloves. It's not my fault.

I hate you, she said, looking in my eyes. You fucking bitch.

I can't believe you just said you fucking hate me, I choked.

And like a stoic linguistics professor, Chris said no, I didn't say fucking hate. I said I hate you, you fucking bitch.

I felt sick and knelt on the floor. I took off my gloves and cried into my hands. Chris put her cracked phone into her pocket.

I'm going to Sydney to get a new phone, she said calmly. I could barely hear her over my obnoxious keen, leaking out of me like air from a hole. I heard her go out the door, start the car, and roll down the crunching gravel. I lay on the floor like it was my bed and stared at the dust under the refrigerator. I stared until my tears stopped and my breath slowed. I thought about getting up, but couldn't. My body was too tired, too leaden, too hated. All the workers were lying down too, on the floor of my brain.

After a while, Della came over and pushed her cheeks into my head. I was jealous of her. What was her trick for incurring no wrath? Not talking, maybe. Being a cat. A couple of weeks ago she'd knocked Chris's water glass off her bedside table and it broke on the floor. Chris said Del-LA in mock exasperation as the cat scampered from the room. Then she picked up the pieces, sopped up the puddle, and got back into bed like nothing had happened. It wasn't fair. But then I thought maybe it was a good sign, because if Della doesn't drive Chris up the wall like I do, perhaps our future baby would get a pass too.

CHRIS CAME BACK HOURS LATER. I had put all the dishes away and was making sweet potato ravioli, folding the pasta up like prayers. Please be kind to me, please be kind, I thought into the little pockets before I pinched them shut. When Chris came up behind me my shoulders rose as if to guard my neck, but she wrapped her arms around my waist and kissed my nape. I got a nice Sangiovese, she said. It'll pair perfectly. I allowed myself a small smile. My prayers appeared to be working.

The ravioli were amazing. Chris said so. And the wine was delicious. As we ate, I looked across the table and said so what about names? We hadn't thought of any yet. Chris's mouth was full so I said what about Ryan, or Robin? They'd work whatever the baby's gender. Chris swallowed and said that was very modern of me. What about family names, she suggested, like after my parents.

There was no way I was going to grow a human being inside my body, rip myself open squeezing it out into the world, and name it Nick or Janet. But I thought one fight was enough for a Saturday so I said maybe.

ON WEDNESDAY NIGHT CHRIS DOUBLE-CHECKS our shared suitcase. We'll only be gone four days so we're packing light. The list she prepared reads, for each of us: *two pairs of pants, one sweater, three shirts, three pairs of socks, three pairs of underwear, pajamas.*

While Chris takes inventory of our clothes, I clean. I put away the dinner dishes that I washed immediately after we ate. I run a cloth along the countertop. Under the shelf holding my last precious jar of jam, I see a soft shape affixed to the corner where the wood meets the wall, a gossamer sac of what must be baby spiders. I tear a sheet of paper towel from the roll and step toward the sac, but I can't make my hand reach up and wipe it away. I don't really want a hundred baby spiders in the house, but still I can't.

We'll fly to Toronto from Sydney. It feels strange to be headed so close to my parents' realm. If Bonnie got wind I was travelling to a fertility clinic with my lesbian partner, she'd probably arrange for a pop-up exorcism. So I haven't told anyone who might tell my mother. I haven't told anyone at all. The disgruntled worker in the back cubicle of my brain keeps telling my thumbs to text Ruth, but I won't let them.

I stand in the kitchen with the damp cloth in my hand and look down at my stomach. Not flat, but not pregnant. I run my hand over it and imagine it as an incubator. Ruth would be pleased to know I'm no longer considering picking up drunk men as a source of free sperm, that I'm using fancy tested sperm, as she said I should. However, she would not be pleased to know I'm doing it with Chris.

I've tried to understand my want with reason, but the thing about wanting a baby these days is that it's not reasonable. I have no desire to carry on my family name. I don't require multiple small hands to help with farm chores. I don't believe in a god that mandates me to be fruitful and multiply so as to have dominion over the fish of the sea and the fowl of the air and every living thing that moveth upon the Earth. I want a baby because I want one. My body wants one. And also, I'd like to try to make a family that doesn't feel like a punishment. I'd like to try my hand at parenting that doesn't run on fear.

I rinse out the cloth and find Chris in the bedroom. The suitcase is zipped and standing by the door. Chris is typing on her laptop. I ask if I can make her some tea.

She scrunches her eyes shut and rubs her hand over her face. That'd be nice, she says, thanks Sorch.

I return to the sink and fill the kettle. Chris works so hard. A few days away will be good for us. A time to rest and reconnect.

BUT THE RECONNECTING DOES NOT happen as we drive along the shores of the Bras d'Or on our way to Sydney, and it does not happen while we wait in the airport. It does not happen on the plane. Across the aisle from us, another couple sits side by side. The woman rests her head on the man's shoulder and he kisses her forehead. I watch them peripherally. They can't have been together long, that's just new dating stuff. But then I see a gold band glinting on the man's hand as he angles the book he's holding toward the woman so they can read it together. Well, whatever. Maybe it was a quickie marriage, or maybe it's just easier for straight people. Maybe definitely. What must that be like? Mass approval of your love, not being excommunicated from your family, et cetera.

Beside me, Chris scrolls her phone.

What are you reading? I ask.

A report, she says, without looking up. It's confidential.

Maybe we need counselling. Maybe we're in a rut. Though I don't think the rut is supposed to come this early. Isn't this supposed to be the easy part? Not even a year and a half in, no kids to sap our energy, nights all our own for board games or shared baths or sex or whatever happy couples do together. We run together, I guess. We share a bed, eat our meals across from each other. We have sex at least once a month, usually.

The mewling of a very young baby a few seats ahead cuts through the static of the plane. Two women awkwardly stand, crouching beneath the low ceiling, one cradling the crying babe and the other reaching into the overhead compartment to pull out a diaper bag. Maybe that's the best way to raise a baby, I think, with a sister or a friend. Maybe doing it with a partner is just too hard. They're so caring with each other, these sisters or friends. Look at them shuffling out of their seats and touching each other's arms so kindly and smiling at each other tiredly, and kissing each other on the mouth.

Oh. Well, good for them. I'm so glad everyone on this plane is in love.

IN THE HOTEL NEAR THE clinic, Chris and I ride the elevator up to our room. I ask if we can go out for dinner as a special city treat. It's been so long since we have. The closest restaurants with vegan options on the Island are Papa's Pub or the China King Buffet in Port Hawkesbury. The buffet does a good almond vegetable ding. But in the Big Smoke, vegan options are endless and I feel that this is our time to live.

Chris looks at her phone, swiping, swiping. Mm-hm, maybe, she says. But I have to catch up on some work. I missed a few emails during the flight.

Baby, I say, we're only in the city for one night before I'm knocked up.

Let's order in, she says.

Because it's Toronto, you can order everything in. The bike courier zips the food over to the hotel and we sit across from each other at the small table by the window of our room, eating jackfruit tacos, still hot. Chris types with one hand and eats with the other. I chew and try to think of what sort of thing I could say that she might like to hear, something worthy of her attention. Something clever, or maybe funny. No, something serious, like something I read in the paper. Except I didn't read the paper.

Did you know, I try, that the Gaelic word for small is beag?

One second, Chris says and types a few more words. What?

In Gaelic, small is beag.

Chris looks at me. You read that in your book?

Yeah, I say. I just thought it was cute.

Has that woman been back in the store?

Linda?

Yes, *Linda*, your crush.

Chris, I don't have a crush on Linda, I say. Though since she first suggested it, this has become sort of a lie.

So she has been in?

No, she hasn't.

Chris takes a bite of her taco. I try again.

Maybe there's some live music we could check out tonight, I say. You know, before we're parents and never get to leave the house.

Chris looks up from the computer screen and I smile.

Sorcha, she says. I have to work. My job is the reason we can afford to do this.

Aren't you supposed to be on vacation? I wheedle. What sort of urgent emails do you need to send about paper milling?

Can you give me a break? Jesus. She stares at her screen, chewing.

The muscles that had been holding up the corners of my mouth and eyebrows and cheeks are cut like tiny strings by tiny knives and my face settles into loose disappointment.

Do you even like me? I ask quietly.

What? Chris looks up from the screen.

I feel like you don't like me. You used to like me.

Sorcha, Chris says, what are you talking about?

I don't know. I don't know what to do to make you happy. I try to be good. I do all the things you ask me to do.

Jesus, Sorcha, Chris says. All I said was I have to work. That I can't go out and fucking party. This is what it means to be a grown-up. I thought you wanted that. To be a grown-up, to have a family. Do you want to have a baby? she asks, like she's about to take it away.

I do, I say. More than anything.

She returns to her food, but it's hard for me to swallow. I wake my phone up for company. I see a little red dot, a message request, and I open it.

Sorcha, is this you? My friend's daughter is good with computers, she did some searching and told me Bonnie had two daughters. I've written your mother and your sister as well. I hope I have the right Sorcha, I think I do. You look like me a bit.

I'm not sure your mother wants to know me. Perhaps you don't want to know me either, but I'm here, if you want.

With love,
Agnes

I choke on my jackfruit but Chris doesn't look up.
Agnes Blair. My runaway aunt. My patron saint.

We have your sperm, says the nurse. It's pre-washed and we've thawed it out. I'll give you a minute to get into this, she says, passing me a johnny shirt. Then you just climb onto the bed and I'll be back with the swimmers.

The swimmers, I say to Chris after the nurse leaves the room. Chris smiles and takes my clothes from me as I undress, folds them and places them on the chair beside her. I turn around and she helps me tie the shirt.

We had a pretty nice morning. I peed on the ovulation stick and a smiley face materialized in the little window. When I showed Chris she smiled back at it. There's a cute breakfast place between the hotel and the clinic and we stopped there on the walk over. I had the best last latte I could hope for, at least in Chris's presence, and fancy avocado toast. Chris had tofu scramble. Pale sunbeams filtered through the restaurant windows, fogged with everyone's breath and the steam rising from our food. Chris didn't send any emails, and we read our horoscopes out loud from the city's arts weekly. They were all lyrics. Hers said *I wear my sunglasses at night so I can watch you weave then breathe your storylines.* Mine said *no promises, no demands, love is a battlefield.* What the hell is that supposed to mean? she asked. I said I didn't know, but thought I might.

The nurse knocks and re-enters the room with a smile. She's very nice. I mean, for the price of all this, she'd better be. She asks me to please lie down, put my feet in the stirrups, and scoot my bum to the edge of the table like at every pap I've ever had. She tells me the speculum is warmed up and shouldn't be a shock. She says now you'll feel my hand on your leg, okay take a breath, in and out, now you'll feel the speculum, and I'm opening it up slowly, there.

Chris sits in a chair next to the bed, holding my hand. I look over at her and she brings my hand to her mouth and kisses it. I look at her handsome face, her sharp jaw and beautiful brown eyes and perfect hair. I think that maybe I hate her.

The nurse holds up a vial. The swimmers. She draws them into a syringe and pushes a thin bendy tube onto the end of it. She says and now you'll feel the catheter being fed into your cervical opening and into your uterus. There may be some light cramping.

I do feel something, a twinge. For a second before she pushes the plunger I think of telling her to stop. Like when my ex Jen and I were drunk in the tattoo shop and the gun was about to make its first indelible mark on my arm and I was somehow suddenly sober and thought to say no, but Jen was looking at me so I said nothing.

Here they come! says the nurse. Chris squeezes my hand.

I can't feel them, I say.

Well they're very small, says the nurse.

She pulls the catheter out, closes and removes the speculum. Okay, she says, you just lie there for ten minutes. I'll knock when the time is up and then you can get dressed. She leaves the room and closes the door.

I start to cry. Chris says what's wrong like nothing had better be wrong.

I just can't believe we finally did it. Happy tears, I say, as I wipe my eyes.

Chris smiles. She leans over and kisses me on the forehead. We shouldn't get too excited, she says. It almost never works on the first try.

Right, I say, feeling a bit reassured that maybe I didn't just stitch myself to Chris for life. I think of all the tricks I heard in high school for how to not get pregnant post-sex, like douching with Coke or taking a handful of aspirin or drinking parsley tea or punching yourself in the stomach. I wonder where I could go on the Island to get an abortion.

Chris asks what I want to do for the rest of the day. She says she'll take it off, that she won't do any work. Maybe we could go to a museum or something, she suggests. That would be nice, I say. She takes out her phone and looks up places to go. I stare at my feet in their mismatched socks, both black but one shorter than the other. I think about the message from my aunt. I haven't written her back yet. But in the bathroom of the restaurant this morning I studied her profile. She only has one picture, a kitchen selfie. The wall behind her is yellow and there's a blue kettle on the stove. She looks like my mother, and like me. I've been told I look more like my mum, Aileen more like our dad. But Bonnie, Aileen, and I all have the same squinty green eyes, the same heart-shaped face. In her picture, Agnes wears a brown sweater and thick-frame tortoiseshell glasses. Her hair is short and grey. She has five earrings in her left ear and three in her right. She looks cool, as I always expected she would.

The nurse knocks on the door and says I can get up. Chris unties my johnny shirt and hands me my clothes. I wonder what the swimmers are doing, if they've found the egg. I feel like I should know, that I should somehow be able to tell. It doesn't seem fair that something so pivotal could be happening or not happening inside my body at this very moment and I have to wait nine to fourteen days and pee on a stick to find out.

We go to the art gallery. Chris takes a call from her boss and I stare at Tom Thomson's lonely pine trees. I put a hand on my belly. Don't let them in, I whisper to the egg.

We *stop in Sydney on our way home, for groceries and cat food and* an armful of pregnancy tests. Marg had agreed to drop in on Della while we were away. She left a note on the kitchen table to say Della was a real sweetheart and she hoped we had a nice visit to the big city. I love Marg. Della rubs her cheeks against our legs and meows up at us while we put the groceries away.

What do you think, Della, says Chris. Is Sorcha pregnant?

I pick up the cat and kiss her head and whisper don't tell into her fur. I'm sure there's nothing to tell. The chances are slim, and I feel the same as I did before I was injected with swimmers. Though I do feel like I could drink a whole carton of milk.

CHRIS AND I WAKE UP at 6:15 on Monday morning, on schedule. It's not so bad in the summer when the sun rises early, but in the winter it's dark and punishing. The house is frigid and my feet are numb, even in my slippers. We get ready fast, we have a routine. I pull on black jeans and one of my many grey shirts and a thick brown sweater, like my aunt's. I pee and brush my teeth at the same time. I make coffee and eat a bowl of cereal as fast as I can without choking. Then I pour coffee and almond cream into Chris's travel mug and put it on the table beside a bowl of cereal for her, take our lunches out of the fridge, put on my coat and boots, and go out to start the car. I blast the heat and scrape the ice off the windshield. Then I sit in the passenger seat in the dark until Chris comes out and drives me to work. It all takes about thirty minutes and feels like it should be an Olympic sport. The sun won't be up for nearly an hour.

Chris usually doesn't like to talk in the morning, but when she gets in the car she leans over and kisses me on the cheek and says thanks for scraping off the ice. She turns the heat down and throws the car into reverse, then forward, and we roll down the crunching gravel toward the dark ocean. We should get you some prenatal vitamins, she says, just in case.

She drops me off at the bookstore and I unlock the door and haul in the stack of newspapers under the ringing bell. I was only off for two days plus my usual weekend, but it feels like forever, like the bell is heralding my long-awaited return. I turn the thermostat up to eighteen, the highest Marg will allow, and walk to the back room to switch on the electric kettle. I deposit my lunch in the fridge and make my milky tea. The mice run in the ceiling and I feel better than I have since we left for the city. I breathe out into the quiet.

At the seafoam counter I drink my tea and stare at the glowing screen of my phone in the dark store. I want to text Dana, to ask how early she could tell, but I don't want to confess what I've done.

I read Agnes's message again. *I'm here*, she says, *if you want.*

I type *Hi Agnes*, then change it to *Hello Aunt Agnes*. I'm not sure which is best. How do you hail your long-lost aunt, your patron saint? I change it back to hi and add an exclamation mark. I write *I'm so glad you found me, thank you for looking. I think I look like you too. I would love to know you. Will you tell me about yourself? Where do you live? What do you do? What has your life been like? I live in Cape Breton with my partner and our cat. My mother doesn't talk to me either, and I don't talk to her. It goes both ways. I would love to visit Scotland someday.* And I ask her how she would pronounce my name. I look at the message for a few minutes and then tap send.

I unlock the door at eight and am happy to see all my morning regulars arrive soon after, in their usual order: Mme Comeau and Sophie, Lorraine, Glen. Lorraine says she missed me. Her hair is freshly red, a welcome shot of colour in the winter light. Glen brings me a bag of shortbread cookies from the batch Joanne baked to mail to their grandkids for Christmas. Extra buttery, he says.

After Glen leaves I put a whole cookie in my mouth and let it melt. I look at my phone. Agnes has already messaged me back.

She says:

> *You can't know how much it means to me to hear from you. What a gift. It's hard to know where to start, telling you about myself. I'm 77, retired, but practiced for years as a midwife. I live in Balnain, in Inverness. I have a cat too, Alastair, but no partner. I mostly spend my time in my garden and around the loch, though in winter I watch a lot of bad TV. It's beautiful here though, even now. We have a bit of snow but who's to say how long it will last. You're welcome to visit anytime. I'm not sure how to send a video but perhaps we can talk on the phone and you can hear how I say your name.*

I cry and this time they're happy tears for real. I write that I can't wait to meet her, that I heard only a bit about her when I was young. I write that I would always think about her, that I still think about her, when I, too, want to run away.

Is that what they told you? she replies. *That I ran away?*

It's been a week and my body feels the same, looks the same. *Apparently* you can't tell this soon, not even the tests would know. But Della has been sleeping curled against my belly at night like she's protecting something. Or maybe it's because it's been so bloody cold. Why did we think it was a good idea to move to an ancient house metres from the ocean? The wind pushes in through the cracks in the windows and sounds like someone struggling to breathe.

I texted Ruth yesterday to wish her happy Hanukkah, but Hanukkah came early this year and was already over. I felt like such a WASP. I mean, I am. I asked how she and George have been, how her mom is doing. She didn't write back until this morning, but she said good, we're all good, how are you? I said good good. I didn't say I might be pregnant. I didn't say I found my runaway aunt who, it turns out, didn't run away. I didn't say that I want to run away. After I betrayed Ruth this time last year, and then almost came to Halifax on the bus in October but bailed, I feel like she's finally given up on me. I feel like that's probably fair.

I drink my steaming tea at the counter in the dark and wait for the store to warm up. What will I do with my free hour today? I could read the little book again. Agnes says she speaks some Gaelic. We've probably sent each other twenty messages this week. I wish I could teleport to Balnain to drink tea in her kitchen and practice my phrases. I need someone to talk to, since Linda hasn't returned.

What will I do, what oh what? I am rather hungry. I could eat a buttermilk scone. I could eat a molasses cookie. I could eat an oatcake.

I could take a pregnancy test.

Marg keeps them under the counter. People don't ask for them often because it's such a small place. No one has ever asked me. Better to buy them discreetly in the city like Chris and I did, or order them online. Maybe these ones are expired. I take a box from the drawer and look at it with the light from my phone. Not expired. I still have time before I have to unlock the door. And I get a thirty percent discount.

It feels like an afterschool special, except I'm not sixteen. I'm thirty-one. Though what are the chances, getting pregnant the first time? The sixteen-year-old probably said the same thing. I look the chances up on my phone: 10 to 20 percent. Higher than I'd like. I walk to the bathroom at the back of the store and open the package and pee on the stick. I set my timer for three minutes. I'm sure I'm not pregnant. I'm 80 to 90 percent sure.

And then the timer beeps and I look at the stick and it shows two pink lines.

No no, it's not supposed to detect it this early. It's probably a false positive. So I do another test and it says I'm pregnant too. I do a third, the last of the boxes under the counter, and it tells me the same.

I think I picked the wrong door to the future. The worker was right—I can't have a baby with Chris. But if the afterschool special teen can handle it, so can I. I'm a feminist. And a scientist. I can get a fucking abortion.

I flatten the boxes and put them in a bag with the plastic oracles. I tie it up and stuff it into the bottom of the bathroom garbage can, under balled-up tissues and toilet paper tubes. I wash my hands for a long time under the hot water and stare at myself in the mirror. Maybe I do look different. I try to determine whether I have some sort of glow. I pay full price for the tests so Marg won't know it was me who bought them all. I flip the sign, turn on the lights, and unlock the door.

Bon matin, says Mme Comeau as she enters with Sophie. T'es jolie aujourd'hui.

Do I look different? I ask.

Oui, she says. Peut-être un peu.

After Mme Comeau leaves I look up where on the Island you can get an abortion. The answer is nowhere. I would have to go to Halifax. Maybe I could hitchhike to Port Hawkesbury and get the bus. Maybe I could stay in Halifax forever. But if Chris found out, what would she do? Yell at me until I cried so hard I had a heart attack? Sue me? I can never predict what she'll do when she's mad.

I would have to leave today. I would have to leave before she finds out. It's 10 a.m. now. I look up the bus. It departs at 10:20 and it's the only one running. If I left the store now it would still leave without me. It's probably too late to douche with Coke. I laugh at myself for thinking for a second that might work. And then I cry and pound my head with the palms of my hands because how the fuck did I get here, a bundle of cells building inside me against the odds that I can't scrape out, and me living in a house with the meanest person I know and I can't scrape myself out either. How funny I thought I could make a family that doesn't feel like a punishment. How so very funny.

ON SUNDAY, CHRIS ASKS ME to take a test. I go into the bathroom shaking like I'm a spy about to be discovered. Where's my cyanide pill? I lock the door but quietly so she won't hear the hook in the eye. I dip the end of the stick into the toilet water and then take it out, then pee extra hard so she can hear it. I stare at myself in the mirror and practice looking disappointed. I bring the test out to the kitchen table so we can look at it together once the timer is up, hoping it won't somehow tell her I cheated. Fingers crossed, I say.

She was pretty nice to me this weekend. She said I didn't have to go for a run with her, maybe worried it would dislodge something.

I feel fucked up about lying. Maybe she's not so mean after all. Or maybe she is mean but I deserve it.

When the timer goes off, Chris reaches over and holds my hand. She turns the test over and looks at the one pink line in the window. Her shoulders slump. Oh, I say, geez. I blow out my breath. We'll try again, I say.

Do you want to take another test to make sure? Maybe you didn't do it right.

I try to calm my blood so it doesn't rush to my cheeks and give me away. She'll probably want to oversee the next one. She loves making sure I do things right. Why don't we wait, I say. It's still early. I can try again in a few days. I'm out of pee, anyway.

Yeah, Chris says, yeah. She runs her fingers through her hair and flips it to the side. I wish she wouldn't do that. I feel nostalgic for it already.

She goes upstairs to fold laundry and I peel carrots and sweet potatoes for dinner. We're getting closer to the longest night of the year and the sun is already down, but the sky was so thickly grey today that I barely missed it.

I think that if I stay here I'll die. Not right away, but slowly, like a houseplant in a windowless room. Maybe I could ask Glen to drive me to the bus, go to the hospital in Halifax and ask them to hollow me out. Beg my friends to forgive me, beg for my job back. I wish I had a time machine and could rewind the last year and a half and just not go to the market that day. Or go but not invite Chris for pizza. Or do all that but end things after the show. Or after the Seahorse. Or after any number of other Times. After last Christmas. How am I this person? Where is my spine? I feel like I'm shrinking. Like if I don't go now I won't be tall enough to reach the doorknob when I finally get up the nerve.

I decide to message Agnes. I usually only write to her at the bookstore so Chris won't see, but I need her counsel now. She didn't run away, ultimately, but she knows how it's done. It was her parents who left her, she said. My gran and grandad packed Bonnie up one day without telling Agnes, and were gone. I almost couldn't believe it. How could they do that to her? I asked why and she said she would explain it to me one day, but not yet.

I scoop the vegetables into a dish with garlic and oil and put them in the oven. And then I write to my aunt. *Agnes*, I say, *I'm pregnant. I can't have a baby with Chris. I have to leave. If she finds out it worked I'll never get away from her. Please tell me what to do.*

She writes me back within the minute. It's 9:30 p.m. in Scotland. She's probably watching TV with Alastair. *Oh my dear*, she says. *You were trying to get pregnant?*

Yes, I say. *I wish I hadn't but it worked.*

Do you want to have a baby? she asks.

I cradle the phone in my hands and stare at the question. I think about the tiny cells, working so hard, diligently dividing.

Who are you texting, Chris says from behind me.

No one, I say. I shut off the screen and put my phone on the counter.

Then what were you doing, she asks.

Looking up a recipe.

For what?

Um, vegan cheese sauce, I say.

Let me see, says Chris.

Well, I decided not to make it.

No, she says. Prove to me you were looking at a recipe and not texting Linda.

What?

Prove it.

Chris, of course I wasn't texting Linda. I don't even have her number.

Show me.

Can you just trust me?

Show me, she says, and I'll trust you next time. She holds out her hand. Give me the phone, Sorcha, she says.

God I hate her.

Don't look at me like that, like you fucking hate me, she says, and grabs the phone from the counter behind me. Unlock it, she demands.

No, I say.

She grabs my wrist and pulls my hand toward her, trying to press my thumb to the button. I twist my arm away.

You cheating fucking bitch, she spits. You fucking bitch.

I'm not, I say. I'm not.

I'll believe you when you prove it, she says, and shoves my phone in her pocket. She stomps to the door and pulls on her boots and coat and grabs her keys from the hook. I'm going out, she says. I'm not eating your fucking food. She slams the door.

I'm shaking, but for once, I'm not crying. I feel like a worker pulled a lever and filled a moat around my heart. Don't worry, I say to the cells, we're getting out of here tomorrow.

I eat dinner alone and eventually pass out with Della on the couch, mittens duct-taped to my sleeves, just in case. The fire burns out while I sleep. When Chris comes in at midnight, she slams the door again and drops her keys on the floor. I wonder where she went for six and a half hours. I wonder if she's drunk. She kicks her boots off and fills a glass of water at the sink. I can see her staring at me through my fake sleeping eyes. Fuck you, she says, and stomps up the stairs.

I think about how to leave, where to go. I think about it until I fall asleep again around two. I dream that Realtree comes in for a bun of bread and I get on the back of his ATV and he drives me across a Mario Kart rainbow bridge to Scotland, and Agnes and Alastair meet me at their front door, and Alastair is as big as a panther and can talk, and he says wake up.

I open my eyes in the frozen house and Chris says I'm leaving in ten minutes, if you don't want to miss work go scrape off the car. I scramble off the couch and rip off my duct-taped mittens. I'm already dressed because I slept in my clothes. I grab my toothbrush and three pairs of underwear and two pairs of socks and stuff them in my sweater sleeves. I wrap my neck in a scarf and pull on my coat and put a banana in my pocket.

Chris is eating cereal at the kitchen table. I pick the car keys up off the floor where she dropped them last night. I almost forgot that I know how to drive. Maybe I should just take her car and go. But she'd probably call the cops on me, so I just warm it up and scrape it off like I was told. Then I eat the banana in the freezing dark with my breath clouding around me. The thermometer says fifteen below.

Chris doesn't say a word to me on the drive. I don't feel anything about it. When she pulls up to the store I ask if I can please have my phone even though I'm sure she'll say no.

No, she says.

Okay, I say. Goodbye.

She doesn't look at me. I get out of the car and close the door and she drives away.

In the black of the predawn I feel like I did under the ocean: perfectly, blessedly alone. Though in a way, this time, I'm not.

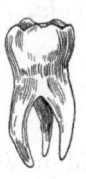

might believe in divine intervention after all, though I'd never admit it to Bonnie. Not God necessarily, but something must have told Linda it was a good day to come to the bookstore for a Coke and scones. She walked through the door at eleven, after the last of my morning regulars. As I rang Mme Comeau, Lorraine, and Glen through, I thought of asking each of them to help me run. I wondered who was most likely to say yes, who was safest to ask, who gossiped the least. Mme Comeau only recently seemed to have come around to my queerness and I wasn't about to change her mind with my tale of woe. And Lorraine is a real loudmouth. Glen was my best bet, but I wimped out at the last second and then he was gone.

Maybe Realtree really would roar up on his ATV and spirit me away. Maybe my dream was a premonition. My plan was to get to Port Hawkesbury and then bus or cab or hitch my way to Halifax. But then, my plan might have changed. Because maybe I do want to have this baby. And Halifax is not a good place to have a secret baby.

I thought of calling Marg to ask if I could stay the night with her while I figured things out. But then the bell rang over the door and in walked Linda like a deus ex machina wrapped in plaid, and she said madainn mhath, Sorcha, ciamar a tha thu?

Dona, I said. Did I say that right?

Linda said oh kiddo, like she'd met me more than once. She asked if I was okay.

I don't think so, I said. I'm having—I stopped and took a breath. Say it, the worker commanded—a pretty hard time at home, I whispered.

Is it your man? Linda asked.

Sort of, I said.

Well, as you said, down with husbands.

Yeah, down with husbands, I agreed. If Chris were my husband, I thought, I probably would have left sooner. Out loud I said but really, I need to get away from my partner. Please don't tell anyone.

Oh dear, said Linda. I hoped she didn't think I was being overdramatic. Well, she said, I keep an eye on seat sales to Glasgow and there's one on now. Maybe you could make the trip to Scotland you've been dreaming of. It's plenty far for someone looking to get away. I could drive you to the airport.

I blinked at her. Are you serious? I asked.

Sure, she said. It's only a few hours' drive to the city, and I wouldn't mind going to Costco.

That cracked me up and Linda laughed too.

Really though, she said, I wish someone would have swooped in to deliver me from my husband before he broke my collarbone. It took me another six months after that to leave him. And we have a son, so I had to battle the bastard in court for a year before I could be rid of him, and I still never truly was. At least you and your partner don't have kids.

My hand went to my belly. Yeah, I said, at least there's that. I closed my eyes. I'm sorry, I said, that's horrible.

It was. I got a restraining order but he would still show up at my son's school. Then my son went away to university and Danny died a few years after. A stroke, I heard. I felt a bit bad, though only a bit. Mhallaich mi e. I cursed him, you know.

A spinster and a witch, I said.

It is a bit cliché, said Linda. But listen, I will take you, if you want. I can't help you with the flight though. Do you have money?

I think I have enough, I said.

Linda told me to book it online asap. I told her Chris took my phone.

Danny used to unplug our house phone and lock it in a drawer, she said. Use mine. She held it out to me.

Yeah, I said. Okay. I waited to see if any of the workers would stop me, but they were all quiet. Okay, I said again, nodding. Okay. I booked the flight. Rob from down Shore Road came in for smokes and toilet paper and I rang him through. I told Linda to have a Coke on me while she waited, browsing the bookshelves. Then I used her phone to message Agnes. *I'm coming to Glasgow*, I wrote, and sent the number of my flight. *Can I stay with you?*

Then I looked up at Linda. What about the store? I asked.

I could use a job in the offseason, she said. Tell Marg to give me a call. We go back.

I bought us oatcakes and scones and a block of cheese and a litre of milk for the road. I taped a sign to the door that said *sorry, closing early*. I thought of Chris reading it when she came to get me at six, how she would think I'd run away with Linda, and that I sort of had after all. I called Marg and my prayers to get her machine were granted. I said I had to go away and to please not tell Chris anything. I said Linda was helping me and to call her for shifts, that I had done the inventory and would lock up and leave my key under the big rock beside the ice chest. I asked her to forgive me for the very short notice.

Linda drove me to the house. My heart was a bird. She stayed in the car and kept a lookout while I unlocked the door and ran upstairs with my boots on. I kept expecting Chris to be hiding somewhere— under the kitchen table, beneath the bed. I dug my passport out from under my socks. The bedroom door creaked and I almost died from fear but it was only Della rubbing her old body against it. I picked her up and pressed my forehead to hers. I kissed her three times and whispered goodbye into her fur. I threw shirts and sweatpants, a hoodie and jeans into my backpack, and emptied into it the socks and underwear and toothbrush I'd stuffed into my sleeves. I grabbed the photos of me and Ruth and Dana and Linh that had broken from their frames, and the little Gaelic book. All of my plants would probably die but it felt like a necessary sacrifice.

I took the last jar of cloudberry jam from the shelf, left my housekey on the hook under the dollar store sign, and shut the door.

Linda had the car running and turned around. As soon as I got in she hit the gas and we spit gravel at the house.

You just never know, she said, as we turned onto the highway. Best to get out fast.

I nodded and passed her the jam. I made this, I said. It's for you.

She smiled and put it in the cupholder. We'll eat it on the scones, she said.

MY FLIGHT LEAVES AT SIX, arrives in Glasgow at midnight. Or my midnight, Agnes's 4 a.m. Linda let me check my messages on her phone again before she dropped me off. Agnes had written that she would drink a coffee and drive down to get me. As a retired midwife, she said she's used to being up all hours. It felt unreal. After all those years of prayer, my patron saint was coming to save me.

Linda gave me a hug across the console and told me to take care. I said thank you so many times she told me to stop. Don't, she said. It's selfish, really. Helps me feel less bad about not getting myself out sooner. She unwrapped her plaid shawl from around her shoulders and handed it to me as a warm ball. It smelled of juniper. Tìoraidh, she said, and pushed me gently out of the car.

I drink the last swig from the carton of milk before I go through security. It sloshes in my belly as I walk to the gate.

THE WINTER BEFORE I MET Chris was the last time I was alone on a plane, for a pesticides conference in Maine. Whenever I'm in a massive metal craft, hurtling through the air in a way I hope makes sense to the laws of nature, I can't help but think of death. I wonder who would miss me if the machine were to fail, what I'd regret.

This would be a weird time to die. Almost no one knows I'm on this plane, and the only person who knows I'm pregnant is my runaway aunt. I mean my abandoned aunt. Who would go to my funeral? Where would it be? My parents would probably hold one at the church in Chesley, even though we haven't spoken in four and a half years. Pray for my soul to be accepted despite my trespasses. Maybe my pack would pour an old fashioned out onto the slushy sidewalk, and split a pint of chocolate peanut butter ice cream and say sweet things about me, like that I was a good dancer, and was funny in a salty sort of way, and that they missed the way I hugged them and the way I smelled, even the way I used to hoard all the cups. Would Chris mourn me, or feel that I'd gotten what I deserved?

On the flight to Maine I remember thinking that the thing I would regret most if I died was never getting to be a mother. On my last night there I slept with a very polite man with a thin ponytail and round gold spectacles, a professor I'd met at the conference. Disappointingly, he brought condoms. He and his wife were open, he said, and she insisted. That's fine, I said, but crossed my fingers that the condom would break.

This kind of behaviour is probably why my life is the way it is now. You can't just hope for a condom to break on some happily married professor's dick and expect no comeuppance. Though I am pregnant now, so I suppose I shouldn't complain.

Beside me on the plane, an old man is reading. He doesn't get mad at me for flipping through my little book, or for raising and lowering and raising the shade on the window, or for nodding my head to the music in my earphones. He's not visibly disgusted when I order tomato juice as my drink and cookies as my snack. He doesn't seem annoyed when I ask if he would mind getting up so I can go to the bathroom.

No one on the plane is mad at me and it feels amazing.

And no one is texting me angrily from a distance because the person who does that still has my phone. By now she'd have been to the bookstore and found it empty. I try not to think of the words her mouth might be forming, the things of mine she might be burning in the wood stove.

My body feels like warm dough slowly rising under the juniper shawl. The plane shushes my thoughts. It's dark outside, pitchy blue, and the moon is a scythe again. I sleep.

I *wasn't completely wrong. Agnes did run away from her family at first,* though only to Glasgow. It was later that her family ran from her. Maybe running away runs in our blood.

She's waiting for me in the arrivals hall, under the taxi sign. I catch sight of the heart shape of her face, the grey of her hair, the glint of her earrings. We lock eyes and I jog into her arms. She hugs me tight and fast, like a gasp. Oh my dear, she says, my dear Sorcha. The lilt of her voice and the clasp of her arms, the press of her chest against mine, swells my heart. She smells like Pears soap and Blistex. She pulls back and looks into my face and says well, isn't this something, isn't this something, her eyes welling up behind her tortoiseshell glasses. She takes my arm and leads me to her little white car.

She drives us through the night city to the Gorbals, playing The Yardbirds at a medium kick. She points out where the stone tenement used to be, where she lived sixty years ago, before it was demolished.

With who? I ask.

Oh, she says. Some lad I fancied I was in love with. But I was fourteen, a wee bampot.

Bampot? I say.

An eejit, she explains.

It's hard to picture the stone buildings covered in black soot, as she describes. Now it's all green grass and stolid high-rises lit by shining spotlights, no snow even though it's mid-December.

Famous for its filth, Agnes says as we drive through the Gorbals. Rubbish all through the streets, clatty weans running about.

Why did you come to Glasgow? I ask.

For the lad, she says. We came together from Inverness. He'd been my neighbour. Seventeen and not bad to look at, taller than me. I was taller than all the lads in my class. And he had me pregnant, so that was the main thing.

She looks ahead at the road and I look at the side of her face, lit on and off by passing headlights.

All that to say, I know a bit of how you might feel. Though I don't know much about lesbians. Not that it minds me, of course.

Did you have the baby? I ask.

She takes a breath as if she's preparing to tell a tale, then lets it go. Not a story for half five, she says. Or for our first meeting, I don't think. She glances over at me and smiles. What a shame that I have to face the road and can't just stare at you! I'd say you look like your mother but I don't rightly know what she looks like now. You do look a bit like me, though, or like I used to.

THE DRIVE TO BALNAIN IS three and a half hours from the airport. I fall asleep around six and wake when the car stops. It ticks and pings as it settles from the road. In the twilight I can see a stone cottage and behind it a hill and behind that the sky.

Here we are, Sorcha, my wee bothy. Alastair's been keeping your bed warm, I hope. I bribed him with his favourite treats.

She tries to take my backpack but I insist on carrying it. Maybe if I were fully pregnant I'd let my elderly aunt carry my bag, but not with the cells still just cells and Agnes a bit stooped. If she stood up straight I think she'd be nearly as tall as me. She probably used to be even taller, but time presses us down. I wonder if she has any photos of herself when she was my age. I'd like to see a family resemblance I don't resent.

Agnes leads me down a flagstone path to the front door and opens it without a key. A lamp is lit on a small table by the door and Alastair trots toward us, into the light. Agnes takes off her runners and gives him a pat. I unlace my boots.

He can't meow, she tells me, or perhaps he just won't.

That's funny, I say. I had a dream he could talk.

Isn't that something, she says, and picks him up. Is that your secret, you wee beastie?

Standing in my socks inside the front door of my aunt's house in the Highlands, I feel like I've been teleported after all, to a land that once felt impossibly far, into the home of a person I wasn't sure was even alive, and from a place I thought I'd never manage to leave. It feels too easy, like I should have had to endure a series of trials involving riddles and feats of strength, spend a month as a stowaway at sea, walk into the Highlands alone and starved with no shoes and my hair matted by the wind, and fall against Agnes's door half dead. But I'm here after a brief flight and an uneventful drive, and Agnes is here too and she's offering me a cup of tea.

Come in, she says, come in come in. She sits me down at her table.

I look around at the yellow walls while she fills the kettle at the sink and takes a box of PG Tips from the cupboard. She has photos up on the wall. One a collage of too many babies to count. One a picture of her in a toque and coat, holding a walking stick, at the foot of lumbering hills softened by a blanket of rust and ochre and moss. One in black and white, a group of women in three crisp rows, matching shoes, stockings, coats and hats, legs and hands crossed the same, just so. Demure smiles, no teeth. I look for my own face and find something like it in the middle of the back row: heart-shaped, squinty eyes. The tallest of them all.

Those weans aren't the half of what I delivered, Agnes says, gesturing to the collage of babies. Just the most recent. I have boxes of photos in the closet. Perhaps one day I'll frame them all. I think I could wallpaper the bothy with the lot of them.

Is this you? I ask, pointing to the tallest woman in the black-and-white photo.

'Tis. See, we do look alike, you and I.

When was it taken?

It would've been '58, the year I qualified as a midwife. I was twenty-two. These girls and I did our training together in Glasgow. I've lost touch with most of them, but Mary on the bottom left there's on Facebook and we play Scrabble on Saturdays.

Did you have to go back to finish high school first? After you left Inverness?

Agnes leans against the kitchen counter, Alistair pushing his cheeks into her shins. High school? Ah, no. The leaving age was fourteen then. So I worked until I could put myself through training. And then I worked as a midwife the rest of my life, until oh, nearly ten years ago. I can't think of a better job. I quite miss it.

I want to ask again about her baby, but I don't. If I had a cousin somewhere I think she would have mentioned it. But if Agnes had to give up the baby or abort it on a greasy kitchen table in the Gorbals, I can't imagine how she could go on to spend her life delivering too many babies to count.

Can I be hollowed out in a hospital here? Perhaps it won't even take. It's only been eleven days. Aren't you supposed to wait over eleven weeks to tell anyone, in case it doesn't work?

The kettle whistles and Agnes moves to get it.

What's my plan? Which door should I choose—yearned for baby plus eternal tether to the meanest person I know? Or hollow, heart-crushing freedom? The choice feels impossible. Maybe my body will decide. Rabbits absorb their litters in times of stress.

Agnes brings two mugs and two spoons to the table.

It's decaf, she says, so we can both get a bit of sleep. I've added the milk already, I hope that's all right. Sugar is in the wee pot just there.

Just milk is perfect, I say.

I'm so glad you're here, says Agnes, you can't know. Her eyes are wet behind her glasses. Don't mind me, she says.

I'm so glad I'm here too, I say, and squeeze her hand across the table. Thank you.

I don't ask about her baby and she doesn't ask about mine. We drink our tea and she shows me to my room, a single bed under a small window looking out on trees and a field and a rising hill, still green. I draw the curtains and put my backpack on the chair beside the door.

Go sleep with Sorcha, beastie, she says to Alastair. Keep her feet warm.

But Alastair won't.

It's okay, I say.

Agnes closes the door gently. She says my name like Linda does. Sorcha, I whisper to myself. I still can't say it quite right.

WE WAKE AT NOON. Agnes makes us ham sandwiches. I apologize that I don't eat meat and she says oh feed it to the cat, so I do and just eat the bread and cheese. I hope it endears me to him. Then she sets me up with her laptop at the kitchen table and goes to start a fire.

I wish I could just disappear, even from my pack. I'm not sure I can call them that anymore, anyway. I think I need to establish a sort of policy before I sign in to my email, and I think it needs to be Don't Read Anything From Chris. Yes, I agree with myself, I won't. I key in my password and see fourteen new messages: one from Marg, one from Ruth, nine from Chris. Three from listservs I keep meaning to unsubscribe from. Bed Bath & Beyond is having a sale on knives.

Marg says *Dear Sorcha, I got your message. You left me in a bit of a lurch, love. It's OK but I wish you would've talked to me sooner. Linda will pick up most of your shifts, and I'll send your last paycheque if you give me your new address. Chris came to the shop to pick you up at close. I said you weren't feeling well and left early but that I didn't know how or with who. I hope you're all right.*

Ruth says *Sorcha, where are you? Are you okay? Chris messaged me and asked if you were with me, and I told her no but I don't think she believed it. What's going on? Call me girl, please.*

Don't read Chris's emails, says a worker in my brain. Remember, they say, remember just a second ago how you said you wouldn't? But I'm already reading them. The first one says *You cheating fucking bitch, I know you're with Linda. Thanks for proving me right and leaving like I knew you would.* The next says *Sorcha are you with Ruth? I'm sorry I took your phone. Please call or write me back.* The next says *Fuck you Sorcha, if you don't write me back by tomorrow I'm calling the police.* The next says *I'm really worried about you baby, please call me. I can't sleep without you in my arms. I love you so much. I need you.* The next says *I've called the police.*

Suddenly my arms are so heavy and my finger joints won't bend. I don't read the rest. I slump in the wooden kitchen chair. Will the police track me down and pick me up like a delinquent teen? Will they put me on the first plane back to Canada and deliver me to Chris with my hands cuffed behind my back like an international criminal? I hope I can at least get an abortion first so I don't have to be bound to her forever like Linda to her piece of shit ex-husband. Maybe Agnes knows of some potent Highland herbs that will do the job. I apologize to the cells and shut my leaking eyes and feel everything closing in around me again.

Oh my dear, says Agnes beside me. Are you all right?

I look at her through a blur of tears. Her cheeks are ruddy from lighting the fire.

Oh, I say, I'm fine.

Let me get you a tissue, she says. Can I make you some tea?

Ah, no, I say, embarrassed. No thanks. But I take a tissue from the box she holds out to me and blow my nose loudly.

Does your mother know where you are?

No, I say, but that's normal.

And does Chris know?

No. She says she called the cops.

Oh dear, Agnes says. Well, I suppose we should ring them.

Who?

The police. And tell them you're fine.

Can you do that? I ask. And they'll leave you alone?

I expect so.

You don't think they'll tell her?

I can't say for sure, but I should think not.

I sit in the chair and stare at the screen through my swelling lids. I wish I could just disappear, I say.

Let's close this, Agnes says and shuts the laptop. She sits across from me at the table. You can stay here as long as you like, Sorcha. And I can help you do whatever it is that needs doing. Whatever you decide is best.

I press the snotty tissue into my eyes. Agnes slides the box over and I pull a fresh one.

I don't think that's true, I say from behind the tissue. At the airport they told me I could only come as a visitor. I said I was just here for a couple weeks.

We'll cross that bridge when we come to it. For now let's ring the police so they don't come searching for you. She pulls the computer over to her side of the table and types something in. All right, she says, and taps a number into her phone. We'll keep it quick, long distance and all. Just tell them you're with a relative and you're safe. Hopefully that should do it. No crying on the phone now.

She smiles gently at me and I nod, sit up straight, and sniff decisively. After a few rings a deep voice answers. Cape Breton Regional Police, the voice says.

Hello, I say. I, ah, broke up with my partner yesterday, and left our house in Creignish. I think she's reported me missing, so I guess I'm just calling to say that I'm not.

Ohhkay, says the voice. I'm not sure we've had a missing person's report lately, ma'am. What's your uh, husband's name?

Um, not my husband. My partner. Her name is Chris.

Right, says the voice. Rrright. And your name?

S-o-r-c-h-a, I spell, Sorcha. I hear typing, clicking, breathing.

No report about a Sorcha, and no calls yesterday from anyone named Chris.

Oh, I say.

Yep, says the voice.

Well, uh, if anyone calls in to say that I'm missing, I'm not.

Okee doke, says the voice. I'll make a note.

Okay, I say.

Okay, says the voice.

Well, thanks. Bye then, I say.

Bye ma'am, says the voice.

I hand the phone back to Agnes.

That wasn't quite so bad now, was it? she says.

No, I say, closing my eyes and shaking my head. It wasn't so bad.

Agnes gives my shoulder a squeeze and returns to the couch to watch TV with Alastair. I write to Ruth. I takes me fifteen whole minutes to type *Hello, I'm safe. I left Chris. I'm staying with my aunt in Scotland. Please don't tell anyone. I miss you.*

Then I watch *Hamish Macbeth* with Agnes on her orange couch. Alastair slinks over and curls his small body up on my lap and purrs like a machine.

On the day my sister was born, I asked Bonnie about her own sister. I don't remember doing it, but Bonnie told me the story when I asked about her sister again years later. She said that when I held Aileen at the hospital for the first time, I turned to her and said where's *your* sister, with the lisp I had until I was ten. My gran and grandad were there to see the baby too and were furious with Bonnie for telling me she had a sister, because how else would I have known to ask? Bonnie said she hadn't told me, that she didn't know how I knew, but they didn't believe her and left without holding Aileen.

After they'd gone, Bonnie asked me why I had asked about her sister, and I pointed at the baby and said my sister, mine. Then I asked my dad where his sister was. Pittsburgh, he said. Bonnie figured I'd just assumed everyone in the world had a sister and I had finally joined the club.

When we were older, Aileen took one of the puppies out of my Puppy Surprise and buried it in the yard, which was especially upsetting because mine only came with three puppies inside. Our neighbour got five out of hers and we both knew it meant she was better than me and favoured by God, who controlled everything.

At the time I thought it was practical to use the mother dog as a sort of duffel bag for the babies. When it was time to clean up I could just stuff her puppies back inside her velcroed body. I wonder if it messed me up in some Freudian way. Like if, theoretically, I gave birth to the baby these cells could become, would I wish from time to time that I could just stuff them back in when they're too heavy to carry around outside my body, or when they're bawling with no reprieve? Or would I just leave them to cry it out until they finally slept, alone in a dark room, like my parents did with me and Aileen?

After Aileen buried my puppy and forgot where, I ran to Bonnie and said I wish I never had a sister! And Bonnie said something like, you'd better not say such things because if you don't love your sister it will poison your heart and turn you to a life of sin.

I was eight. I said what do you mean.

Bonnie told me she had a sister once, Agnes. But when Bonnie was born, Agnes became so jealous that she tried to steal Bonnie away to sell her to a rich foreign family or a Columbian drug lord or some other racist fairy tale. She's told me and Aileen a few different versions over the years and I can't remember them all.

Where's your sister now, I asked, still with the lisp, and Bonnie told me I'd asked her that before. She said her sister was crazy and probably living in a harem or dead. She said that after Gran and Grandad foiled Agnes's attempt to kidnap Bonnie, Agnes ran away in shame and they moved to Chesley without her.

My grandparents had died by the time Bonnie told me this story, so I was never able to fact-check it. I haven't found a time that feels appropriate to run it by Agnes.

Agnes told me how she found me. Her Scrabble friend, Mary, who lives in Aberdeen, has a daughter, Kim, who like many other people under fifty is reasonably competent at using the internet. Agnes gave her Bonnie's last name at birth, Blair. Kim was initially thrown off course by a flood of images of the spandex-hooded

American speedskater by the same name. But on the fifteenth page of search results was a post from the Chesley High School Alumni Facebook page: a scanned clipping from the local paper, in which Bonnie Blair is not a speedskater but a teenage girl with an unusually high forehead, wearing a turtleneck and embroidered vest, seated between a mop-haired boy with a light moustache and a beehived girl, Bonnie's own hair long and brushed flat. They had each been awarded top marks in their years and were wearing their medals around their necks, seated in front of the mural on the wall of the school gym, featuring a ferocious cougar and the school's motto, *Clawing our way to purrrfection.*

The mural was still there when I was a student, but it had chipped and been repainted so many times that the cougar's eyes had become a bit wonky, its teeth rather round.

Kim searched archived editions of the Chesley paper until she found Bonnie's marriage announcement, Bonnie Miller née Blair. Luckily the town's population is under two thousand and there are only a few other Millers aside from us, and they are all very old. She found Aileen on the high school alumni page, too.

Aileen loved high school. It's only been twelve years since she graduated and she's already been to two reunions. She organized them both. But for me, high school was a beige slog. I was good at it without trying, but not the best. I received no medals. I went to no parties because I wasn't allowed. I smoked with Angie between classes in the copse of beech trees beside the parking lot, and managed to avoid the discovery of my secret gayness, though some of the cool girls with cars and braces took to calling Angie and me The Ellens until Angie got a boyfriend, so maybe I'm wrong about that part. Kim didn't find me on the alumni group, but rather on Facebook through my sister. We are "friends."

I asked Agnes if Bonnie or Aileen had responded to her messages. They hadn't. I can give you Bonnie's number, I said, but couldn't help wincing as I made the offer, and Agnes declined.

WE'RE GOING INTO DRUMNADROCHIT TODAY, the closest town. It's fourteen degrees out and I'm not even wearing a coat. There's no ice to scrape off of Agnes's little white car. It seems winter doesn't really exist here. I could get used to that.

To get into town, Agnes drives us down a narrow road, bordered by high hedges and stone fences and trees. This time, as I'm not charged with the rush of having just run away from the person whose name I've been trying not to say, and foggy from drifting in and out of sleep across time zones, I am preoccupied by being on the left side of the car and not driving it. When the speed limit drops, my foot presses for a brake that isn't there. We take a right after Nessieland and I lean into it. We pass the post office, the fire station, a field of cows.

Can you drive, Sorcha? Agnes asks.

Um, I say, technically yes.

Technically?

I haven't for a while.

Well, Agnes says. We'll have to teach you to drive here, on the proper side of the road.

Sure, I say, as if I'm confident I won't crash her car and leave Alastair orphaned.

We pull into the parking lot of the Drum Takeaway, which is attached to a Scotmid Co-op. I follow Agnes into the Scotmid and down the short aisles as she grabs Light & Low milk, old white cheddar, a loaf of bread, frozen mini steak pies, sliced ham, oat crackers, apples, potatoes, and a box of PG Tips.

I always get the same things, she says, so I don't have to think too hard about it. But what can we get for you, hen? What do vegetarians eat?

It's a question that always reminds me of the other question I've been asked too many times to count: how do lesbians have sex. Agnes hasn't asked me that one.

I'm already holding a jug of whole milk with cream on top that I snatched from the cooler like a sticky-fingered kid. I put it in Agnes's cart and stalk around the store, trying to think of food that doesn't remind me of the person whose name I'm trying not to say, even in my head. No sweet potatoes. No squash. No pears. No pasta. Pretty much nothing I know how to make. I choose the vegetables I would ordinarily ignore, cauliflower and green pepper and parsnips, as well as a box of minute rice, a bag of oatmeal, raisins, and an engorged tube of vegetarian haggis.

Agnes is at the cash and tells me to put my armload on the counter, that she's got it. I say oh no no and she says oh yes yes, and I let her because I didn't plan this escape very well and only have about three hundred dollars to my name.

Agnes asks if I want to drive home but I say I don't think I'm ready. She says sure you are, hands me the keys, and gets into the passenger seat. I stare at the door handle. Get in! she calls. I open the door and sit down behind the wheel where I haven't been permitted for the past year and a half. It does help that the driver's side of this car would be the passenger's side of Chris's, where I'm accustomed to sitting. But now that I've said her name in my head and I'm thinking about her sitting beside me and staring down the road with her jaw shut like a trap, not letting me drive because I'm immature and have shit reflexes, my throat is starting to swell. Probably it's true that I don't know how to drive and can't be trusted. Probably I am a fucking bitch and should just cuff my own hands behind my back and deliver myself to her and lie at her feet until she's forgiven me. What makes me think I deserve to have cream at the top of my milk, or to not have a baby with someone whose name I can't think of without wanting to escape my body the way I did our house?

I'm crying, and Agnes is apologizing for pushing me to drive. She gently takes the keys from my hand and passes me a tissue from the glovebox. Adult women always seem to have tissues at hand. My mother keeps them in her sleeves. If I were really an adult woman I would have tissues too. I tell the part of myself that thinks it could have a baby that it is stupid, that I would be a bad mother who never had tissues and whose child was perpetually snot-nosed and chap-faced. I'm crying loudly. I'm embarrassing my aunt in her tiny town. I gulp a breath and blow it out slowly. I blow my nose. I press the heels of my palms into my eye sockets.

I'm sorry, I say, I'm sorry.

It's fine dear, says Agnes. No apology needed.

We switch places and she drives us home in silence, but not the silence I'm used to being driven home in. This one is more like a thick blanket and less like a deep hole.

AFTER A LUNCH OF TOAST spread with veggie haggis, which Agnes glances at skeptically while she eats a ham sandwich and sips tea, she asks me if I'm sure I'm pregnant. She says she doesn't think she could've managed to eat sheep's heart, liver, and lungs when she was.

Well, I say, it's fake haggis.

Right, says Agnes, but still. How far along do you think you are?

Twelve days exactly, I say.

Right, she says again, of course you would know, having done it at the clinic.

It must seem stupid that I got pregnant on purpose with someone I hate, I say.

That's not what I meant, hen. People get pregnant in all kinds of complicated situations. I've seen many.

Did you want to be pregnant? I ask.

She takes off her glasses and rubs her eyes like the question has made her instantly very tired. Ah well, she says. I did and I didn't. I loved the lad at the time but I was very young. By the time I had the baby, he was gone. I heard he took up with a switchboard operator across the river in Finnieston. I was quite sad to be left on my own, and felt every bit the dolly my parents said I was. But in a way, I preferred it without him.

So you had the baby?

I did, but that's a story for another day. You may like to take another test, though. Twelve days is still very early.

I nod soberly. It would be an easy out, I think, if my body said no. A relief, in some ways, if the tether was cut. But what if this is my one chance? What if I never manage to get pregnant again?

If you are pregnant, says Agnes, you still have plenty of time to decide what you want to do.

I look down at the crust of bread and crumbs of spiced mash on my plate, and the grime beneath my fingernails, which have grown longer than I like.

I support whatever you choose, Agnes says, and reaches for my hand across the table as I heave myself out of my chair and rush across the kitchen to throw up into the sink.

THREE DAYS LATER, WE'VE EATEN all the cheese and bread and crackers. There's only a swig left of Light & Low. I would've thought a pregnant body would crave fresh things from the earth and as many colours as it could absorb, but the only foods I can stomach are white or beige. I had to put the green pepper in a bag at the back of the fridge because every time I opened the door and saw its thick shiny skin and inhaled its bitter smell, my mouth would juice with spit and I'd have to run to the sink again.

Agnes is making herself a plate of ham tubes run through with toothpicks, pickled beets, and mixed nuts. When she unzips the lid of a tin of kippered herring, Alastair gallops into the kitchen and prays to her with his tiny paws and I retreat to my room and crack the window. It's internet Scrabble day with Mary.

Could I walk to town? I wish I had a phone to look up the distance. I wonder if The Person, no I said PERSON, is still trying to crack my password, or if she's given up and tossed my phone into the ocean, or backed over it with her car. I haven't checked my email since the day I arrived. Not because the Highland air has caused me to grow a hale sense of self-control. I asked Agnes not to let me use the laptop again for a while and she obliged.

I change my socks and trade my sweatpants for jeans and pull on a hoodie. I go to the bathroom to brush my teeth. I see myself in the mirror, wearing all black amongst the yellow tiles and crocheted green tissue-box cover and tufted green toilet seat, and feel like the most angsty teen. I spit into the sink and rinse my mouth. I bare my teeth at myself, then lean forward and inspect the pores on my chin. I try to look at my face as a whole thing to determine if, objectively, I'm pretty, but it keeps dividing into parts to examine for transgressions. My nose is slightly bent. The crease between my brows is deep. My jaw continues to soften such that I can't help but pull the skin back toward my ears with my thumbs to see how much prettier I could be. It's too bad I wasted the last year before gravity began to claim my face on Chri— Fuck. The Person.

Another thing is that my bangs have grown too long. I look like a potato in a wig. But while I can't do plastic surgery on my own jaw,

I can cut my own bangs. I find scissors in a leather case under the sink, tie back my hair, and begin to snip slowly across my forehead.

I've had a professional haircut exactly once in my life, for my high school graduation. Before I moved away, Bonnie would cut my hair, and by hair I mean only the bangs, because the church she grew up in, and which my grandparents attended until their death, was very, very strict about hair. About everything. Doth not even nature itself teach you that if a man have long hair, it is a shame unto him? But if a woman have long hair, it is a glory to her, for her hair is given her for a covering. Don't all kids know that one? Bonnie wasn't even allowed bangs as a child and told me I should be grateful.

Gran and Grandad would trundle into the Free Presbyterian Church of Scotland on 4th Street, and me, Mum, Dad, and Aileen would be around the corner at Geneva Presbyterian, a two-minute walk away. If you were so inclined, the Presbyterian Reformed church was also a two-minute walk away, as was the Lutheran. The United and Roman Catholic churches were a bit further, three minutes at least. The Baptist and Community churches were across the river.

I complain about the god I grew up with, but it could have been worse. Dad was United and Mum was FPCS when they met, and before they married they negotiated the Geneva as a compromise. I'm aware it's not standard practice for split-sect couples to just meet somewhere roughly in the middle, but Bonnie was thirty by the time she met my dad, so, ancient by FPCS standards. My dad felt that FPCS was too strict, and to Bonnie, United was practically Woodstock. I gather they were in some type of love at the time, so they managed to sort it out. And while my grandparents may have otherwise exiled my mother from the family for even considering leaving the church, they were down to their last daughter, which may have dampened their zeal.

Bonnie's conversion meant I was allowed to listen to music and dance and play UNO and watch *The Fresh Prince of Bel-Air*. I was allowed to wear pants, but not at Gran and Grandad's house. I recall being told at six that denim was the Devil's material and being very suspicious of my jeans for a time. And though our church didn't consider it unchristian for me to cut my hair, Bonnie couldn't overcome her lifelong conditioning so permitted bangs only.

For graduation, though, as a gift, she said I could get my hair cut at the Head's Up Hair & Wig Salon in Hanover. Below your shoulders, she said, a commandment. Angie and I rode our bikes for an hour on the side road to get there. She wanted to hit up the Sally Ann and Trudie's Thrift for something cool to wear to prom— specifically, something cool and blue to match her boyfriend's tie. Wouldn't it be easier if he just matched you? I asked. But the tie had been his dad's and his dad was dead. His dad probably owned more than one tie, I said, and Angie glared at me like I had no soul. I apologized. But she stayed mad until we stopped at Pearl Lake to swim, and then she laughed and screamed with me because it was early May and the water was cold as a witch's tit. We dunked ourselves under and ran back out as fast as we could and wrapped ourselves up in one towel and kissed, because even though Angie had a boyfriend, she was still my secret girlfriend.

Angie read hair magazines in a chair by the door while a woman with metallic lipstick and a Rachel cut combed out my wet mop.

What are we doing today, hon? she asked.

Pixie, I said.

She tied my long hair in a ponytail, lopped it off without ceremony, and handed it to me. I thought maybe I should save it in case I regretted my choice, that I could hot glue it to the back of a baseball cap or something. Angie said the cut was cute but Bonnie was livid. She banned me from prom. She had stopped slapping me in the face when I surpassed her in height the year before, so I felt bold enough to tell her I'd never forgive her. I shut my bedroom door and cried face down on my bed for an hour, but it was probably for the best. Angie would never have slow danced with me in public.

Sometimes I think about chopping my hair again, especially now, as an attempt to shear off what I'm trying to leave behind. But I need the hair to hide my beginner's jowls.

I lean over the sink and brush the clippings from my cheeks. In the mirror my face looks a bit more familiar, perhaps not so hideous after all.

I hover in the doorway to the kitchen, as far away as I can keep from the kippered herring, to ask Agnes in a whisper if there's a way for me to get into town, a bus or something. She asks if I'd like to try the car but I say no thank you. She tells me there is a bus, I just have to walk ten-ish minutes west to the primary school to catch it. It only runs a few times on Saturdays, she says. The next is, let's see now, and she looks it up.

Then a voice from her phone says is that Sorcha, pronouncing my name the way Agnes and Linda do. Agnes turns the screen around so I can wave at Mary.

Hello dear, Mary says. How lovely you're visiting your gran for Christmas.

My aunt, I say.

Oh, right, says Mary.

Agnes turns the phone back around. The next bus leaves at just past one, she tells me. And the only one you can catch back leaves from the Drum post office at twenty past six, so be sure not to miss it. One moment, Mary, she says to her phone, and digs for change in her purse and writes her phone number on the back of a receipt. She hands me both.

I grab my backpack and put on my coat and hat even though it's above zero, and walk west on the grassy shoulder of the road, set down in a gentle valley between the low hills and along a narrow river. The clouds hang heavy and I walk under them, hoping they won't burst. I see stone walls and a wooden playset with a metal slide and a greenhouse and behind that, the school. The bus shelter is just ahead. I look at my watch. I still have a few minutes.

I walk up the street beside the school to where the walls are topped with ivy, and evergreens I don't know the names of rise up taller than you'd ever see in Cape Breton. The painted birdhouses in the trees' low branches, the Gothic windows of the stone school, and the green picket gate between the walls, only wide enough to admit children in single file, make me weepy. I'm glad it's Saturday and no one is around to see.

What if I let the cells divide into a baby? What if we stayed here, and Agnes delivered that baby, and the baby grew into a kid, and I walked that kid to school every day and picked them up after? My kid, who would look a bit like me and a bit like someone I've never met. My kid, with hair at whatever length they pleased, running in a pack with other local kids within the stone walls of the stone school, across the road from the green field and low hills. My kid, who would talk like the locals and pronounce all the Gaelic words right. What if I changed my last name to Blair and we just stayed here forever and The Person forgot I existed. What about that?

It starts to rain and I look at my watch again. The bus should be here soon. I run back down the street and into the bus shelter and gaze out at the field. An antlered deer emerges from the trees at the edge of it and stares back at me, but then the bus comes rumbling and the deer runs off. I get on and pay the fare and sit on the right side of the aisle so I can look for it, but it's gone. We pull away.

The bus passes Agnes's cottage, then Nessieland. At the post office I get out. It's raining harder so I put up my hood. The building is old and made of stone, like most things around here, and the staunchness of these structures, the cottage, the primary school, the post office, makes me feel soft and impermanent but also protected, like how can I go back to where houses are made of sticks and so much more prone to being burned up or blown down?

This post office is also a tearoom because everything here is ridiculously charming. I go inside and stare at the desserts in the glass case from under my dripping hood. The plump woman with bleached hair behind the counter says what can I get you, love, and I say I think tea and maybe something to eat, and she says you're just in time for afternoon tea, I can make you up a stand. I don't know what she means by stand but I say yes please and pay £14 on my Visa, which seems like a lot but in this moment I feel brash, since I'm on vacation from my entire life.

I take off my coat and drape it on a chair, and sit across from it at a table by the window and watch the rain. The woman brings over a tier of plates covered in tiny crustless cheese and egg sandwiches and tiny cakes and a massive scone and little pots that she says are filled with apricot jam and lemon curd and clotted cream. She sets it down before me, along with a teapot, milk jug, and gilded blue cup on a tray. Nothing is a vegetable. Everything is made from milk or eggs or flour or sugar, and I know that even though a single person probably wouldn't, I will finish it all. The words *clotted cream* sound so unhealthy together it's almost a turn on. When the woman turns her back, I dip my finger into the pot and suck it off.

As the rain patters its final drops onto the wet ground, I drink the last of the cold tea at the bottom of the pot. I feel pleased with myself, like instead of being bad by eating so much dairy and sugar I'm being very, very good.

Well done you, the woman says when she comes to collect my empty dishes, and I think to the cells, you're welcome.

I walk south toward the Scotmid, past white stuccoed houses and a field of cows, under a sky whose impenetrable grey makes me think of Creignish. I wonder what she's doing right now. The Person. It's Saturday, so she isn't at work. What would she be doing for fun? Or is she in mourning? Maybe she's found some bicurious divorcée in the Cape Breton Highlands to woo. Maybe she's staying with her parents to recover and hate me in concert.

I thought I'd be sadder about leaving. I've cried so much these past months that I expected to shed a good few cupfuls over the split. But by the time I had my feet in the stirrups and the swimmers were shooting down the tube, I had already been stripped clean of love. I thought there was a chance it could grow back but it hasn't. Turns out it's more like a coal mine and less like a red, red rose.

At the Scotmid I buy two jugs of whole milk with cream on top and a jug of Light & Low for Agnes, two bricks of old white cheddar, two loaves of bread, oat crackers, and a box of decaf PG Tips, which I cram into my backpack, crossing my fingers the zipper won't split.

On my way out I pick up a sweet potato from a bin near the till, the only vegetable that doesn't make me want to retch, and whisper fuck you to Chris. Yeah whatever, Chris, I can eat a sweet potato. I can say your name in my head and not perish. Though I can't stop from checking over my shoulder, as if just thinking it could alert her to my location.

I return to the till and buy the potato and put it in the wet pocket of my coat. Then I walk to the pharmacy down the road as directed by the Scotmid cashier. I wander the aisles like I'm not sure what I need. I casually take a pregnancy test off the shelf. Beside the tests are prenatal vitamins, several different brands. I pick the ones in the form of gummy bears and try to pay like I have no idea what I'm purchasing.

You all right? says the teen behind the counter.

Um, I say, because somehow this youth with braces and the tightest ponytail I've ever seen knows I'm essentially not.

Jumping the gun, yeah? she says, shaking the vitamins.

It's for my friend, I say.

Well if your friend keeps the receipt she can bring 'em back if she ain't up the duff.

Thanks, I say, and drop my purchases into my other pocket.

Outside, I look at my watch. I still have three hours to kill with my enormous backpack and bulging pockets and soggy mantle, and the winter sun is already setting. I walk back north, wondering if the blond woman will let me wait out my bus in the teahouse. But I'd probably have to eat another scone to justify it and I'm still full and nearly broke. So I detour down Kilmore Road, walking by a public hall and a bar and then some woods and on the other side, a cemetery, which seems a bit YA thriller, a cemetery on Kilmore Road. If I were sixteen maybe I'd wander through and sit up against a headstone and read some Plath, but I'm thirty-one and very damp and my pockets are full of potato and prenatal vitamins and I really, really need to pee. I step over the crumbling rock wall along the side of the road opposite the church and walk a few metres into the woods, where I take off my boulder of a backpack and unzip my jeans. I rip open the pregnancy test and hope not to startle some wholesome family out for a walk now that the rain has stopped.

I put the test back in my pocket with the vitamins and rehoist my bag. The road intersects with another and I follow it, crossing my fingers I won't get lost as I walk past hulking stone rowhouses and then a squat white building with a red door and a red sign that says Cobson's Bakehouse. The setting sun finally burns a hole through the quilt of clouds. I turn my face to it and close my eyes before it goes down. The air smells like blueberry muffins, and I take the test out of my pocket and check it and it tells me, again, that I'm pregnant.

Okay, I say to the test, and to the cells, and to myself. I nod and inhale. Okay. I'll jump through this door. I eat a prenatal gummy bear and walk back to the main road in the low light.

Near the fire station, Agnes drives past me in her little white car, turns around, and pulls in.

Have you had enough of trudging about Drum? she asks. I nod and get in. You should've rung me, hen, she says, I'm happy to get you.

I reach over with both arms and give her a tight damp hug and tell her I'm making us sweet potato ravioli for dinner.

I open the laptop with a chaperone. *Agnes is across the table from me reading* The Da Vinci Code *with Alastair in her lap. We drink tea from matching yellow cups.*

It's been a week since I checked my email, a week since I left. I only have four new emails from The Person, an improvement over the first nine. Two have no subject and one is entitled *Coward* and the other *Bitch*, which I know is meant to make me feel bad but actually takes the edge off, to know that in the midst of an angry tirade, she paused to consider an appropriate title for her rant, and capitalized it.

I delete all thirteen and feel like I control the weather.

I read the emails from my friends. Dana sent a picture of Oscar eating cucumber with his new teeth. She and Linh both ask where I am, if I'm okay. Ruth is a perfect vault, she probably didn't even tell George. And her own email is kinder than I deserve. I want to tell it all to her, write her a novel of every fucked up thing that happened as an excuse for how I became a horrible friend, but the catalogue is a mess because I never had a proper filing system and pretty much just swept it all off the floor and into a closet. You can see corners and edges slipping through, down by the hinge and there by the knob, and an unravelled strand like a tail beneath the door. If I open it up who knows how long it will take me to shove it back in again. It's not really an excuse, anyway.

So I write to each of them, *I love you, I'm sorry, thank you, I'll write more soon.* Agnes passes me the plate of oat crackers. I email Marg my address so she can send the cheque. I beg her to tell no one where I am.

Agnes says she wants to take me to the castle. It's the day before Christmas Eve. Though I'm mostly sure I don't believe in God, I've attended Christ's birthday party, such as it is, twenty-six times, including the years I travelled home for the holiday before I came out and was banished, or banished myself, I guess. Co-banishment.

Christmas, for most of my life, has been heavy on rejoicing, though my mother's discomfort with it was always palpable, and we had to tone it down while my grandparents were alive. They were the sort of Christians who believed true Christians should celebrate nothing, and certainly nothing remotely proximal to a Pagan solstice. And besides, there's no proof Christ was born on the twenty-fifth and there's no place in the faith and life of a true Christian for deliberate falsehood. As Gran would oft remind us, the Devil is a liar. The beeswax nativity figurines my father brought to the marriage from his childhood were blasphemous for their flagrant breach of the Second Commandment, re: graven images, and had to be melted into candles. Given my associations with my family and Christmas, I have a residual confusion regarding how to properly rebel. Is it by not celebrating or by celebrating extra hard?

My poor aunt. If I think I got it bad for coming out in a blended FPCS/United family, Agnes certainly had it worse for getting pregnant out of wedlock at fourteen in the undiluted glare of an FPCS God.

I wonder how she rebels during the yuletide.

We boil another kettle of water and make a thermos of tea. Agnes puts it in her purse along with a bag of salted crisps, and we drive past Nessieland, the post office, the fire station, the Scotmid, through the roundabout, across the River Coiltie, and along the loch to the castle. In the winter it closes at four but because Agnes delivered the manager and all three of his sons, he turns a blind eye when she sneaks past the gate after hours.

The sun has set and the wind off the loch is sharp. I zip my coat up past my chin, tuck my hands into my sleeves, and follow my aunt down the path and across a stone bridge in the twilight. With no one else here, it feels as if we've discovered the ruin ourselves. We pass under an archway between two huge broken cylinders, white with lichen. We climb the steps toward the ruins of a tower, the remains of walls. Agnes says the manager made her promise to only go up to the third floor, and to be careful for the love of God. I ask her if she comes here often. She says you might say that. The tower's south wall looks as if it was chomped by a medieval dragon. We climb the wooden stairs, built for tourists, and look out over the remains of old halls and rooms on the ground below, open to the air and carpeted with grass, and beside them the loch, reflecting the dark sky.

Agnes spreads a blanket on the stone floor, sits down and pops open the crisps as the gibbous moon emerges from behind a cloud. Sit, hen, she says. She wraps another blanket around us both and offers me the bag.

I take a crisp.

I've decided to have it, I say.

Well dear, says Agnes, you've come to the right place.

It's true, I think, and say a silent thanks to whoever arranged it.

Do you pray? Agnes asks, as if she heard me.

Not to God, I say. But to something, every now and then. Do you? She rubs the salt off her fingertips and puts on her mittens.

No, she says. I put in enough time praying as a child to last me a lifetime. It reminds me too much of my parents.

What did they do, I ask, when they learned you were pregnant?

Well, Agnes says, well. She stares at the moon for a minute, as if it might speak for her. I knew they'd toss me out so I saved them the trouble. But when I realized I couldn't do it alone and came back to Inverness from Glasgow with wee Bonnie, they took her. They didn't tell me they were leaving. They sent me to the shop for milk and when I returned, they'd gone. Eventually I got it out of a neighbour that they'd sailed to Canada.

What do you mean, you came back with Bonnie?

Oh my dear, she says. I thought you might have sorted it by now.

I stare at her. I haven't.

Bonnie was my baby, she says. I gather they told you otherwise.

They did, I say in disbelief.

So I'm your gran. Though I'm partial to Aunt Agnes, as it doesn't make me feel quite so old. She looks at me with wet eyes and a small smile, as if she hopes I don't mind.

I find her mittened hand and hold it. I like you even better as my gran, I say.

And then I cry too, because I have a living gran who doesn't believe I'm destined to be cast into hell to endure conscious torment forever, and who has five earrings in her left ear and three in her right, and who took me to a castle to eat crisps under the moon, and who could deliver my baby, and who seems like she could maybe even love me.

We decided not to do presents, which is for the best because I'm broke. But we've put on the radio and are singing along blasphemously while we roll out a Christmas pizza with rosemary and cranberries and sweet potato, plus cold cut turkey on Agnes's half. She is tipsy from eggnog and rum and I wish I was too.

I've been looking at her birth books. I read in one of them that the cells are now an embryo the size of a grain of rice. According to the developmental diagrams, it looks like a salamander: tiny jewel eyes, permeable skin. And a tail.

I'm so tired all the time that I fall asleep while sitting at the table shredding mozzarella for the pizza, and wake up when "Jingle Bell Rock" comes on and Agnes drops a few more ice cubes into her glass. She asks if she can top up my cup and I nod dozily while she glugs in some eggnog.

Happy Christmas, hen, she says.

Happy Christmas, I say, and smile.

I feel insulated from everything. The only person who could find me right now is Marg. I hope she's sent my cheque. Most of the time I don't feel lonely because I have Agnes, and because she's retired she'll hang out with me whenever, except during Saturday Scrabble. We've watched the first two seasons of *Hamish Macbeth* together already. She has the episodes memorized. She says that even after all these years, Scrabble and television feel like a rebellion, and you can tell she relishes the wickedness. She holds the remote like a child with a cherry bomb. I'm not one for cop dramas but I do like Isobel, and of course Wee Jock, the dog.

I've also been talking to the salamander, so that makes me feel less lonely. As an incubator, you're never really alone.

I miss Ruth though. This time of year my guilt feels extra sharp.

After Agnes and I have eaten the pizza and watched Hamish and Anne uncover the murderous plot of the local laird's glamourous new wife, Agnes passes out on the couch. I cover her up with a blanket and tuck it under her feet, and Alastair resettles himself against her stomach. Outside the kitchen window, the full moon lights up the first falling flakes of snow I've seen since I arrived. I wrap my arms around myself and wonder if it's snowing in Halifax. It would be six there now. My friends are probably eating their own Christmas dinners with their families and partners. Ruth usually goes to George's parents' house on Prince Edward Island.

Every year, after bits of wrapping paper are picked off the carpet and cranberry sauce washed off the plates, I get this lonely, mortal feeling. Maybe because I know I'm supposed to feel full and tranquil, basking in the glow of a fire or at least a candle, cozy with my loved ones, and because it seems this is what everyone else I know is doing, or at least their social media posts suggest so.

My twenty-six Christmases with my family were pretty consistent. My sister would be piously silent yet palpably annoyed that Bonnie had bought her the cheaper version of the doll/curling iron/cellphone she had specifically requested. Bonnie would be marinating in guilt for celebrating Christmas at all, discreetly wiping away angry tears while she stirred gravy at the stove, for another year in which her ungrateful daughters didn't appreciate the presents they should not have received in the first place, gift-giving having originated with festivities for the queen of Babylonian heaven and having nothing to do with Christ. I would be feeling sad for the turkey but would eat it anyway so as not to anger Bonnie. And my dad would be watching hockey, quietly drunk on the couch. Even when I'm not in Chesley, the bitterness of cranberry seeds in my molars and the glow of little coloured lights in the dark remind me that there are only so many more Christmases left before death.

Ruth is probably busy drinking organic wine and eating free-range turkey in Charlottetown, but just in case she's not, I take the laptop into my bedroom and video call her. She picks up on the third ring and it takes a few seconds for her face to emerge from the pixels, but there she is, cheeks rosy, hair in a ponytail and eyebrows up, looking worried.

Sorcha? she says. Sorch?

Hey, I say. How are you? Are you at George's folks' place? Sorry if I took you away—

I am, she says, but don't say sorry. I'm so glad you called. How are you?

I'm good, I say. I'm...weird, but good. It's snowing here. Is it snowing there?

Not yet, she says.

I just, I wanted to say again how sorry I am, about what happened last year. About everything. I should've listened to you.

Yeah, she says, you should've. But no one listens when they're in love, and I already forgave you anyway. Are you okay?

I think so.

When are you coming back?

I don't know, not yet. Has she messaged you again?

No, says Ruth. I haven't heard anything since the first time. Have you spoken to her?

Fuck no. I pray if I'm gone long enough she'll forget she ever knew me. Maybe someone can lure her to a hypnotist. Eternal sunshine of the spotless mind.

Wouldn't that be nice.

Wouldn't it?

You can talk to me, Sorch, if you want. About whatever happened.

Yeah, I say. Yeah. I don't know if I've figured it out yet, whatever it was that happened. Or how it happened. I'm still, like, climbing out of the hole.

I hear you, Ruth says.

Thanks, I say. I miss you.

I miss you too. What's your aunt like?

Oh, I say, she's cool as hell. And she's actually my gran but I'll explain that later. I wish you could meet her.

What? Okay well, yeah, into hearing that story. Look, girl, I should get back to dinner. But I'm so glad you're okay, and I love you.

I love you so much, I say. Tell George I say hi and happy Christmas.

Taken up the local dialect, I see.

It's cute, right?

You're a dork, Ruth says. Call me soon.

I put the laptop on the floor and get under the covers. My hands are cold so I slide them under my sweater and onto my belly. I feel like it's a bit rounder, but that's probably just the Christmas pizza.

You would love Ruth, I say to the salamander. I'll take you back to meet her, someday.

Then I fall asleep. I dream that we're locked in the basement of the Creignish house, and when it's time for the salamander to be born Chris comes down wearing a headlamp and rubber gloves that smell like lemon soap, and she pulls it out of me in a gush of salt water, and takes it upstairs and locks the door again, and I try to run up the stairs to catch them but I'm so weak, and the basement is flooded from the watery birth and I swim and swim like Alice in a sea of her own tears but I can't reach the door.

When I wake up my watch says 5 a.m. I'm slick with sweat. It's raining and all the snow has melted.

Sometimes *I sit on the couch with my tea and stare into the fire and* ponder how absurd my life is. I just sit and have a good think about it. Especially when Agnes has gone out on an errand and isn't here to entertain me with midwifery anecdotes or soothe me with her calm company. When it's just me and the workers in my brain. They dig through filing cabinets and pull out other lives and hold them up to the light, side by side, to compare. Ruth and George. Dana and Liam. Linh and Emma. Meet-cutes. Inside jokes. Twin tattoos. Cozy homes. Steady jobs. Good love. Wanted babies born into interwoven arms.

And then me. My life, like a bad reality TV show. Like, that would never really happen, the producers must have nudged things askew. The director must have cut and rearranged the scenes to create more drama. Surely that character is a plant. No one could be so cruel. Surely the main girl is putting it on. No one could be so green.

But I've been living this life for the past year and a half and I can attest: I really am so green. I really did give up my friends and home and job for a noxious love because my body yearned for a baby. I really am knocked up and on the lam. And I stare and stare and stare into the fire and wonder what it is about life that I don't get, which part of the instructional manual I skipped, which of the workers in my brain deserves to be fired.

And then when my mood is turning especially bleak, Alastair begins to knead my legs and looks me in the eyes like okay, enough. And I lie back on the couch and he sits on my chest and purrs at me until Agnes comes home and pulls me out of my wallowing.

I can't wallow around Agnes because she had it worse. Not that I pity her, she would hate that. But she does help put things in perspective. Like, Chris probably won't steal the salamander and sail across the sea to a country where I've never set foot, and raise it in a life that's a lie and leave me reeling in the dark for decades before I finally track it down to find that it won't return my Facebook messages.

Agnes says I can have ten minutes of wallowing/worrying each day. I say what if Chris hires a fancy lawyer and gets full custody? Agnes says she won't get full custody, hen, and sets the timer. I say what if she gets split custody and I have to see her every week for the next eighteen years? I say what if I'm forced back to Creignish? I say what if I never get to take the salamander to visit my friends? What if I'm never happy again? What if no one ever loves me? What if the salamander doesn't love me? What if I become my mother? What if I die in childbirth? What if the salamander dies? What if Chris dies, I ask, but I'm kind of smiling when I say it so I knock on wood to cancel the thought lest the universe return it to me threefold and kill me so hard I can't even come back to haunt Chris in the way she so deserves, or watch my tiny amphibian grow into a real human child.

When the timer goes off, Agnes makes tea and stacks digestives on a plate. We sit at the kitchen table and eat our biscuits and she asks me to name three things that are good. Sometimes it takes me a while. Sometimes all I can think of are things I can taste or touch, like milk and tea and cats. Sometimes I say Ruth and Linh and Dana, and then I cry. Sometimes I say you, meaning Agnes, and that makes me cry too. Sometimes I say the salamander. Once I said me, and it surprised me.

Agnes has been trying to get me to do yoga but I keep falling asleep. She says I should meditate. She says I should drink more water. She says I should eat pumpkin seeds. She says I should look on the bright side. What's on the bright side, I ask. Milk and tea and cats, she says. Ruth and Linh and Dana. You. Me. The salamander. The miracle of life.

I used to think the miracle of life was a religious thing, but now that I'm building a person inside my body, I get it. It doesn't need to be religious to be miraculous. And even though science can explain it, it's still magic.

Even though my life is absurd, it's still magic.

My cheque came. Even with the deductions Marg made for milk it's over a thousand bucks, so I feel rich. It's Friday, which means the buses run more often. I caught one into Drum to look for the cheque at the post office. All the shops were closed yesterday for Hogmanay, the Scottish new year. Agnes and I cleaned the bothy from top to bottom, as is tradition, before tuning into the countdown on TV and watching the neighbours' fireworks through the windows, which Alastair did not enjoy.

I splurge at the Scotmid on lemon curd, clotted cream, flour, baking powder, butter, milk, and mini steak pies for Agnes's virtual Scrabble tomorrow. In the little yellow kitchen I turn the ingredients into buttery scones and arrange a cream tea for Agnes and me on the coffee table, while we watch the last episode of *Hamish*, in which Ava and Kenneth steal the Stone of Destiny and Isobel and Hamish finally get it on in a snow cave, and the ghost of TV John's father visits Hamish and tells him Isobel is pregnant. I suppose it's not your typical cop show.

I tell Agnes I need a job. She says she can look after us, but I insist. We look online and learn I'm too old for the youth visa and too poor for the ancestry visa and ineligible for the work visa because I have no sponsoring employer. But the way one becomes not poor and finds a sponsoring employer is by getting a job, so it's all rather backward. Agnes tells me to leave it with her, that she's sure she can dig something up.

The next day after Scrabble, she makes some calls. I hear her talking on the phone from the couch, cheerfully asking after kids and grandkids, playing the midwife card to find me something illegal but not terribly so. While I'm peeling potatoes for dinner she emerges from the living room and says would you bake?

The potatoes? I ask.

No you numpty, as a job.

Oh, I say. Of course, but I don't have any experience.

Your scones were grand. I'm sure you can learn whatever else.

I'd try my best.

Perfect, she says. I'll drive you to Cobson's on Monday.

COBSON'S IS THE BAKERY ON Kilmore Road. The last time I was there it smelled like blueberry muffins. This morning it smells of oats. I've tied back my hair and I'm pretty sure I won't throw up, though I might fall asleep.

It's six and still dark. Agnes parks the car alongside three others in front of the squat white building. She comes with me to knock on the door and the manager, Gerald, answers. He looks about fifty and wears a white cotton chef's coat and flat white cap and white apron dusted with flour. He owes his life and limbs to Agnes, who saved him as a newborn, blue with meningitis. She delivered his daughter as well, so in light of all that, an under-the-table job seems like no big deal. They hug hello and Agnes wishes me well on my first day before getting back into her little white car and driving off.

Gerald takes me on a tour of the bakery. It's long and narrow with few windows. Even though the sun won't be up for another three hours, two bakers are already slicing trays of shortbread into fingers and popping cakes from their tins.

This is Sorcha, Gerald says to the bakers. She'll be helping us out.

One of them looks up from the shortbread and gives me a quick smile. Glad to have an extra set of hands, she says, as she cuts a sheet of cookies with an enormous knife.

The other baker tilts his head at me. Sorcha, he says. That's a good Scottish name. Same as my gran. Where you from?

Halifax, I say.

West Yorkshire? But you sound American.

Canadian.

Ah, the colonies.

I suppose, I say.

Sorcha, this is Iain, and this is Gemma. Stick with them and see if you can learn a few recipes. I'll be in my office dealing with orders for a couple hours should you need anything.

Have you a coat or cap? Gemma asks.

Afraid not, I say.

Not a worry. Lisa's are in the back. You can borrow them.

She leads us farther down the narrow building to a room full of cardboard boxes and a deep-freeze and a row of hooks on one wall holding winter coats and, at the end, a white cotton coat and flat white cap.

You can hang your stuff up here and put these on, Gemma says.

Where's Lisa? I ask.

She had a baby a month or so ago, poor thing. Says getting up at half four to come in here and bake seems like a sleep-in now. Have you any kids?

No, I say. Do you?

No, though my mother and mother-in-law won't get off my arse about it. I told them I'll only squeeze one out if they'll each babysit half the time, because we all know my husband would be useless.

I smile.

Do you have a boyfriend? she asks.

No, I say. I don't know anyone here other than my aunt. I mean, my gran.

Mix them up, do you?

It's early, I say with a laugh.

Actually, says Gemma, it's late. I've been here since five.

I WATCH GEMMA SLICE UP another tray of shortbread. Then she talks me through the recipe for oaty vanilla creams as she mixes the wet and dry ingredients in two stainless steel bowls, and combines them. All the recipes are contained in a book that's kept under the kitchen counter, though she and Iain have them memorized. She says I can borrow the book to study and practice a bit at home, but that I mustn't share the recipes with a soul as they're top secret and much coveted. The bakery supplies Nessieland and the hotel, as well as a couple cafés in Inverness, she says proudly. People trust the name, so consistency is key. Everything has to taste as the consumer expects.

I nod, intimidated.

Is that a manifesto? asks Iain from over by the oven.

Quiet you, says Gemma. He's quite the pest, as you'll quickly learn.

Iain winks at me and I try to remember the last time I had sex. And then I think of the last time I had sex with a man—in Maine, with the bespectacled professor. My first, I would have thought of as more of a boy, an eighteen-year-old virgin from Petite Rivière who was good at kissing but nervous about everything else. We were both new to Halifax and in the same class. He cheated off me on a test so I told him he owed me a beer for it, and we had half-drunk sex that wasn't half bad. But then I met Jen and fell into a deep hole of love and when he asked me out again I said I had to study, and he said what about next week and I said I was busy then too, and after that he sat on the other side of the classroom. What an asshole I was. In retrospect I probably should have dated him, or at least given it a try. Then I wouldn't have this morbid heart tattooed on my arm.

I've never dated a man. I tried in high school after Angie got a boyfriend and I figured that was how it was meant to be done: secret girlfriend, public boyfriend. Maybe I should have tried harder. It does seem, I don't know. Easier. Based on my stellar history of dating women, perhaps I should give men a go. Though Iain is stubbly and I've never kissed anyone with stubble. What if it gives me a rash?

Oi, Sorcha! Iain says from beside me. You gonna stare out that window all morning, or you want to learn to make cranachan cake?

Sorry, I say with a blush.

I don't suppose you can pronounce it?

Cranaken, I say.

Iain shakes his head smugly. Say the ch as in loch, or Sorcha. Or can't you say your own name either? He winks at me again. Good grief.

I can't say it very well, I say. But I'm practicing.

Well, he says, keep it up.

I watch as he mixes up a sponge cake with a handful of raspberries tossed in. While it bakes, he toasts oats in a pan over the flame of the gas stove. He gives me a bowl of huge, pale raspberries to crush with a spoon.

Imported, he says with distain. In summer I grow them in my garden and they're deep red, juicy and sweet. Scottish raspberries are the very best.

I can't wait to try them, I say with a smile. And then Iain blushes. Ha.

He whips three tablespoons of whisky in with the buttercream, then folds in honey drizzled from a spoon, followed by the oats.

This has to chill in the fridge until the cake is cooled, he says. I'll show you where it is.

I follow him through the kitchen toward the room where I hung my coat, but we turn left and pass Gerald in his office, typing on an ancient tangerine iMac, the balding back of his head looking vulnerable without its white cap. The fridge is next to the office, an entire room behind a stainless steel door, which Iain heaves open and holds for me chivalrously. It's full of jugs of milk and cream and foil-wrapped bricks of butter stacked into silver walls. Heaven.

Iain sets the bowl on a wire shelf and says so this is where we store all the dairy, and where we put anything else that, you know, has to keep cool.

Yeah, I say. I've heard of fridges.

Cheeky, he says.

You can't dish it out and not expect to get it back.

Fair, he says. He tilts his head again and looks at me with a little smile. The hat suits you.

Thanks, I say. Though I'll need a toque if I'll be spending much more time in this fridge.

A toque?

Like a warm hat.

A beanie, he says.

No, I say, a toque.

Listen, if you want to be a Scot you're going to have to lose the Canadianisms. What brought you here, anyway?

My gran, I say, which is partly true. I'm staying with her in Balnain.

How nice, he says, and it's so earnest and free of any impishness that I have to just say brrr! and turn around quickly and exit the fridge. I see a bathroom on the other side of Gerald's office and tell Iain I'll find my way back to the kitchen. Then I lock the door and look at myself in the mirror and try to decide if I'm pretty enough to reasonably assume Iain is flirting with me.

I help Gemma make a marmalade cake, and then she lets me try my hand at the scone recipe myself. By the time they're out of the oven, Gerald is back from his office. He takes a scone from the floury baking sheet, breaks off a chunk, and examines it. He crumbles a piece between his fingers. He eats a small bite plain, and another with butter.

Not bad for your first day, lass. Though I'd say you overworked the dough a bit.

I nod. Sorry, I say. I'll remember that next time.

Not to worry, says Gerald. A better first go than Iain at least. You remember those, Gemma?

Aye, says Gemma. Good projectiles.

Wheesht, says Iain.

I'M DONE BY TWO, but Gemma and Iain will bake until three. I can't imagine being on my feet for any longer, and I'm only six weeks. I wonder for how many hours I'll be able to stand at six months. I'll probably need orthotic shoes. I wonder if Iain will still flirt with me then.

Gerald let me take my overworked scones home. Agnes says they're delicious and that he's just a perfectionist, not to worry. We eat them with the lemon curd and clotted cream. She asks me what series we should start next. Perhaps *Queer as Folk*, she asks, or *The L Word*? Oh my gosh, she is so sweet I can barely not cry about it. But actually I feel like I could use a break from gayness.

I've been without a phone so long that I feel I should just shun technology entirely. I find an old fountain pen in a drawer and Agnes fills it up with blue ink. If I write my friends by hand, I don't have to see how many more emails Chris has loosed into my inbox.

I buy postcards at Nessieland with my bakery money. I only work three shifts a week so it's not much, but it's enough for groceries and treats for Alastair and a decent bottle of whisky for Agnes every now and then. I feel guilty about not paying rent, but she says not to be daft.

I write Linh about the bakery and how I've mastered the recipe for oat crackers. I write about watching the moon over the water from Urquhart Castle with Agnes, and how after two months of living in the bothy, I've still never heard Alastair meow. I write Dana about veggie haggis and the stone schoolhouse in Balnain and how it barely ever snows here. And I write Ruth about being secretly nearly thirteen weeks pregnant but still looking like I've just had a large lunch, and ask her whether I should disclose this fact to a person who I could, hypothetically, have sex with. I ask what she thinks it means for my queer cred if, hypothetically, the person is a cis man. I put Ruth's postcard in an envelope before I mail it, in case the posties are feeling nosy.

Time feels elastic. It's a good thing I have this gelatinous advent calendar. I've now eaten all sixty prenatal gummy bears. The twelve-week belly in Agnes's book looks more pregnant than mine, and I ask her why. She says not to compare too much, that all pregnancies are different. But if I still don't look pregnant in a couple weeks, she'll see about getting me an ultrasound. She asks if I have travel insurance and I laugh like fuck, I wish.

It was Valentine's Day last Friday. I worked an extra shift at the bakery to help prepare. We made heart-shaped cranachan raspberry cakes and heart-shaped shortbreads dipped in chocolate and chocolate cakes crowned with despicable imported strawberries. Gerald says my baking has much improved. He only picked out one slightly wonky shortbread heart from my stack before we wrapped them up in pink cellophane. Iain wrote *xo* on the bad cookie in chocolate icing and handed it back to me with a wink. So much winking, Christ. I try to watch him sometimes to see if he winks at Gemma as well, but he seems too pleased with himself when he catches me looking.

THE TEEN AT THE PHARMACY remembers me.

You all right? she asks.

God, is it so obvious? I think. Though I have been feeling much more all right these days.

Do I not look all right? I ask.

The teen laughs. It's just what we say, she says.

Oh, I say.

Your friend preggers after all? She looks up at me like we both know who my friend is.

Looks like it, I say.

Well congratulations, she says. Babies are grand. My mum and stepdad just had another and he's the sweetest wee thing.

Thank you, I say, meaning it. It's the first time I've thought of this as something to celebrate rather than a barely managed crisis. The teen flashes me a peace sign and a bracey smile.

I pop open my new jar of vitamins in the parking lot and eat one. There you go, I say to the salamander. Though it's not really a salamander anymore. Agnes's book shows an illustration of a bobbleheaded creature the size of a lemon with eyelids and little bones in its arms and legs.

I'm off today and tomorrow but back at the bakery on Friday. Gerald scheduled me for an afternoon shift to help Iain make a cake for a Sunday wedding. I can't imagine who would want to get married in February. Or at all.

BACK AT THE BOTHY, Agnes and I play Scrabble. She's so good it almost makes me grumpy. I had thought I was smart, or at least moderately literate, but my seventy-seven-year-old gran keeps killing it with words like *quixotic* and *wheezy* and *flapjack*. She lets me borrow her Scrabble dictionary. In exchange I lend her my book of Gaelic phrases. She says she can understand a bit but rarely has cause to speak it anymore.

What do you know? I ask.

Oh you know, the usual. Ciamar a tha thu?

Tha mi gu math, tapadh leibh, I say.

Well done you! she says. An dèan mi an tuilleadh tì?

Oh, I don't know that one, I say.

It means shall I make more tea?

I smile. Nì, tapadh leibh.

Agnes says there are a few speakers around Balnain, and in Inverness, but most live in the Outer Hebrides. She says she spoke better when she was delivering babies, using Gaelic with parents and grandparents, many of whom are now long gone.

ON FRIDAY AFTERNOON I walk to the bus stop. The primary school kids are still running off the energy from their lunches, screaming in the absolutely piercing way I'd forgotten children can scream. Sliding down the metal slide, pumping their legs determinedly on the swings. Digging holes in the earth with sticks like it's their job, collecting rocks and pine needles as precious treasures. I wonder what the salamander would be doing. I myself was a collector, quiet and weird, storing moss and rocks in old egg cartons, pressing flowers into books. I hope the salamander doesn't turn out to be a jock. Maybe we shouldn't have chosen Andrew the runner as its donor.

It's too bad I have to spend this afternoon in the kitchen. In Nova Scotia it's snowstorm season, but here it's a balmy ten degrees and the trees look like they're thinking of sending out their buds. The sun is setting later now, 5:30 rather than 3:30, and it's a gift.

I run into Gemma and Gerald on their way out.

I left a sketch of the cake with Iain, Gerald says. Cranachan raspberry but with pound cake rather than sponge, and six layers instead of two.

I give him a thumbs up. Weddings are stupid but I love making cakes.

Afternoon, Miller, Iain calls from the far end of the long bakery, where he stands texting in the coat room. He puts his phone back in his jacket pocket.

Afternoon, Buchanan, I say as I come in. I unbutton my sweater and hang it beside his jacket.

You're looking well, he says.

I brushed my hair.

For me? I'm flattered.

You should be, I say.

After a month and a bit, our banter is well baked. I ask if he's been studying the blueprint for the cake and he says he's way ahead of me and has measured out most of the ingredients. He says he wanted to get it done in advance so we'd have more time to waste together. I roll my eyes at him. I feel obliged to act as if I don't like his attention, some deeply socialized hetero hard-to-get roleplay. But I look at him and see that he's clean shaven and decide that I would like to kiss him, and that to make this more likely I'll try to stop being so salty.

I crack eighteen eggs into a large steel bowl, careful not to miss a speck of shell among the orbs. Iain brings over the milk and vanilla and stands closer than necessary while he pours each into the bowl.

Is this a two-person job? I ask before I can stop myself.

You're still in training, ye wee besom.

Excuse me?

Upstart, he says, glancing at me with a smile.

I force my eyes not to roll. Straight flirting is cheesy as hell.

I whisk the eggs and milk and vanilla with a fork until just combined while Iain knocks flour, sugar, baking powder, and salt into the giant electric mixer and blends it on low. I bring over the sloshing bowl of whisked eggs and another heavy bowl of softened butter, and watch as he adds the butter and half the eggs slowly into the mixer, and the paddle folds them in. We're really not supposed to but I always scoop a taste when no one's looking.

So who's getting married? I ask, as Iain cranks up the mixer to medium.

Someone in Inverness, he says. No one I know. He turns it back down and adds the rest of the eggs.

Six tiers. Sounds like a real party.

Iain laughs. Have something against weddings, do you?

I just don't think they do what people want them to do, I say.

What do you mean, he asks.

No party or gold ring or six-tier pound cake is going to preserve your love.

You divorced, then? he asks.

No, I say, never married.

Well, weddings can be fun. You know, get dressed up, get sottered with your mates.

If you like weddings so much, why aren't you married? I don't see you wearing a ring.

Ah, well, he says. Good bakers never wear rings.

We butter the cake tins and I hold them still while Iain scrapes batter into each. Again, not a two-person job, again standing closer than necessary. We carry them to the enormous oven, slide them in, and set the timer.

What shall we do now? he asks. Fancy a drink?

I shake my head at him and smile. We should make the icing, I say.

Ah, that takes all of fifteen minutes. We can do that while the cakes cool. Gerry doesn't mind if we take a wee break.

I don't drink, I say.

What're you, pregnant? A nun?

I laugh and hope not to be punished by the universe for lying by omission. I haven't yet heard back from Ruth about what to do, and am afraid if it gets out that I'm pregnant, I'll never have sex again.

How about tea? I ask.

Good grief, woman. You're spending too much time with your gran.

She's the best, I say.

Aye, I hear she is. He fills the steel kettle and puts it on the stove to boil. But truly, you need to get out. Go for a beer at the Inn or something. You've been here how long?

Just over two months, I say.

And have you made any friends?

I smile. Aren't we friends?

Iain looks at me and says, ah, well, I'm not very good at being friends with beautiful women.

This is cheesy too, but I haven't been called beautiful in a good minute and I need to be touched. We're sitting on wooden stools, pulled up to the stainless-steel counter by the window with the sun shining through, and I let myself look directly at him for more than a second, long enough that if one of us doesn't look away or say something, this will turn into something else. But I keep looking and because we're sitting very close, much closer than necessary, he doesn't have to move far to bring his face to mine. And I kiss him.

He tastes like cake batter, he must have licked the spoon. He puts a warm hand on the side of my neck, his thumb on the hinge of my jaw. We kiss with the sun on our faces, glowing though our eyelids. He stands and pulls me up with him, and even though I'm tall, he's taller, and I wrap my arms around his waist.

He walks me backward to the coat room with his hands on either side of my face.

The cake, I say.

We'll hear the timer, he says.

He pulls my shirt over my head and kisses my swollen breasts. Christ but aren't you lovely, he says.

I sink into it like a hot bath, his touching and sweet, generic compliments. I think for a second that I shouldn't let him fuck me in the coat room on the first date and almost laugh into his mouth, because who do I think I am—a twentysomething straight girl with some sort of reputation to uphold and not a bad dyke in a foreign country, secretly pregnant and dying to come via anything other than her own hand?

Iain throws his jacket over the deep-freeze and I let him unzip my black polyester kitchen pants and lift me up onto it. He presses against me, his basic, unmysterious desire. And though sex with cis men can be alternately scary or boring, after enduring a year and a half of Chris's wildly unpredictable desire and layers of ire and so many nights in a row spent sleeping in the same bed without touching at all, I feel very fine about fucking Iain on top of the freezer. Though I do have to use my own hand to come in the end.

Agnes pretty much runs this town. I wonder who over the age of ten she hasn't delivered or midwifed. She says that when she retired, the firefighters spelled out *THANK YOU AGNES BLAIR* on the notice board in front of the station. They were colleagues of a sort, called to the same emergency births.

Agnes mentored Kirsten, a midwife who looks younger than me but who's been practicing for thirteen years, and therefore makes me feel like a real underachiever. I try not to think about my abandoned career as an environmental researcher as she calmly asks me questions about my last period, and acts perfectly unsurprised when I say I know my dates exactly because I conceived by insemination.

She agreed to see me on a Saturday, her usual day off unless someone's in labour. I'm lucky she agreed to see me at all as I'm very much uninsured. But, she says, she's happy to do a favour for my gran. She says she didn't know Agnes had a granddaughter, or a daughter, for that matter, while she pumps up the blood pressure cuff velcroed around my arm. I start to say neither did I, but instead I just shrug and smile.

Agnes makes tea in the kitchen while Kirsten sits with me and Alastair on the orange couch. Alastair sits between us, actually. He seems rather protective of me. What is it with cats? How do they know? When Kirsten asks me to roll up my shirt so she can palpate my belly, he gets up from his spot and sits on my lap. I kiss his head and lift him down to the floor. Kirsten rubs her hands together to warm them while I roll up my shirt and sweater, unbutton my jeans, and lie back. From this angle I look more pregnant than usual. Standing up I just have a little Renaissance belly, like back when they were in style. It's hard to tell whether it's the salamander or all the dairy I've been freely consuming.

Kirsten presses gently but intentionally, and runs a paper measuring tape to the top of the little mound. Agnes comes in with tea on a tray while Kirsten squeezes a blob of gel onto my skin.

Sorry, she says, it's nearly frozen from sitting in the car.

It's five degrees out and nearly spring. I'm not sure Scots know what cold is. Agnes sits in the orange armchair, close to the fire, and pours us each a cup of rooibos. She wears her thickest wool sweater. She'd probably need to wear five sweaters to survive in Nova Scotia. Even with my belly bare and this goop on my skin, I'm perfectly warm. Kirsten holds a small machine corded to a wand and turns it on.

Okay, she says, let's see if we can find the baby.

And don't be alarmed if we don't, hen, says Agnes. Fourteen weeks is still a bit early to hear a heartbeat.

Kirsten smooshes the gel around with the end of the wand, pressing into my belly until it picks something up, a fast fuzzy thump, kapow kapow kapow.

There it is, she smiles up at me.

Really? I say, looking over at Agnes. Her face is like the sun, glowing at me from the orange armchair.

Oh my god, I say to the salamander. You're real.

I CHECK THE POST OFFICE every day except Sunday, but I still haven't received a reply from Ruth. So I have sex with Iain on the freezer again while another special order bakes in the industrial oven. This time, one hundred chocolate whisky retirement party cupcakes, a recipe I helped create for the retiree's wife, who refused to choose from the menu. I tasted the batter several times. I hope the salamander's not drunk.

I show Iain how to move his fingers. I tell him to use his mouth. And it takes a good fifteen minutes but I finally get there just before the timer goes off, and he runs to the kitchen to haul the cupcakes out of the oven and then runs back to me, my legs splayed on the deep-freeze and tits out, and he snaps on a condom and fucks me like he's seventeen, which is to say fast and very earnestly. He comes quickly and looks abashed, so I kiss him on the cheek and say no, it was good, it felt really good, and he hugs me tight and smells my hair, and I feel guilty about not telling him I'm knocked up.

Iain told me we should keep things under wraps.

Oh, I said, I shouldn't mention to Gerald that we've been tupping on the clock?

He poked me in the side and said Gerald doesn't like when bakers date because it messes with the kitchen dynamic.

But we're not dating, I said, we're fucking.

He called me a wee besom again and kissed me in the coat room doorway.

Maybe I do want to date him.

I can still be queer if I date Iain, I think. Though it's a position I've always secretly judged, and feared: the queer cis woman with the straight cis man. In the early days or even years of it, I think I could still call myself queer in earnest, but after a while I worry it would start to feel put-on, a clung-to title. Like oh, the glory days! A dancer who hasn't danced in years. An artist who can't bring herself to paint. An environmental researcher who never reads about amphibians anymore. I want to be queer not only in theory, but in practice. Why is that so hard? Why can't the Highlands be swimming with charming rugged lesbians? Or bookish cottagecore enbies? I'd even take a bicurious divorcée.

Iain is easier, I'll give him that. He comes with no trauma, no drama. His parents never shunned him or threatened to. He doesn't seem to know what it means to be confused about who he is or who he wants. He doesn't seem to understand real fear, or shame. So that's nice, I guess. Though it sure gives us less to talk about.

He's good to kiss. He runs his thumb along the bone of my jaw. He holds the cage of my ribs in a way that makes me weak and steady at once. He tastes like butter and cream. He sucks my tongue like it's delicious.

When we can't fuck in the coat room while we bake, we have sex in his hatchback after work, parked by the cemetery on Kilmore Road. He puts the seats down and lays out a blanket so I don't bruise my spine, rocking back and forth with my legs over my head.

When we're done, we wrap the blanket around us like a cocoon and look up at the pines through the moonroof. Sometimes I can see that he's staring at me in the periphery. But I don't look because I can't risk them. You know, feelings.

inh's letter comes first. They moved with Emma into a yellow house on Falkland with shingles like crooked teeth. I know the one. They say there's no shower because the slant of the bathroom ceiling is too low, so they have to kneel in the tub when they come home sweaty from biking all over town and rinse themselves off with a jug like it's the 1800s. Emma is making them wear knee pads and elbow pads and got them a dorky new helmet with built-in lights. They're pretending to be grumpy about it, maybe to temper their sweet news for my benefit because I'm still fresh from domestic failure. But I can see through their complaining. The house sounds charming, and Emma lovely.

I'm so curious about how that happens, healthy love. Like, where you go to find it, and what you're supposed to do to deserve it.

Agnes's book says the salamander is now the size of an onion. Who decides which vegetables to choose for these comparisons, I wonder. Why not an orange, or a pomegranate? And why are my boobs so big already, Jesus. I almost resent the attention Iain pays them because they feel borrowed. The book says it's normal. It also says the salamander has fingerprints.

I look at myself from the side in the bathroom mirror and try to decide if I look pregnant or still just Renaissance. I ask Agnes if she thinks I should tell Gerald, though secretly I mean Iain. I know the answer is yes but I'm really going to miss this extremely convenient sex. And when I'm not trying to be cool about it, I would call it quite sweet sex, quite sweet kisses. Iain wrote me a poem on the back of a napkin and left it in my coat pocket yesterday. I read it on the bus. It was unoriginal and too rhymey but the crux of it was so charming, Iain wanting to eat raspberries with me in the sun, that I allowed myself to imagine raising the salamander with him for the whole ride home.

Agnes says I should tell people when I feel ready. She sips her tea and spells out *CREAG* (rock) on the Scrabble board. Gaelic Scrabble has been good practice, and it helps that Agnes can't use all the high-point letters she usually employs to wipe the floor with me, being that there's no J, K, Q, V, W, X, Y, or Z in Scots Gaelic. There are no accents on the tiles, of course, but we make do. The best I can think of this turn is *TÌ* (tea). I swear a vow to Alastair, who is sitting on the couch beside Agnes, that before I have this baby I will beat my gran at Gaelic Scrabble at least once. Agnes reaches over and pats my knee, then lays down *UISGE* (water), and I pretend to cry.

I STOP AT THE POST OFFICE on my way to work on Thursday, and because I've been working all these extra afternoon shifts and feel flush with cash, I order a decaf latte to go. Blond Jeanette grabs my mail while the milk steams and hands it to me across the counter. On top is a letter from Ruth and I say YAY so loudly that it startles Jeanette. I apologize and tear open the envelope. I missed Ruth's handwriting so much, she has the nicest little O's and does this sweet loop between her T's and H's. The way she wrote bathroom on the chore wheel was so pleasing that I didn't mind when it came my turn, though she did always have to remind me a few times before I finally cleaned it.

Ruth says I should tell Iain when I feel ready. I wonder if she and Agnes had some sort of subconscious conference. I guess it's the answer I expected. But if I don't tell him soon, my body will do it for me.

Her letter is long and I read it while I walk to the bakery. She asks how I'm feeling and if there's anything she can do. She asks if my feet are swollen and if I've been eating pickles on my ice cream. She asks what will happen when people find out that it worked. By people she means The Person, but she does me the favour of not writing out her name. She asks if I'm coming home. She asks if Iain is kind. *Meet his friends*, she writes. *That's one of the best ways to tell.* And she wants to know all about Agnes. *Video call me with your gran and the cat, and we can have virtual tea.*

I kiss the letter and slide it into my jacket pocket. It's twelve degrees and officially spring. Everyone is out with their babies and dogs, squinting gratefully into the sun. The cows in the field across the road swish their tails like they're waving at me.

I wish I could transport my pack here so I could stay insulated in this new life but miss no one. Or go back to Nova Scotia in disguise, with a new name and a new face, move in next door to Ruth and George, or Linh and Emma, or Dana and Liam, into a house big enough for me and Agnes and Alastair and the salamander. Or maybe Chris could just be swallowed up in a vortex and shipped to some parallel dimension. That would be good. That would be best.

I don't know, maybe she doesn't care anymore. Maybe she's over it and is step-parenting the bicurious divorcée's kids, or just like, running so hard all the time that she's worked through her anger and is full of endorphins.

I cross the road and flip through the rest of the mail. There's a bill for Agnes, and a seed catalogue. We could send away now for dahlias and chrysanthemums so they'd be in bloom when the salamander arrives at the end of summer, and we could nap together in the garden, lulled by bees. The salamander will be a Virgo—I forgot to tell Ruth. She'll be so pleased.

Under the seed catalogue, there's a letter for me with my name typed on the envelope.

Which is weird.

I stand at the corner of Kilmore and stare at it. Of the few people who know I'm here, who would type on an envelope? The government? Maybe I'm being sent back. Or has Kirsten somehow discovered something's terribly wrong with the salamander? Maybe it's from Gerald, who's learned of the tryst and has decided to can me in a very formal manner.

I swallow and look at the sun as if it knows. I open the letter.

It says *Sorcha, as you refuse to answer my emails I had no choice but to gain entry to your phone. I understand the insemination was successful. I expect you to return to Nova Scotia in advance of the birth, sign an agreement recognizing me as the intended parent, and file a statutory declaration acknowledging same so I can be registered as such. I will be applying for joint custody. Regards, Chris.*

The hills and the sky fall away and the sun mutes. I'm in the dark alcove praying to be swallowed. I'm in the car pummelled by rain, gripping my wet shoes in my lap. I'm in the cold basement and my sleeves are crusted with snot. I sit down and vomit my latte onto the sidewalk. I sit there for who knows how long until a worker in my brain drives my body to the bakery, and somehow I'm inside but I don't recall coming in through the door, and I say something I can't hear and Iain drives me home.

Alastair *has been sleeping with me, right up by my head. I wake with* black fur in my mouth and threaded through my eyebrows. He seems to know I need his purring directly in my ears.

I stare at the ceiling and feel the room pressing in on me. Four thousand kilometres wasn't far enough. She found me. I feel like Frodo when the blazing Eye of Sauron sees him at the Inn. Like what the fuck. How many combinations of passwords did Chris tap into my phone before it finally opened for her? How late did she stay up? All night every night for the past three months? And now she sees all.

What are the rules here? I used Agnes's computer to google whether it counts as kidnapping if the baby is the size of an onion and lives in your body. I googled what happens if you give birth in Scotland when the other parent lives across the sea. I googled whether queer non-bio parents can get custody and ended up on a site that said no, but it was Focus on the Family so I felt like a monster. And I googled if seventeen weeks is too late to get an abortion.

I don't know what the right thing is, the best thing. The least fucked up thing. I could have another salamander, a different salamander, one day, maybe. This salamander isn't a baby, yet. Not really. I haven't felt it move. It's not a person, legally. It doesn't have an opinion about its future.

Though I've sort of tricked myself by calling it a salamander. Because it doesn't look like one anymore. It looks like a baby.

But even though it looks like a baby, and even if I were to call it a baby, and even if I had felt it move and even if it did have an opinion about its future, I still believe, deeply believe, that its rights don't trump my own.

I can't remember what I said to Iain on the drive to the bothy, if anything. Nothing about abortion, I hope. Gerald left a voicemail on Agnes's phone saying he hoped I felt better soon and to ring him on Monday.

I showed Agnes the letter after Iain dropped me off. She said oh dear, oh dear dear dear. And then we burned it in the fireplace.

AGNES RAINCHECKED SCRABBLE WITH MARY. She says she's taking me to Skye. It's drizzly but she says better to start with rain than be surprised by it.

We drive past Kilmore Road and I look to see if my vomited milk is still on the sidewalk, but there's a bird in the way. We drive past fields of sheep and the vast grey loch. I leave forehead prints on the window from staring at it. I imagine myself at the bottom, ears filled with water. I ask Agnes if she believes in the monster and she says no but it's nice to imagine.

We drive past the castle, the road set into the hill, bending around the shore and overhung by bare trees, then cutting along sheer boulder walls. My stomach makes a sound like an opening door and Agnes hands me a hard-boiled egg from her purse. My throat is too thick for swallowing, but the egg is still warm so I hold it in my hand.

When I asked the internet if seventeen weeks is too late to get an abortion, it told me it wasn't, but that due to the fetus's size, the procedure is done using forceps to remove its body in pieces. The doctor keeps track of the body parts to ensure none remain, so as to prevent infection.

I believe in abortion. I do. But I can't stop thinking about the salamander—the baby—in pieces.

We turn west toward Invermoriston and pass a whitewashed cottage selling antlers and sheepskins. We follow the river and the bare trees give way to looming pines, and then open onto fields of sheep and more sheep.

How are you, hen? Agnes asks.

I unstick my forehead from the window. I don't know, I say.

The trees and the low hills rolling ahead look too much like Cape Breton. I try to remind myself that's not where I am.

Would you like to talk? asks Agnes.

No thank you, I say.

ANGIE'S PARENTS WERE DIVORCED. Bonnie would say Angie came from a broken home, and give her a bigger helping when she was over for dinner as if she were a starving orphan. Her dad did something to her mom when she was little that no one would tell Angie about, but it meant he wasn't allowed to come to their house to pick her and her brothers up for their weekend visits, or even wait at the end of the driveway. Instead, her mom would drive them to the hockey arena, where they would stand with a neutral hockey mom until their dad came to get them fifteen minutes later, so Angie's parents' paths would never cross. Her mom would give them a dollar each to spend in the vending machines while they waited, those crusty plastic capsules full of sour gum and BBQ peanuts, but sometimes she and her brothers would pool their money and buy an extra-large slushee at the concession with three straws and see who could drink the most before tapping out with brain freeze.

I wonder if I'll be forced back to Creignish so the salamander can be close to Chris. Would we do the custodial exchange at the community hall? I can't think of a neutral third party, so maybe the kid would just have to walk alone across the gravel lot between our cars like a hostage. What about before they can walk? Would we get a remote-controlled stroller? A zip line? My brain is trying to be funny to cheer me up because the prospect of seeing Chris every week for the next eighteen years makes me want to drown myself.

Suddenly we're small at the base of rising hills, driving alongside another loch, long and narrow.

This is Cluanie, Agnes says.

It's beautiful, I say, grateful it doesn't look like anywhere I've been with the Great Lidless Eye.

You know my dear, she can't take your wean from you, Agnes says, as if no one ever took a baby from her.

I stare at the placid water, stretching on and on beside the road. The hills are ochre and olive and rust, muted by fog in the distance but seeming never to end.

Maybe not completely, I say. But half the time. And I'd be tied to her for the rest of my life.

Perhaps not, says Agnes. Though if it can't be helped, there are ways to make it more bearable.

I remember last night's dream. Chris and I were married, but instead of sliding rings onto our fingers the officiant sewed our hands together, and every time I tried to protest, water poured from my mouth. The salamander had been born but it was such a small, slippery thing that it kept falling through my fingers, and Chris picked it up by the tail and dropped it into her pocket. In my own pocket I found a knife, and slowly began to cut off my sewn hand, hoping Chris wouldn't notice until I was done, but I woke up before I got through the bone.

My eyes start to well and I open the window a crack, hoping the wind will dry them.

What would you have done, I ask Agnes, if you had known your parents' plan?

Agnes sighs. She taps her thumb against the wheel.

I've thought about that thousands of times over the years, she says. Imagined what would have been if I'd returned home sooner from the shop, if I'd somehow known. She looks over at me. I'm sure I'd have done what you've done, she says, taken the babe with me and run again.

And now she's crying, too. She reaches over and turns on the radio.

I'm sorry, I say.

Ah, she says, and waves it off.

An eerie violin sings through the fog around us as we become smaller and smaller among lumbering hills. A dense forest of firs hedges us in on the right and a thin river runs on our left.

Agnes pulls off the road, parks the car, and closes her eyes.

In the end, she says, I can't regret anything.

The wind gusts through my cracked window and nudges the little car as the violin becomes frantic. Agnes turns the radio down.

I can't regret, she says again. All what happened, and what didn't. I've done my best to live a good life, to not let despair rule me. She reaches over and squeezes my hand, and we look at each other. If it were otherwise, you wouldn't have been born, Sorcha, so I can't regret.

I close my eyes and close my fingers around the egg in my other hand.

Let's get a breath, says Agnes. She pats my knee and unbuckles herself.

We climb out of the car and into the damp spring air. It beads on my hair and the fibres of my sweater. I follow Agnes through the wet grass and down to the little river.

You know, she says, they say if you dip your feet in this water you'll always find your way home. And if you dip your hands they'll never shake in battle.

Really? I ask.

Agnes smiles. No, she says. I made that up. But isn't it nice to imagine?

We take off our boots and socks and hold each other up while we step into the freezing water. We plunge our hands in and wipe our salty faces clean.

When we get back to the car, Agnes asks if I want to drive.

Okay, I say.

It's just as you would've done before, hen, only on the other side. And you've dipped your hands in the Shiel, so you've nothing to fear.

I look over at her in the passenger seat and she winks. I buckle myself in, adjust the seat, and check the mirrors. I take a breath. Fuck you, Chris. I turn the key and pull out onto the empty road with the radio playing softly, piano in a minor key. The road curves between the hills and I take it slow.

I drive us along Loch Duich and through a little village and my hands don't shake. A car zips around me and Agnes says not to worry, the locals drive fast but just take your time. She points out a castle on the left, sitting on the water and connected to the land by a stone viaduct. I drive us along Loch Alsh, and across the bridge to Skye.

Now hen, says Agnes. We're coming to a roundabout. Not to worry. Just enter calmly when there are no cars coming and take the third exit.

I hold my breath as Agnes counts out loud one, two, three, and exhale as we turn off.

Well done, you! she says.

I smile and turn the radio up.

We roll through grassy flatlands with the sea on our right, the Highlands soft and smoky in the distance. My stomach groans and Agnes picks the hardboiled egg out of the cupholder where I left it.

Can I peel this for you? she asks.

No thank you, I say.

My dear, she says, will you please eat something?

I haven't been able to eat much since the letter, due to the enduring lump in my throat. And because I feel fucked up about feeding the salamander while considering its eviction. And because I feel sick when I think about the forceps.

We drive through a small village of white stone houses and Agnes points to a sign that says *Fresh Seafood*.

Pull in here, she says.

We're the only customers, early for lunch but the server says not a worry. Agnes looks briefly at the menu and orders pan-seared scallops and langoustines in lemon pepper butter. Urged by her insistent eyebrows, I agree to sweet potato soup.

From the window beside our table we can see the water surrounded by low hills, and a bright spot in the clouds where the sun is trying to split them.

Even if you were to choose not to go on with it, you still have to feed yourself, Agnes says, as if she can read my mind.

I say I don't know what I'm going to choose. That I'm terrified of a future in which I'm bound forever to the meanest person I know. But, I say, I've been talking to it.

That does make it harder, Agnes says.

And I've sort of named it.

Oh?

Salamander, I say, and Agnes bursts out laughing.

That's unique, she says.

I smile. It's temporary, I say. But still.

The server brings our food. It smells like roots and the sea. I eat all of my soup and a thick slice of wholemeal bread with plenty of butter. Agnes cracks apart her langoustines and sucks out the meat. She offers me a scallop.

It doesn't have a brain, she says when I shake my head.

I think about how mad the Great Eye would be to know the salamander isn't vegetarian, and open my mouth. I chew the sweet muscle and swallow it down.

AFTER LUNCH, AGNES TAKES THE WHEEL. Slices of light cut through the clouds and sweep across the fields and hills ahead. Sheep pick at the yellow grass and rusty brush in their pastures. I feel better, filled up with food. I put my hand on my belly.

Agnes slows for unfenced sheep, who have little regard for roads and their perils. The herd dots the shore on our right and ranges across the asphalt. She gives the sheep a beep and they trot on, their wool dense and grey, stuck with twigs and burrs.

The road winds through rock cuts and climbs slowly into the hills. We pass through Portree and Agnes says not too much farther, and turns inland and then along the western coast. We drive through Uig and around the tightest hairpin turn as the little white car climbs above the sea. We roll down a narrow road, unmarked and only wide enough for one.

What do we do if another car comes? I ask.

Agnes nods at the passing places, little spots on either side of the road where you can pull over to allow oncoming cars to pass. But there are no other cars. Beyond the curve of the hill there's nothing but sky.

I often thought I'd one day bring Bonnie here, she says.

I look over but she's not crying. She meets my eye and grins.

What a gift, she says, that I get to take you.

We park and climb out. From the slopes of the great hills ahead jut rock towers like ancient ruins. We bundle into our coats and hats and mitts. The wind is strong but the sun is burning up the fog.

The wind beats at our ears as we hike the path with our hoods up. We pick across boulder falls and cross a small wooden bridge. I can see how the land was heaved up and where it fell, the flat slabs and sweeping drops, the sunken pools and jagged spires, its drama made gentler by a blanket of heather and grass. And as always, dotted across the wild hills are our friends, the sheep.

The ocean stretches out beyond the slopes as we climb higher, and becomes bluer as the fog lifts. Agnes outpaces me, but at least we aren't running.

At the highest point of the trail we look out, over the surging earth and sculpted shoreline, across the water to the mountains on the other side, blue in the mist.

A worker in my brain says listen, Sorcha, you've already chosen.

I nod. I won't let despair rule me.

Agnes takes my mittened hand and we turn for home.

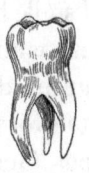

On *Monday I call Gerald and tell him I'm feeling better. He says to* rest for the morning and come in the afternoon to help Iain with the tray bakes for a function. I roll up my shirt and check my belly in the bathroom mirror. I can barely pass for not pregnant and I feel like a spy. Or maybe the salamander is the spy, I don't know. But the sun is bright and it feels like a good day for honesty.

I've been running this scene in my head where I tell Iain I'm pregnant and he says he loves babies, how wonderful, and our secret sex turns into secret dating, and then into real dating, and when the salamander is a toddler and we've passed Ruth's two-year threshold, we move into a little stone cottage in Balnain, walking distance from Agnes, where we bake our own bread and grow raspberries in the garden. Or maybe we don't wait to pass the threshold and he just adopts the salamander at the moment of birth and I marry him for citizenship but also for love, and Chris fucks off forever. I have to say I enjoy imagining this second scenario even though it makes me a bad feminist and a very bad dyke.

I arrive at Cobson's early and listen to Gemma gripe about how she needs a bloody holiday and how her husband had better take her to Paris before she goes off her head. I hang up my jacket and button the loose white coat over my little belly. Iain is pulling a double, finishing up by packing cooled scones for delivery before we start the tray bakes. He looks up at me with the sweetest smile, his eyebrows up as if to ask if I'm all right. I smile back and blink, meaning yes. I hope he doesn't come to hate me within the hour.

I set blocks of dark chocolate in a double boiler on the stovetop to melt, and begin crushing biscuits for the chocolate tiffin as Gemma and Gerald make their way out. Gerald says he's glad I'm feeling better and Gemma tells Iain not to slack off and leave all the work to me as usual.

I feel like I'm about to give a high school speech. I crush the biscuits with all my might to stop my hands from shaking. And then I realize, they're not.

You've pulverized them right proper, says Iain from very close beside me. I turn to look at his cheeky grin. You all right? he asks.

In a way, I say.

That's rather cryptic, he says.

I wipe my clammy hands on my coat and turn to face him, and he closes the space between us, runs a thumb across my cheek, and kisses me softly.

I thought we only did that in the back room, I say.

I'm happy to see you, he says. You had me worried.

He wraps his arms around my waist and tucks his head into the slope of my neck. His hot breath on my skin makes me want to take a nap with him.

I have to talk to you, I say.

He pulls back, looking worried. I ask if we can sit down.

Jesus, Miller, he says, what's up?

Please, I say, let's sit.

We balance ourselves atop the stools at the steel counter and he squeezes my hand. I look at him, and then out the window at the hazy sky, and then at my grimy kitchen sneakers.

Come on now, out with it, he says gently.

Okay, I say, and look him in the face. Okay. I'm pregnant.

He drops my hand and stands up so fast he knocks the stool to the floor. He squeezes his head between his palms and says oh god oh god, and I realize like a dope that he thinks it's his, but before I can clarify he says:

My wife will kill me.

Pardon? I say.

Fuck, he says, fuck fuck fuck. He kicks the metal leg of the steel counter and it reverberates up through my arms.

Jesus Christ, Iain, I say, it's not yours.

He stops squeezing his head.

I was pregnant when I got here.

His arms drop to his sides.

And you didn't think to tell me? he shouts.

Your wife? I say.

Yes, he says, quieter.

Well, I say.

Well what? You let me pump you while you're fucking pregnant? What's the matter with you?

What's your wife's name?

Why? You want to ring her?

No, I just want to know.

He rubs his face hard like he's trying to wake up. Helen, he says with his eyes still closed.

This is a small town, I say.

Yes, he says.

You thought I wouldn't find out?

He stares at me. I'm thick, all right? Is that what you want to hear?

I let out my breath. Can I see a picture of her? I ask.

He sighs deeply and stares at me some more, then goes to the back room to get his phone. He shuffles over to where I'm seated by the counter and holds up a photo of a pretty woman with a long face and sweet mouth and curly blond hair, about to eat a plate of pasta.

How long have you been married? I ask.

Nine years, he says.

Have you done this before?

He closes his eyes and scrubs his face with his hand again. Yes, he says.

Why?

For Christ's sake, he says. I don't know why. Because I wanted to. Why are you pregnant?

I don't know, I say. Because I want to be.

f I weren't working under the table solely by Gerald's good grace, I probably would've quit. But I don't expect Agnes to hustle me an unlimited number of illegal jobs. And really, what did I expect from someone who was interested in me? History suggests I send out a *please fuck with me I'll take it* beacon, so I shouldn't be terribly surprised. I cried a little, in the privacy of my room. Mostly out of shame. I can't believe I let myself imagine we would grow raspberries. How embarrassing.

But you know, I roll on. I've been through worse. The book says the salamander is now the size of a banana, and I've started to feel it move. At first I thought it was indigestion but I described it to Agnes and she said no, the wean is exercising. So now when I have to stand beside Iain to cut up trays of shortbread or pack scones, I do my best to close off the rest of my senses and feel only the tiny fist pummelling my bladder. I think to it, hell yes kid, use my organs as your baby gym, build your strength. May no one fuck with you.

And anyway, I have bigger concerns than philandering men. For example, in less than two months I'm supposed to leave the country. So I've been crying about that too. I thought I might be able to apply for an ancestry visa for me and the salamander and just stay here forever, outside the realm of the Lidless Eye, but according to the government FAQs, I can't. That is, despite my illegal baking gig, I'm still too poor.

To distract from all of this and fill the void left when we finished *Hamish Macbeth*, Agnes and I have resumed watching Scottish crime dramas. Agnes likes *Rebus* while I prefer *Field of Blood*. Normally I wouldn't tolerate the violence, but my seventy-seven-year-old gran beside me on the couch and a purring cat and endless milky decaf tempers it somewhat. Plus I love a strong female lead.

Agnes will be seventy-eight next month, five days before I turn thirty-two. We've been talking about how to celebrate both of our births in a way that doesn't feel funereal. Because two and a half weeks afterward I have to be on a plane back to Canada or risk never being allowed to return. No matter how cheerful the party, I know it will feel like a death, of a life I really liked imagining I could have.

I CALLED RUTH A FEW weeks ago, after Iain and I made our respective confessions. She raged and then lamented and eventually laughed with me about it because men are such garbage, how can you not? (We both know George is not garbage but in moments like these you're allowed to make sweeping generalizations without footnotes.) Then I brought the computer to the kitchen and introduced her to Agnes. They got to chatting so well that when I took a break to pee neither of them even noticed I'd gone, and when I returned they were onto the after-effects of Thatcherite terrorism and I felt laden with nostalgia for the childhood I never had, a family not fiercely rooted on the opposite side of a deep and echoing chasm.

I told Ruth the salamander will be a Virgo. I told her I have to come back in June. Months ago, she and George filled my old room with a social work student who is chore-wheel compliant and doesn't hoard all the cups or leave empty Häagen-Dazs pints on the bathtub ledge. Despite all that, Ruth said, she'd kick them out in a heartbeat if it didn't go against her principles. She told me that she and the pack will find me a place.

WHEN AGNES AND I TALK about me leaving, it's still in the hypothetical. She says she doesn't think the Home Office would come looking for me, all the way out in Balnain. But to be extra safe, she says we could sell the bothy and pack the wee beastie into his crate and move to the Outer Hebrides, where we'd buy a flock of sheep and become experts at Gaelic Scrabble. She says she's been here long enough that she could do with a change of scenery. I tell her I think I would be a decent shepherd. But we both know I have to go back.

I ask if she thinks I'm evil and she says whatever do you mean.

Well, I say, I'm trying to do to Chris what your parents did to you.

No, she says, it's not at all the same.

It is, I say, sort of.

She says again that it's not. You're like me, hen, she says. You're not like my parents. You're not stealing anyone away.

Aren't I though? I'd do anything to keep the salamander for my own.

It is your own, says Agnes.

I put a hand on my belly. Even if it's not Chris's by blood, I say, it was meant to be hers too.

Even if it was related by blood, I'd say the same, says Agnes. If it was some coarse bastard who'd knocked you up instead, I'd say you were right to do your damnedest to keep him away. The wean hasn't been born. It doesn't know Chris. It knows you.

And you, I say.

I BREAK IT TO GERALD on Friday that I'm with child. He jokes that he thought I'd just been nipping butter from the fridge, and I turn red because that's also true. My belly is too big to hide now, even in the loose white coat. I keep catching Iain eyeing it with a mixture of deference and fear, and it makes me feel like I'm wielding an ancient weapon or a secret power.

Gemma says she thought I didn't have a boyfriend and I look at her like, come on girl, use your imagination. Then I tell her my ex-girlfriend paid to get me knocked up with the sperm of a runner who likes to cook Italian food, and that I'm hoping I can reimburse her so I never have to see her again. After that, Gemma doesn't ask me any more questions.

I had thought that by now I'd be so heavy I'd have to quit, but I feel full of vigour. Agnes says to enjoy it while I can, before the backaches kick in and my sleep wanes. I work all the shifts Gerald throws at me, even alone with Iain, my belly a forcefield blocking the *please fuck with me* beacon. Agnes's book says I should use my energy to nest, which feels a bit cruel given I have no idea where my nest will be.

*A*t *the bakery I pipe vanilla buttercream between oat biscuits until my* forearms are sore, like my feet, like my back, as Agnes promised they would be. Baths have become my saving grace. I prefer them scalding but Agnes says not too hot or the babe will be poached. She loaned me her thermometer to be sure.

After checking the temperature of the bath I lie back and let my ears fill with warm water, my heartbeat and Agnes's footsteps in the kitchen echoing around me. I imagine I'm in a womb. I'd rather not think of being in Bonnie's womb, so I'm just some creature waiting to be born. A small mammal with sharp teeth and a strong sense of self-preservation.

The surface of my belly heaves and rolls because I'm not the only one who likes baths. This lump feels like a knee, or maybe a little bum. I like when the salamander moves like this, confirming it's still alive. Now that I've promised not to let despair rule me, now that

I'm hauling the door open with both hands, jumping through it with both feet, I fear this will all be taken from me. A sickening plot twist in the awful reality TV show that is my life.

I manoeuvre so my mouth is under the faucet and turn the cold water on low. I could lie here for hours if not for the heartburn burbling up my throat. These days I pop Tums like I'm in a Mentos commercial. Agnes and I went in on a jumbo bottle and are already halfway through.

We've decided to celebrate both of our birthdays on mine, the last day in May, with a castle picnic under the moon. Agnes says it will be a waxing crescent, connected to the womb. I said are you a witch and she said she looked it up on the internet, you can find anything on there. I need to think of what to make. Something involving cheese. God I miss wine. Sometimes when Agnes opens a bottle for herself, I take a swig and hold it in my mouth for a minute just to remember the taste before spitting it into the sink. The book says it's okay to have a sip now and then but I'm so scared I'm going to fuck this kid up just by being its mother that I'm avoiding all avoidable fuck-ups.

The book says the salamander is now the size of an eggplant. I bought one at the Scotmid the other day, but not to eat. Just to hold.

WHEN I WOKE FROM MY nap yesterday I overheard Agnes in the kitchen, talking to Scrabble Mary on the phone. She sounded like she was crying. She said whatever will I do with her gone? And who'll help her with the wean? It's not right, Mary, it's just not right.

I went back to my room and sat on the bed. It's not right, I agree. But it turns out that's irrelevant. Many things in the world are very wrong and go on happening all the same. I wanted to give Agnes a hug but didn't want to embarrass her. So I sat on my bed for a while longer. When I got up again, she was standing at the sink, staring out the window. What are you looking at, I asked. My reflection, she said.

What would Bonnie be like if Agnes had raised her, I wonder? Kinder, likely. Calmer. Less prone to yelling. Less prone to shunning. And what would I be like? Less neurotic. Less of a sucker for punishment. More Scottish. Though of course there would be no me, if Bonnie hadn't ended up in Chesley.

What would Agnes be like? Would she have become a midwife? Would she have managed to escape the church? Would she have five earrings in her left ear and three in her right? Would she eat crisps in a castle under the moon?

I think the thing about life might be that it's just hard, for no divine reason, and it will change you, with no preordained end, and it's for you to decide whether the hardness hardens you or cracks you open. I try to figure out which it's doing to me. I press my fingers in around my heart, feeling for bulwarks, or openings.

ON SATURDAY KIRSTEN COMES to see me again. I can tell she's trying to be nice about it but she gives me a bit of a lecture. She says, you know, most pregnant people see their midwife or doctor at least once a month during pregnancy, and biweekly in the third trimester. You should have had at least two ultrasounds by now, as well as blood work and urine tests. She says she's happy to visit informally when she's able, as a favour to my gran, but where I'm not a proper patient she can't send me for these things.

I say haven't people had babies for hundreds of thousands of years without ultrasounds and tests?

Yes, she says, with significantly higher fetal and maternal mortality rates.

That shuts me up. *Fetal mortality rate* is my least favourite phrase. I knock on wood every time I encounter it in Agnes's birth book. I knock on wood now. Then Kirsten squirts cold goop onto my belly and we listen to the fast little heartbeat through the machine. It sounds louder this time. Stronger. I wish my uterus had an intercom I could press whenever I wanted to check in, to assure myself the salamander is well. How are you feeling today, I would ask. And it would answer with its tiny, persistent kapow kapow kapow.

Kirsten measures my fundal height and takes my blood pressure. Everything seems fine, she says, but you really should be properly followed. I nod yes but I've looked it up and one ultrasound would cost me more than my flight home and first month's rent put together, so it's just going to have to wait. I sit up and eat two Tums from the bottle on the table beside the couch.

To be honest, I'm nervous to see it. I still think of it as more of an aquatic pet than a baby, something that will live inside my fishbowl belly forever. I still think of it with a tail.

It's booked. I'm leaving June third on a seat sale. If I'd had the sense sooner to consider grown-up concerns like visas and the Home Office and that I couldn't just melt into the Highlands without a trace, perhaps I could've found a flight mid-month. But I was somewhat distracted by the sentient being growing ever larger inside my body, and my stupid daydreams about stupid Iain.

Agnes had to help me fill in my info on the airline website. I was too weepy to be trusted with the details. And we had to use my old address in Creignish, which put me back there for a few minutes, on the couch in front of the burnt-out wood stove with my mittens taped to my sleeves.

Put your feet on the floor, Agnes said. She walked over to the counter to switch on the radio. I thumped my heels on the wood like a heartbeat and ran my thumb along the metal edge of the kitchen table until I was in the bothy again.

I went to the pharmacy last week and bought a pack of extra-large socks, as my own were leaving furrows in my swollen ankles for hours after I peeled them off. My new post-work ritual is to eat five Tums and lie in a lukewarm bath with my feet up the wall. I can't believe I still have three months of this to go. I've read that wolves only gestate for sixty-four days. Human pregnancy feels a bit much in comparison. It almost makes me believe we really are being punished for listening to that snake. Though elephants gestate for nearly two years, so maybe a sexist god is punishing us all.

Yesterday Iain's wife dropped his keys off to him at the bakery. She looked quite lovely in a tweed blazer, her curly blond hair in a loose knot. I should have had an affair with her instead. God knows she deserves one. Iain gave her a chaste peck and wouldn't look in my direction for the rest of the day. Bakers don't wear wedding rings. How thick am I?

Ruth says the salamander will do me good because it will make it harder for me to date for a while. The book says that by now, it will have started to open its eyes.

I've returned to the internet, out of necessity. I changed all my passwords. Looking at my emails and messages knowing Chris's eyes had been all over them was like coming back to your house after it's been robbed. I trawl Kijiji for Halifax apartments and wonder if "no pets" includes no babies. There's a 300-square-foot carpeted bachelor with a two-element stove tucked behind the front door that I could afford, but there's no bathtub. Everything else is either out of my budget or a room in a shared house. The muscles of my neck and jaw are strung so tight. Each scroll is like the turn of a winch.

I think of the nest I'd imagined I would bring my baby home to, in Creignish. A quiet house by the ocean. A clawfoot tub to soak my sore body in after birth. A crackling wood stove to sit by and nurse, Della purring at my feet. A little room painted yellow with a handmade crib and an antique rocking chair and a sheepskin rug.

But even when Chris wasn't yelling, the quiet felt loud. And despite the wood stove, the cold reigned. And two floors beneath what would have been the sweet yellow nursery was the basement, where I would surely still retreat to sit on the concrete and cry.

TOMORROW IS AGNES'S BIRTHDAY. Though we've planned to celebrate together at the castle on mine, I'm making her a cranachan raspberry cake. It's full spring now and the ground is thick with flowers. My ankles and I are going for a walk to pick some as a garnish.

The sun shines unveiled and birds party in the trees all around the bothy, chirping and trilling. I once read a study by scientists who hooked electrodes up to the tiny skulls of finches to see what they dream about, and found that they dream of singing.

What does the salamander dream of, I wonder?

I walk down the flagstones to the dirt driveway and then to the narrow road. I pick chickweed and mouse ear along the shoulder and drop them into a jar. Everything is so lushly green I can feel it in my pores. The road is empty and my ears are full of birds and the rustling hush of thousands and thousands of leaves and blades of grass brushing against each other in the breeze. Yesterday I trimmed my bangs and cut my fingernails and sloughed off all my old skin in the bath, and today I feel freshly myself. My shirt is stretched tight over my belly and the sun heats it like a solar panel. Despite the discomfort, I think I'll miss it when it's gone.

I get my shoes wet picking feathery white flowers shaped like stars from the ditch. I walk along the grassy roadside, tapping heads of Queen Anne's lace, and turn up the street toward the school. The playground is empty, but I can still see the salamander at the top of the slide, nervous to come down but doing it anyway. So brave, I whisper. I lean against the ivy-draped stone wall and look at the old building. Maybe we'll come back. I twist off a tendril of ivy and put it in the jar with my flowers.

I cross the road and walk quietly alongside the grass field, hoping to see the antlered deer emerge again from the trees, but he doesn't come. Further on, the asphalt is canopied by overhanging limbs, and in their shade I find purple flowers that remind me of violets, but with deep wells that suggest they're carnivorous. I pick two. And then I come to the river.

I shuffle through the ferns and the fence of narrow trees to the water's edge, and squint my eyes against the sun, shining on me twice, from the sky and again from the river's surface. I sit on a rock and take off my shoes. I scan for frogs, but they must have heard me coming. The water is frigid. I sink my hot feet and fat ankles into it until it sends an ache through my bones.

The salamander rolls and stretches against my ribs, and I sit up straighter to give it room to move. Then it gets the hiccups. I didn't know this was a thing babies did in the womb until it started happening. I asked Agnes about it and she said oh yes, it's common. It's such a funny feeling, but I love it. Another confirmation the salamander is well.

It hiccups all the way home, under the leafy canopy, past the field and the school. It hiccups up the dirt driveway and down the flagstone path. Agnes is reading the little Gaelic book at the kitchen table, preparing to school me in Scrabble again. I tell her to feel my belly and just as she touches it, the hiccups stop.

Funny wee thing, she says.

I empty my jar of flowers onto the table and we look at them together. Butterwort, Agnes says of the purple carnivores, and bogbean of the white stars. I fill the jar with water and leave the ivy in it to root. Then I unwrap a brick of butter, cut it into chunks over a ceramic bowl, and cream it with sugar.

What is it you're making? Agnes asks, looking up from the book.

Cranachan cake, I say.

Lovely. And good pronunciation, hen.

I smile to myself at the counter. I've recently got the hang of my name, too.

I add the eggs one by one, sift the flour and fold it in, toss in a handful of crushed raspberries, and pour the mix into a buttered tin. I slide it into the oven and shake oats into a pan on the stove to toast. I whip vanilla, cream, honey, and a splash of whisky together until it's thick. I let Agnes lick the spoon.

Math agus blasta, she says.

Blasta? I ask.

Delicious, says she, and points to the page in the little book about food.

These days the sun doesn't set till nearly ten. It beams through the windows as we sit on the couch with our noodles watching *Rebus*. When I'm done eating, I paint Agnes's toenails blue, and she does mine to match though she doesn't have the steadiest hand. I can barely bend over my belly to do them myself though, so I shouldn't complain.

By the time it's dark, the cake is cool. I slice it lengthwise and lay down thick icing and a jumble of raspberries in the middle, replace the top and ice that too. I craft a crescent moon from the chickweed, mouse ear, purple butterwort, and white bogbean. Months ago I would've taken a picture of it to post, but I'm glad I can't. I like knowing that the only people to see it will be the ones to eat it, Agnes and me. She snores softly from her room. I put the cake in the fridge and turn off the lights.

IN THE MORNING I PRESENT the cake to Agnes and she decides we will have it for breakfast. Her birthday, her choice. She adds whisky to her tea and pulls a cigarette from her purse.

I didn't know you smoked, I say.

Just once a year, she says.

I'm working this afternoon so I ask what she wants to do this morning. She asks if I'll cut her hair. She says she wants to look cool.

We sit in the wrought iron garden chairs in front of the bothy with the chattering birds, drinking tea and eating our breakfast cake. When Agnes is done she moves her chair away from me and smokes her cigarette. She says she started secretly at twelve and quit when she was forty. If she makes it to ninety she says she'll take it up again full-time.

After she stubs out her smoke, I ask her to take off her glasses. She holds them on her lap in her knobby hands, and I drape an old towel over her like it's an ermine robe. Her eyes look much smaller without their magnifying lenses, squinty like mine and watery green. She sits up as straight as she can. I cut her hair short on the sides to show off her earrings. She's changed them for the occasion, all pearls.

I remove the towel and shake out the silver hairs for the birds to add to their nests. I hand her a mirror and she turns her head from side to side and smiles.

Cool, she says, very cool.

I start to cry. I ask if she'll come visit me in Halifax.

Of course I will, hen, she says, and holds out her arms to me.

If you can't manage to talk to a person in real life, you shouldn't sign their goodbye/baby card. Between Gerald's *Blessings to you and the bairn* and Gemma's *Safe travels and congratulations!* Iain has written *Best regards.* It feels a tad disingenuous. Just write *regards*, Iain, if you must write anything at all.

Gemma hands me a sparkly gift bag along with the card. Inside is a tartan onesie and a little stuffed Nessie. I give her a squeeze and shake Gerald's hand. Iain is busying himself at the stove, cleaning more thoroughly than ever before. I call out see you from the doorway and he half turns and gives me a loose wave. I let myself feel ashamed one last time on the walk from the bakery to the post office, and then decide that's enough.

The salamander is the size of a cauliflower and everyone can tell I'm pregnant. I get kindly looks from old women. From men I get kindly or leering, by turns. I'm still not used to these boobs.

At the post office I order a decaf latte and a cream cheese toastie to go because I'm always hungry, and because this is my last day of thirty-one so I feel I deserve a little treat. Jeanette hands me my mail. There's a letter for Agnes from Scrabble Mary in a purple envelope, a late birthday card by the look of it. And a letter for me, my name typed on the envelope again.

I sit down in a chair by the window. I take a few breaths. I hate that the Eye knows Agnes's address, probably knows exactly where I'll be when I receive her missive. I open the letter. It says *Sorcha, I write to follow up on my previous correspondence, as you have yet to respond. I ask that you confirm your imminent return.* Then it says something about regulations and that she's retained a lawyer. She writes like she thinks she is one. I wonder if she asked at the post office when to send the letter so it would arrive just in time for my birthday.

I refuse to throw up about this. I tear up the letter and give it back to Jeanette to recycle. I eat my toastie and drink my latte while I wait for the bus. I wonder if I could talk to Emma about the legalities of it all, though part of me doesn't want to admit I'm scheming to deprive a fellow dyke of parental status. What would the community think? I know what the community would think. But another part of me would burn the community down if it meant I didn't have to spend the rest of my days under the surveillance of the Lidless Eye.

In my bed at the bothy I fall asleep with Alastair and dream that I live with the salamander by a tiny pond in Agnes's backyard. We burrow in the mud to sleep. We bump our noses together in greeting and blink at each other with our tiny jewel eyes. We eat snails and I regrow the hand I cut off at the dream wedding. No one can find us.

WHEN I WAKE UP, I'm thirty-two but I feel the same. I don't love when my birthday rolls around because it's a day on which I know my family will think of me and decide not to call. I'm pretty sure I wouldn't pick up if they did, though sometimes I think I might.

Now that I have Agnes, I feel less low. I can hear her singing Led Zeppelin in the shower, about how I don't have to go, oh oh oh oh. I wish it were true.

It's nearly June but the mornings are chill. I stretch my black hoodie over my belly. Soon I'll need maternity clothes. I imagine myself in goth peasant wear, flowy black dresses, flowers in my hair and all that, but I'll probably just get a bigger hoodie at the Sally Ann once I'm home.

Home.

I'll be there in three days but still haven't found a place to live. Linh says they're saving a spot for me on their couch.

When she gets out of the shower, Agnes serves me tea with scones, lemon curd, and clotted cream. She slides one large and two small packages wrapped in tissue across the blue Formica table. A bottle of gold nail polish, with which she says she'll give me one final pedicure, and a tiny tube tied with string, which she tells me to open after I've left. The third is soft and smells like sweet dry grass. I tear off the paper and unfold a thick sheepskin, cream white and brushed soft. For the wean, Agnes says. I lay my cheek against it and close my eyes.

The air is soft and dense, turning the trees around the bothy into spectres. We drink more tea and stare out the windows. We return to *Hamish* for comfort. Part of me feels like I'm not really leaving but another part is already gone, watching all of this like it's a memory. We snack and joke and turn on the radio. For our night picnic we plan a simple meal: crackers, cheese, olives, and hard-boiled eggs with salt, which we prepare and pack. The sun doesn't set until ten, and it could be eleven before it's dark enough to see the moon, though it might be swamped by fog.

We'll see, says Agnes, you never know what the fog will do.

At six sharp she brings me a paper crown, slides it onto my head, and sits me at the kitchen table. Then she tells me to shut my eyes. I can feel the warmth of her leaning over me, smell her Pears soap smell, hear her opening the laptop and clicking, clicking, cursing lightly, clicking. And then she steps back and says okay open your eyes.

SURPRISE! my pack yells from the screen, and Ruth and Dana and Linh and Agnes all start singing happy birthday to me, Agnes speeding up and slowing down to keep time with my friends as the song garbles and pixelates, but ultimately perseveres through the static, across the ocean. It's the best happy birthday I've ever heard.

My friends are sitting around Ruth's kitchen table, wearing paper crowns too, even baby Oscar who isn't really a baby anymore. He stands in Dana's lap holding fistfuls of her hair. She tells him to say hi and he does and we all laugh. Agnes and I drink ginger beer and my friends drink wine. She shows them the haircut I gave her, and they tell her it looks cool and she beams. We talk until we're tired, but before we say goodbye, Ruth says they have a birthday surprise. She holds her phone up to the screen with a picture on it of something blue.

I can't see what it is, I say.

We found you a house! says Linh.

Just a sublet, says Ruth. My coworker is going to BC in August for a few months, so we snapped it up for you.

And you can stay with me and Emma till then, says Linh.

I exhale and my tight-wound muscles soften and the edgy workers cheer from their cubicles.

Oh my god you guys, I say, thank you thank you thank you. I kiss my fingertips and push the kisses through the air to them, through the computer screen. The salamander gets the hiccups and I try to show them but the camera isn't sharp enough to see. Then we all say goodbye, goodbye, and Oscar lets go of Dana's hair to wave at me with both of his hands.

Agnes and I have a nap and wake at half nine to drive to the castle. We wrap ourselves in a blanket and sit in her usual spot among the ruins, watching the fog retreat from the surface of the water like a sheet slipping off a bed. Agnes hands me a hard-boiled egg and the shaker of salt. I crack the egg on the stone floor, peel it into a napkin, and touch its skin to the salt in my palm. We eat olives and cheese. We pour ourselves tea from the thermos.

Agnes says, well hen, have you thought of a name?

I sip my tea and hold it in my mouth to warm up my teeth. What if I give the salamander a name and am punished for the presumption? How can I know it will live long enough to hear itself called? I read the chapter about stillbirth in Agnes's book. I read it several times.

I'm nervous to name it, I say out loud.

Oh my dear, Agnes says, her pearled ears glowing in the soft night air. I can feel her reading my mind again. Less than one in a hundred babies are stillborn, she says, and gives my hand a squeeze.

I nod into my cup. I just can't imagine it on the outside, I say.

Yes, says Agnes. And when it's born you won't be able to imagine it with teeth, but they'll come in all the same.

I nod again.

What if Chris hates the name? What if a judge orders me to change it?

Try to put your worries to the back of your mind, she says.

I think about where in the back of my mind my worries would fit. Maybe between my fear that I'll parent like Bonnie, and my doubt that I'll ever find an un-fucked-up love.

The sliver of moon slips through a thin spot in the fog—a waxing crescent, as Agnes said it would be. She raises her mug. Slàinte mhath, she says. I click my mug against hers, and we drink, and we look up.

I *wrap the rust and ochre shawl around my shoulders. It doesn't smell* like juniper anymore. It smells like cat because Alastair has been sleeping on it. I keep getting his black hairs in my mouth. But I was wrapped in the shawl on the flight here so it feels right to be wrapped in it on my way home.

Let's not review in detail how openly I cried in the airport, or how many people stopped to ask what was wrong, or to glance uncomfortably at my splotchy face and swollen eyes while I waited at the gate. Just sad to leave, I told them, just sorry to go. Agnes walked me to security. We held each other tight before I entered the corral, our cheeks pressed together because she was standing up as straight as she could and it made us nearly the same height. She waved me on, and I kept looking back to see her there, still waving, until security beckoned me through the metal detector and I lost sight of her.

Despite my festering dread about returning to the land of the Lidless Eye, I think that of all the flights I've taken, I would be most sad to die on this one. It would be an easy out, but the salamander would exit with me, and even though I still can't imagine it on the outside, I really would like to see it there. The sky is empty of clouds and the sun sets red. I stare into the glow like I have something to prove, like if it sinks below the horizon, blinks before I blink, I'll win. But before I can prove myself, the woman in the seat adjacent asks me to close the blind.

I open my backpack and eat an oat cracker. Agnes packed me a bag of decaf PG Tips, too, and I'm hoping to smuggle some cheese through customs, and the sheepskin, and the sprig of ivy, rooting in a jar. I wonder what Agnes will do when she gets back to Balnain. Sit in the garden without me I guess, and watch the birds line their nests with the silver clippings from her hair. I wish I could've stayed to see the dahlias we planted come up.

I remember the little scroll and find it flattened at the bottom of my backpack, beneath a brick of old white cheddar. I pull the string and unwrap the tissue. It's a cheque for £3,000. Jesus, Agnes. *For whatever you need*, the memo says. Maybe I'll use it to buy her a plane ticket to Halifax. I think that's what I need the most.

I watch a movie on the tiny matte screen with no sound because I'm too cheap to buy the airplane headphones. It's hard to follow without words, but it's weird enough to distract me from my life, and I like seeing so many things smash in slow motion, and the articulation of the pianist's hands.

How did Agnes feel, travelling back with Bonnie to her parents in Inverness? She said it was her only choice. The baby was sick, the boy was gone, and Agnes was fifteen and too poor to feed herself. I console myself with the thought that, though I'm returning to battle the Eye, at least I won't have to see the salamander swaddled in one of Bonnie's church quilts, laced with prayers.

At the castle under the moon I asked Agnes what birth was like. I admit I'm nervous. She told me it's usually not as fast as in the movies. She said it tends to come on slow, like a stomachache or a cramp, and gets stronger and stronger until you're in a sort of trance, and if you can let it be what it is and remember the pain has a purpose, you can ride it out, push through and come out the other side.

She told me it had never been explained to her. She had heard women in her neighbourhood in Inverness, and echoing down the halls of her damp Gorbals tenement, wailing and straining. So when she was swamped in spasms, alone in her dark apartment and wondering how a person could feel such deep clutching aches, such bright tearing pain, and not die of it, she let herself make the same sounds as those other women and her body took over and pushed the baby out, and she caught it in her own hands. Her neighbours must have heard her, but no one came. She told me she didn't know what a placenta was and at first thought she was delivering her own stomach. She cut the cord with a pocketknife she nicked from her father the night she ran away.

I told her I couldn't believe she had done it alone, that I didn't think it was possible. She said that's why she became a midwife. She didn't want anyone else to do it alone, so long as she could help it.

I wish she could be at the salamander's birth. I told her I didn't think it would agree to be born into anyone else's hands.

WE LAND IN A SOUPY FOG so thick I can't tell whether we're in Halifax or back in Glasgow. I've become so used to anonymity that the thought of being recognized parches me. Could the Eye be waiting? Could she have spies? I pull up my hood and shuffle through the airport like a hobbit on a quest. I make eye contact with no one, try to slow my breath, as I wait at the conveyer belt for my second bag, full of sheepskin and more cheese. I close my eyes and imagine I'm invisible and hope the crowd is convinced.

At customs I pull back my hood and turn on a smile and pretend the salamander is kicking. I laugh and pat my big belly and lie about the cheese and the sheepskin and the ivy and am waved through.

I recloak myself as I enter the lobby. What if my belly gives me away? There's no protection here—no massive distance, no magic forcefield, no Agnes. Chris could just walk up to me, walk up and grab my wrist and drag me to the car, return me to the basement, lock me underground until it's time for the salamander to be born and then leave me to bleed out on the concrete. I can't breathe. I have to get out. My feet start to walk me backward, back from where I came, and then someone taps my shoulder and my heart stops.

Sorch, says my favourite voice, and I whip around and am wrapped up in Ruth's arms, cocooned in her rosemary hair.

EMMA DRIVES US INTO the city in her massive ancient Volvo. Linh is in the passenger seat and Ruth is in the back with me, holding my hand. I can tell that Linh can tell I'm not in a talking mood. They turn around looking like the most compassionate therapist and ask if I want to party. I laugh and say yes and they crank "Y Control" and we bop down the highway in the blurry night, singing of our love beneath the fog, aching to buy back what you stole.

At Linh and Emma's door, Ruth gives me a squeeze goodbye. I hope her rosemary shampoo rubs off on me because it smells like home. Linh and Emma and I climb the steep wooden stairs to their second-floor apartment with its sloped ceilings and uneven floors. You have to crouch to get into a chair at the kitchen table, crouch to climb into the bathtub, and you shouldn't sit up too fast on the couch either or you'll whack your head, Linh warns. The red couch is in the front room beside a bay window crowded with plants, and I drop onto it gratefully. It smells like spilled bourbon and spilled coffee and dust.

Thanks buddy, I say to Linh.

Happy to, Linh says, and sits down beside me.

I'm sorry, I begin, but they say not to be. They hug me like I'm their little brother, a clasp like a pact.

You look different, they say.

Pregnant glow? I joke.

Maybe. Or maybe something else. Em and I work early tomorrow but we'll try to be quiet. Do whatever in the house, there's food in the fridge, you know the deal.

I nod.

And Sorch, they say reluctantly. I'd rather not have to tell you this, but you should know that Chris is back.

I'm underwater. Limbs numb, light dim, sound slow. Linh's hand is on my arm, and they say something about Dartmouth, seeing Chris while on a courier run, asked around, probably she won't, but I might want to just, sure it will be okay, okay somehow. I nod and try to get a breath. My body feels like a shell, clamping down around its pearl. I press my palms into my eyes and thump my heels on the floor to remind myself of where I am.

Linh makes me tea with milk and maple syrup. Lavender, they say. They give my shoulder a squeeze. Try to sleep.

The walls are thin and the floorboards creak. I can hear Linh and Emma getting ready for bed, talking low. I take the jar of ivy out of my backpack, open it up, and nestle it beside the other plants in the window. The salamander rolls under my skin. I unclamp my body and lie out on the couch to give it room to stretch.

The crescent moon hangs high over the rooftops. It glows through the window, turning the leaves of the plants silver, and my mind turns to death. I consider telling it to stop, but let it run. It conjures ravenous cancer, or a drunken fall into the dark harbour. A workplace accident involving some massive grinding machine. A heart attack mid-run. I take it as a good sign that the death I'm imagining is for once not my own. Maybe that's the part of me that looks different. Survivalist glow.

Maybe I do need plastic surgery after all. It wouldn't be frivolous because it would be for stealth. I could get a new nose and shave off my eyebrows, dye my hair black. I could choose a new name, though I'd be sorry to let this one go now that I've finally learned how to say it right.

I've been back in Halifax three days and have yet to leave Linh and Emma's house. I'm afraid to go outside. I lie on the red couch and stare out the bay window. I drink cup after cup of decaf PG Tips and try to imagine myself back in the bothy. I feel like I'm at the Black Gate of Mordor, dragging myself around under the weight of the ring, dreaming of the Shire, hiding from the Great Lidless Eye. Except the Gate is the bridge to Dartmouth and the ring is a baby.

Ruth told me I should probably start thinking of the salamander as such, because that's what's going to come out of me in twelve weeks: a human person but very small. She's right. It's been months since the salamander had a tail. I mean, I assume. At this point no one knows for sure.

At Agnes's urging I have booked an ultrasound. This means the salamander is in the system, on the grid, the fantasy that we could disappear into the hills now properly crushed. But as much as I like to think the establishment is of no use to me, I am ultimately afraid to die. And even more than that, I'm afraid the salamander could die. So we have a doctor who we will meet next week, and we have an appointment to peer into my womb.

IT'S FRIDAY AND RUTH IS over for dinner. Linh and Emma are out for post-work drinks because of their fun and functional love. I ask Ruth how she thinks I should disguise myself. What shape of nose should I get, I ask. What colour hair?

Ruth says no. Hiding is not the answer. I kind of thought she might say that. Listen Sorch, she says. Do you even know for sure she has any right to the kid? Have you asked Emma?

No, I say.

You should ask her.

The question makes me feel evil, I say.

Ruth tilts her head at an earnest angle. You don't volunteer to share custody with your abusive ex just because she's a dyke, she says.

Don't you?

Sorcha, no.

We eat our chana masala in silence.

You know I know non-bio parents are parents, I say.

I know, says Ruth. But paying for sperm doesn't make someone a parent. She gestures across the table and I pass her the raita. Can't you just, like, pay her back? she asks.

That seems a bit crass, no?

Who cares, Ruth says. Chris sucks. Maybe she'd take it and fuck off.

Maybe, I say.

The mango pickle must have reached the salamander. It squirms and kicks me in the ribs.

Sorry, I say to it, and give it a pat. I ask Ruth if she wants to feel. She reaches over and I put her hand over the persistent foot.

ON WEDNESDAY WE MEET the doctor. He is young and handsome and before we get started he says now I don't want you to feel uncomfortable because I'm young and handsome.

Okay, I say, and actually it does help because now that I know he thinks he's handsome, he's not that handsome anymore.

He weighs me on the scale and takes my blood pressure. He gives me a cup to pee into and a swab. For your vagina, he says. At least I get to do the swab myself, I think as I squat in the bathroom, but then I accidentally slip it into my urethra and regret my righteousness. When I return, humbled, he measures my fundal height and we listen to the salamander's heartbeat, which, despite its techno speed, is wonderfully calming. He presses his hands into my belly. This is the bum, he says, squeezing a lump up by my ribs. And here, he says, is the head. I reach down and feel the salamander's round head, pressing into my bladder.

Hopefully he stays this way, says the doctor. He? She?

I don't know, I say.

I PULL MY HOOD UP even though it's sunny and makes me sweat, and keep my eyes down on the sidewalk as I exit the doctor's office and walk to the bus stop. My shoulders stand sentry on either side of my neck, and I hold my book up to shield my face from the other passengers. Not that Chris would ever take the bus, but you never know, she could have spies.

A few seats ahead of me, an old man sits with his arm around a little kid with a brush cut, who sucks loudly on three of his little fingers. A woman across the aisle holds her earbud mic between her lips and talks quietly into it in a language I don't understand. Two boys in the row behind me make lighter-fluid fireballs between their clasped hands, down low where the driver can't see. I decide these passengers are probably not spies for the Lidless Eye. I lower my shoulders, and my book, and my hood. I look out the window at the passing trees and let the sun touch my face.

Back at the house I try to video call Agnes on Linh's computer, but she doesn't answer. Maybe she's out in the garden. She wrote me last night to say she misses me fiercely, that Alastair has been mooning about my room. She asked if anyone has painted my toes. The gold polish she laid down before I left has chipped into little islands, a nail polish archipelago.

She asked if I've been baking. I haven't. But it would be a good way to spend my seclusion, paying Linh and Emma back in scones. I survey the fridge for ingredients, sour the milk with a squeeze of lemon, and put the butter in the freezer to harden. I press my fingers against the round lump of the salamander's head. Maybe you are a human baby, I say, and it kicks me in the ribs. I'm not sure whether that means yes or no.

I sift the flour with a sieve and a spoon. Six months ago I would have skipped this step, but now I know it's worth it. I cut the cold butter and rub it into the mix, slowly pour in the soured milk, and stir it with a dull knife.

WHEN LINH AND EMMA get home I offer them scones with jam like a stay-at-home mum. I feel so wholesome. Like I should pour them juice too, in matching cups. I tell them about the stupid handsome doctor and the whereabouts of the salamander's head. They each eat a second scone and I beam.

How did it feel, Linh asks, leaving the house?

Scary, I say.

Emma rubs buttery crumbs off her fingers. I know you haven't asked, Sorcha, she says, but I can see how worried you are. Linh asked me to tell you what I can about your situation, legally.

I press my lips together and nod.

Before you conceived, did you and Chris make any kind of written agreement that she would be the baby's other parent?

I shake my head and hold my breath.

Okay, Emma says, that helps a bit. To have her listed on the baby's birth certificate you'd need to have that agreement in place, and file a statutory declaration acknowledging her as the intended parent. Or she would have to adopt, with your consent. But, you should know that even if she's not registered as a parent, she could still apply for custody.

Oh, I mumble through numb lips. Do you think she could get it?

I'm not sure she'd meet the test on the facts, Emma says, but I can't say for sure. It would be a rough case to fight, though. A shitty argument to have to make.

Yeah, I whisper. I feel like I'm drowning. I imagine rallies outside the courthouse with placards waving, the crowd chanting rhymes I would have chanted too, if I didn't know the backstory. If I didn't know what it felt like to be pregnant and sick with dread.

I'm so sorry, Emma says. I wish I could give you a clear answer.

I say no, it's okay, thanks so much. But my voice cracks. I stand up quickly and hit my head on the slanted ceiling. Linh stands to try to help me and I say no no, I'm fine. I take my scone and a glass of milk to the bathroom, and let the water rush into the tub so Linh and Emma can't hear me cry. I crouch down while I climb in so I don't crack my head on the ceiling again, and lie back with my big belly and breasts floating, salty tears running down the sides of my face. I eat the scone and wash it down with gulps of milk and pour the rest out into the bath. I sink into the cloudy mix and let my ears fill with water.

Dana and Oscar pick me up in their lime green hatchback. Dana apologizes for the fermented juice smell and the layer of Goldfish cracker dust over everything, but says I should get used to it because soon I'll smell like that too. Oscar screams all the way to the hospital. He doesn't like the car, Dana explains. I turn around to wave at him, I jiggle his little foot in its little shoe, but he will not be consoled. Dana and I have a conversation at max volume about how majestic the Highlands are, how peaceful. I shout to her about the trickling streams, the tiny white flowers, the windswept heather. Wow, she yells, lovely!

We park and Dana extracts Oscar from his car seat and leads me through the hospital and up the elevator. I register at the desk and Dana releases Oscar onto a foam mat to play with a train set. We sit down on the vinyl chairs with a poof and Dana smiles at me tiredly, the circles under her eyes deep and blue.

Welcome to your future, she says, gesturing to the small tornado tearing up the train track on the floor before us. I'm so excited you're having a baby, Sorch. I need cool mom friends. No one else I know has kids yet, and the other parents at Oscar's kindermusic group are so normal it hurts. Liam and I aren't even that weird and I feel like we're constantly freaking them out. She laughs and then closes her eyes for a full minute, and I realize she has fallen asleep.

I don't wake her. I watch Oscar on the floor, bashing the trains together. Train train, he says, and looks up at me.

Yeah! I smile at him, and he looks very proud. I kneel down on the foam, manoeuvring gingerly around my full bladder, and roll a train car down the surviving stretch of track beside him.

Mine, he says, and I hand it over. I pick up another, but that one's his too.

A tech in teddy bear–print scrubs calls my name. I jostle Dana's arm and she wakes.

Whoops, she says. You want us to come in with you?

Probably best to leave Oscar with the trains, I say.

Okay, she says. Say hi to the little bean for us!

I remember that Oscar was a bean before he was Oscar. Maybe that means the salamander will get a human name when it's born, too. I knock on the wooden rail attached to the wall as I follow the tech down the hallway, my superstitions at an all-time high.

She leads us into a small, dim room with TV screens and a vinyl bed reclined like a La-Z-Boy. I'm Paula, she says. I'll be doing your ultrasound today. She tells me to hop up on the bed and I obediently lumber.

Now I didn't see a previous ultrasound on file, she says. Is this your first?

It is, I say.

And you've drunk all your water?

Oh yes, I say.

Perfect. Now, I have my screen here, and there's one for you to look at just there. I can't answer any questions, but I'll send the images to your doctor and he can go over them with you, tell you the baby's gender and all that. Sound good?

Sounds great, I say, focused on not peeing my pants.

She squeezes a cold blob of gel onto my belly. Husband couldn't make it? she asks.

I sigh and wish I was back on Agnes's couch with Kirsten and her tact. No husband, I say.

Boyfriend? she asks.

Nope.

Well that's fine, she says cheerfully. I'm sure you'll do just fine on your own.

Paula doesn't sound like she really believes this. But I might. For a moment I see Chris in the empty chair in the corner, head bent, jaw set, scrolling her phone, radiating anger from all the times I woke her in the night when I got up to pee. Then I blink and she's not there.

I'm grateful I'm not doing this with her. And that I'm not doing it on my own.

Paula turns on the monitors and smooshes the gel around, pressing into my ballooning bladder, the funnel of static on the screen like an alien beam. My pulse is loud in my ears. I'm nervous to see it.

Think you'll have a party, a coloured cake or something like that?

No, I say, looking at the fuzzy grey shapes.

My niece had a big party, with a secret blue cake and blue confetti cannons. It was a hoot.

Where is the salamander, I wonder, my heart speeding. Where is it?

Now, you can see baby's spine here, along your left side, Paula says, and points to a coil on the screen. And this is baby's rib cage, and right up here is baby's bum.

Oh, I say, actually quite surprised to see the tiny bum with no tail.

And here's baby's heart.

There it is, pumping away, doing such a good job.

Wow, I whisper, my hand over my open mouth. Wow.

Baby's head, right down here, she says, pointing to a glowing circle around a Rorschach butterfly. And if we can get a good angle, we'll see baby's profile. Let's see now, just, ah, just there.

There it is. Not a blunt amphibian snout after all, but a tiny human nose and two little lips and a round forehead.

Oh my god, I say.

You can see baby's hand too, tucked under the chin there.

Oh my god, I say again, and stare, finally able to imagine the salamander on the outside.

Here hon, the tech says, and passes me a box of tissues. It's special isn't it, seeing your little one for the first time?

Thank you, I say, wiping my eyes. It really is.

DANA AND OSCAR DROP ME OFF at the yellow house. I ask if they want to come in but Oscar has to nap. He wails while I give tired Dana a hug.

I climb the wooden stairs and hustle to the bathroom and pee forever. The salamander stretches against my ribs. The baby, I mean.

I crouch into a chair at the kitchen table and stare at a blank piece of paper. *Dear*, I write in pencil, and then erase it. *Chris*, I write instead, and then a colon.

See, I can compose letters like an asshole too.

I have consulted a lawyer, I scratch onto the paper. *I do not believe you have a right to be registered as a parent if I don't agree. I won't agree. I won't agree that you can have custody, or that you can have anything. You can't see my baby. We'll cross the street if we see you coming. You'll be an ominous stranger and nothing more. Nothing more. I'll use the moon as a scythe and cut all my ties to you. Cash this please and fuck off forever.*

I find Agnes's cheque, rolled into a tube in my backpack, and flatten it out. *For whatever you need*, it says. I turn it over and write *pay to the order of* Chris's detestable name, and sign my own.

FOR FIVE DAYS I SLEEP on the letter, then I ask Ruth to proofread it. She suggests I take out the part about using the moon as a scythe, in case Chris shows the letter to a judge as evidence I'm crazy and can't be trusted with a baby. The judge won't get it, Ruth says, but I do. She says fuck off forever is probably fine.

I put the letter in an envelope and seal it. When Linh gets home, I ask if they think they could sleuth out Chris's address. Is she staying with her parents? I ask.

Why, asks Linh, are we trashing the place?

No, I say. I have to send her a letter. I'm trying to buy myself back.

I'll find out, Linh says. I'll even deliver it.

They smile at me with such sass and conviction, I believe for a minute that my plan is going to work.

DANA AND LIAM INVITE US all to dinner. Their house is only a twelve-minute walk across the Commons, but the idea of crossing such a wide-open space makes me shake. Anyone could see you out there. Anyone could catch you. Like a mouse, I feel it's best to stick to the periphery. I tell Linh and Emma I'll take side streets and meet them there. Emma says she'll just drive us.

The salamander is now the size of a butternut squash. When it's in these food phases I can't bring myself to eat its comparators. Butternut squash soup would have been nice to bring for dinner, but it'll have to wait until next week when the salamander is the size of a cabbage. I made dessert instead.

We roll into the driveway, where I last sat with my dripping shoes in my lap and begged Chris to let me drive. I thump my heels onto the carpeted floor of the car and breathe out.

It's all good, buddy, Linh says. Look outside. It's summer.

Oscar welcomes us at the door by running right up to us and screaming as loud as he can and then running back down the hall to the kitchen, where he is scooped up by Liam. Liam gives me a hug and Oscar rubs his runny nose on my shoulder. He does that, Liam says, and wipes me off with a tea towel.

Dana thumps down the stairs freshly showered, and gets her wet hair on all of our faces as she makes the rounds. Ruth and George arrive while we're still taking off our shoes, and we're all calling hi, hi! as we hug and shuffle out of the way to avoid chaos in the narrow hall, but Emma falls over and Oscar escapes from his dad and steals one of Linh's shoes and runs away. And I remember that I like this kind of chaos.

We eat mushroom lasagna around the big kitchen table, except Oscar who sorts through the layers and just eats the noodles and cheese, depositing every bit of mushroom he finds with his stubby fingers into Dana's mouth.

My pack brainstorms what the baby will need. My baby. Dana says she and Liam have a bag of tiny clothes and swaddling cloths they've been saving. Emma's sister has a carrier to pass along.

I ask Dana if she was nervous before Oscar was born, or if she somehow knew it would all be okay.

She was nervous, Liam says.

I was very nervous, Dana agrees. And even now when he sleeps I always check to make sure he's still breathing.

Have you thought of a name? George asks.

I haven't, I say. Too nervous.

I serve them marmalade cake. Everyone says they love it, though Oscar picks out all the specks of orange rind and wipes them on his shirt.

At least he's not wiping them on me, Dana says. This morning he walked up to me and handed me the juiciest booger.

Oh my god, Dana, I'm eating, says Linh.

Sorry, Dana says. We live gross lives over here. Nothing is sacred.

I look at my pack seated around the table and it all feels pretty sacred to me.

A ileen and I used to pretend to be pregnant. *We would play wedding* and one of us would have to be the man because that was the only way we understood weddings to work. But we both wanted to be the one to have the baby so we decided that after we were married, we could both be girls again.

We would tuck our shirts into our pants, and take apples from the bowl on the counter for boobs, and use a bear or doll for the baby. We'd walk around the house patting our bellies and saying it's almost time, and oh it's a baby girl, and yes we're very excited! It seemed there was at least one pregnant person at church at any given time, so we had lots of material to go on.

Bonnie saw us playing the game once and made us take out the boobs. She said it was obscene, a word we didn't know at the time but would become quite familiar with. We said how are we supposed to feed our babies if we don't have boobs? She gave me a plastic turkey baster and Aileen a funnel to use as bottles. Aileen liked wearing the funnel as a hat and I liked poofing myself in the face with rubbery air from the baster, and using it to make suck marks on my arms. Once our babies were born, Aileen and I found the bottles too much of a hassle and would just give the babies boob. To give a baby boob you just lift up your shirt and smush the baby's face on your flat kid nipple and rock back and forth and back and forth.

AT MY NEXT PRENATAL APPOINTMENT, the annoying handsome doctor asks if I'm planning to breastfeed. I say yes and he asks if my milk has come in. I tell him I don't know. He tells me probably. Man, that guy is so smug. I don't like him thinking he knows something about my body that I don't. When I get home I go to the bathroom and pull up my shirt and look at my giant breasts. I examine my nipples and realize I don't even know where the milk is supposed to come out. From the very middle like a funnel, or from all around like a tiny colander?

And how am I supposed to tell if there's milk in them? They're two sizes bigger so there's obviously something in there. I give one a squeeze and nothing happens. I press harder and from my nipple emerges a thick creamy drop. I let it fall onto my finger, and I put it in my mouth.

ON FRIDAY I LEAVE THE HOUSE at night, cloaked again. It's the only way I feel safe walking around this city, knowing the Lidless Eye is near. I rub the letter between my fingers, the edges of the envelope now soft. Linh did some sleuthing. Chris is not staying with her parents, they learned. She lives on Pine Street in a purple house. Linh texted me the address. How did you find it, I asked. A combo of small-town queer gossip and bike courier solidarity and good old-fashioned creeping, they said.

I stand before a big red postbox and look up at the crescent moon. Cash this please and fuck off forever, I whisper over the letter like a spell, and drop it through the slot. Ruth was right—I erased the part about the scythe.

I walk to her house. My legs are grateful for the movement. I've been doing laps around Linh and Emma's apartment and some made-up yoga poses, but I'm always restless.

When I arrive, George pops into the kitchen to say hello. He gives me a hug and pours himself some iced tea and returns to the living room. Ruth takes bowls down from the cupboard and unloads a cloth bag of treats.

Healthy treats, she says. For the salamander.

I like that she calls it that too, even though we now know for sure that it's a human baby.

She pours dark chocolate–covered almonds into one bowl, and thin slices of dried mango into another, and deep red strawberries into a third. And from the freezer she brings a frosted tub of Häagen-Dazs.

Healthy treats? I ask.

Yeah girl, she says. Isn't dairy a baby's main food group? And I picked up one other thing, if you want.

She tosses me a box of hair dye in Blackest Black.

Not for hiding, she says. But if you want to pull an Xtina, I support.

Let's do it, I grin.

We eat ice cream in the bathroom while Ruth paints the dye onto my hair. I feed her spoonfuls over my shoulder until my head is covered in an inky cap and the ice cream tub is empty.

She lays towels down on her bed and we spread out our picnic. We watch *The Craft* because it suits my nineties dye job, but only the first half because the timer goes off and I have to wash out my hair. The second half sucks anyway.

In the shower, I watch the blue-black dye snake down my balloon of a belly. I lather my hair with Ruth's rosemary shampoo, close my eyes under the rush of water, and imagine it's two years before now, that I still live here and haven't yet met Chris. But if I never met Chris, I wouldn't have moved to Creignish. I wouldn't have worked at Marg's store. I wouldn't have met Linda, or bought the little Gaelic book. I wouldn't have run away to live with Agnes and learned to bake proper scones. And there would be no salamander. So I decide that in the end, I can't regret.

I wipe a porthole in the steamy mirror and laugh at my reflection. Summer goth mom.

Kind of a Nancy vibe, Ruth says when I return to her room. But not evil. I'm into it.

Thanks, I say. I love you.

I love you too, Sorch. Don't disappear again, okay?

I won't, I say. I promise.

I WISH I COULD CALL AGNES but by the time I get back to the apartment it's half four in Balnain. I write to her instead. I tell her about the salamander's little bum, how its hand was tucked under its chin. I describe the shape of its tiny face. I tell her it's the size of a cabbage. How are the dahlias? I ask. Are they up? How are Alastair and Scrabble Mary? How's Jeanette? I send her a picture of my new hair and big belly. I miss you, I write, so much.

I fall asleep on the couch under the waning moon and dream of floating.

feel like a hamster. I walk from the kitchen to the couch to the bathroom and back. I walk down and up the stairs for something to do. I can see why they gnaw on the bars of their cages. Hamsters just wanna be free.

It's twenty-eight degrees outside and the apartment is a sauna. I hang out the kitchen window to feel the breeze on my face. I put ice cubes in a cloth and let them melt over my head. I wish I had some ice cream.

Agnes calls me in the afternoon, her evening. She says the dahlias have bloomed and Alastair is napping in the catnip. She beat Mary at Scrabble yesterday and is feeling braw. She says she likes my witchy hair.

I tell her I mailed her cheque to the Eye in an attempt to buy myself and the salamander back. I'm sorry, I say. I wanted to use it to get you a ticket to Halifax. I don't know how I'm going to give birth without you here. I'm so goddamn nervous.

As I wrote, it was for whatever you need, Agnes says. I hope she accepts it and lets you be. And you're in luck, because I've bought myself a ticket to Halifax already.

You have?

I have.

She says she'll arrive two weeks before I'm due, just in case. I'll be in the little blue house by then and she will stay with me. We'll nest and cook and paint all of our nails gold.

What about Alastair? I ask.

I'd like to bring him, she says, if you don't mind.

Please, I say. And your Scrabble board. And the *Hamish* box set.

Of course, she laughs.

How long will you stay?

As long as you need me, she says.

I wipe my eyes with the heel of my palm. Forever, then. Maybe you can catch the salamander, instead of the stupid handsome doctor.

Agnes chuckles. I'll be with you, hen, she says.

I LEAN OUT THE WINDOW, eating strawberries and letting the sun singe my shoulders. I wish I was at the beach.

Remember Ingonish? says a worker.

I'd rather not, I say.

But the worker has already fed the reel into the projector and the projector is my brain so I have nowhere to avert my eyes. I see Chris and me walking through the sand, hands clasped and half-drunk by mid-morning, our feet wading side by side into the clear water, and her up-close face, freckled on the temples. I remember how it felt to be held in the water like I was precious, to be fucked on clean sheets like I was precious. I remember my slippery thighs and the invisible tether I wished I could braid between our eyes. I remember how her mouth tasted like strawberries.

Okay, I say to my brain. That's enough. But my mouth tastes like strawberries for the rest of the day, even after I've brushed my teeth. It makes me nauseous.

IT'S BEEN A WEEK SINCE I mailed the letter. I've been wishing I let Linh deliver it so I would know for sure that it arrived. Maybe it's lost, or maybe it was intercepted by some other Chris, who has cashed it and is living large, eating oysters and sleeping on silk sheets. But I asked Agnes and she says it hasn't been cashed.

I can't sleep, and not only because of this leaden unknown. My joints are so slack they overstretch in every position. My hips ache. The muscles of my back are a tight-strung gnarl. The soft red couch has become my enemy. And I'm up to twelve Tums a day, which the bottle warns against but I can't afford to heed. Dana told me that to save money she just ate baking soda out of the box by the spoonful.

Apparently the salamander's skin has turned from transparent to opaque and it's now the size of a papaya. I'm sure I've seen a butternut squash bigger than a papaya, but whatever. The point is it's big, too big to roll around inside me. So it just kicks, and has been kicking my ribs with such verve that my whole left side has gone numb. Linh said it would be the perfect time to get a rib tattoo but I think I'll wait. I'm taking a break from new commitments.

If I'm not counting kicks or the days until Agnes arrives, I'm fixed on the Eye. Whether she got the letter. Where she was when she opened it. How she was standing. What she said. Did she cry? Did she laugh at me for thinking I could buy myself back?

TWO WEEKS PASS, THEN THREE. I've been maintaining my sanity with night walks. Ruth meets me on Citadel Hill after the sun goes down and we lie on our backs and listen to the sounds of the city, rattling exhaust pipes and dinging bike bells, barking dogs, someone giving a blowjob behind one of the hill's few trees. We try to think of names for the salamander, but nothing suits.

Stick with Sal, says Ruth. At least to start.

I WAKE TO THE SOUND of a digital knell. Linh's computer is ringing. I heave my achy body off the couch and pad to the kitchen. I can see through my blurry morning eyes that it's Agnes calling, and I answer.

Good morning hen, she says. Did I wake you?

It's my eight, her noon. I can see the shape of my hair in the screen's reflection and I laugh. Whatever do you mean? I say.

It's a very creative style, she says. Sorry to ring you so early. I just wanted to let you know, the cheque's been cashed.

Oh, I say.

Have you heard whether she'll let you be?

I haven't heard anything.

Well, Agnes says, let's keep our fingers crossed.

Then she says something about Alastair and something about Scrabble but I can't really hear her. The light outside the window catches my eye and I stare into it, stare and then shut my eyes and let it glow through my lids. I hear Agnes say okay hen, take care of yourself, I'll see you in three weeks. I nod at the computer and wave goodbye.

I lean back in the wooden chair and wrap my arms around my enormous belly. The sun heats half my face. I'm not sure whether I can float off or if I'm still bound. I shrug my shoulders and stretch out my arms, trying to feel for the tether. I run a hand over the back of my head to check. I stand.

Go outside, I say out loud to myself.

It's Saturday, and Linh and Emma are still in bed. I brush my teeth and hair and pull on Dana's old maternity jeans and sweater. I look at myself in the mirror and try to smooth out the crease between my brows with my thumb.

It's okay, I whisper to my reflection. I hope.

I open the door. The morning city is dewy and bright and loud with birds. I walk down the sidewalk as if I haven't shut myself in for nearly two months, as if I know where I'm going, as if I'm not shocked by the vivid colours of the painted houses in the daytime. My feet take me uphill, past the flower shop and the convenience store. A dog on a leash with its tongue lolling looks at me like welcome to the world! A pack of runners break around me in a neon surge, their panting breath like the surf in my ears until they overtake me and run on.

Remember running? asks a worker.

Please don't, I say, and duck into a shop before they can start the reel.

Coffee? asks the green-haired kid behind the counter.

I glance at the chalkboard menu. Before me is a glass display, a rainbow of ice cream tubs.

Ice cream, I say.

Ice cream for breakfast, says the kid. Right on. What flavour?

I don't know, I say. Two scoops of something good.

They scoop out a creamy tower and hand it over.

Yeah, I say to the salamander, back out on the sidewalk. We can have ice cream for breakfast. We can do whatever the fuck we want.

I walk to the Commons and lower myself onto a bench. I reach behind my head to pull up my hood and remember it's not there. It's probably for the best. The sun beams into my face like it's happy to see me. I close my eyes and let the ice cream melt in my mouth. The salamander presses a foot against my ribs. I listen to the birds and imagine I'm in Agnes's yard. When she's here we can walk to the Commons together. Maybe we can put Alastair on a leash.

So many runners, up so early in their stretchy pants, pounding the asphalt in their springy shoes, puffing their breath out into the morning air. The opposite of eating ice cream for breakfast. It's so familiar, the breathing. In-in, out-out, in-in, out-out. I hate the sound.

I open my eyes and a worker in my brain says that's Chris.

No it's not, I say.

Yes, says the worker, it is.

My breath is gone. My skin flashes hot and I'm slick with sweat. My legs shake so hard I can't get my heels on the ground. It is Chris, twenty metres away, in stretchy pants and springy shoes, walking with her hand on her hip, sipping from a water bottle. Ice cream foam rises up my throat. Where is my hood? Where can I hide? How fast can I run with my belly so full? In the daytime there's no scythe in the sky and I'm weaponless before the Lidless Eye. I wrap my arms around the salamander. I'll gnaw Chris's arms off if she tries to reach for it. I won't go down without blood on my teeth.

Chris hasn't seen me yet and I whisper thanks to Ruth for my blackest black hair. She takes another sip from her water bottle and leans over to kiss the runner beside her. A sweet, sweet kiss. A new love kiss.

I look closer. I know this girl maybe, though just to see her, just from around. She laughs at something Chris says. Chris is laughing too and they kiss again. I remember this Chris from the beginning. I remember this laugh and the taste of those kisses. I should warn the girl. I should warn her! Warn her that it will be romantic as hell but then Chris will take away all her friends and all her nerve and all her milk, that she will find herself crying in the basement and wonder how she got there. I should warn her.

And then Chris looks over and sees me, my hair black and skin slick and tongue panting, my arms wrapped around my belly, and she stops. The girl looks at Chris and then follows her gaze. And they stare at me like I'm a ghost or a rabid wolf or a crazy woman, like I'm a thing to be feared. I won't blink. I stare and stare. My heart beats so high and fast in my throat I feel like I'll vomit it out but I won't blink no I won't. And then the girl takes Chris's hand and says something to her softly, and Chris breaks the stare and turns, she turns and they walk back together the way they came, the girl's arm around Chris's shoulders.

I blink. The salamander gets the hiccups and it brings back my breath. I slump on the bench and swallow down my beating heart. I think that maybe I've won.

I exhale in a stutter and mash my palms into my eyes. I hoist myself from the bench and drag my feet across the grass. My stomach roils and I heave my breakfast onto the turf. A runner in a bright pink suit asks if I'm all right and I nod and wave her away.

I think that maybe I've won but I'm sick with adrenaline. I stumble down the sidewalk and crawl up the wooden steps to the apartment and lie on the red couch.

Linh is making coffee in the kitchen and comes into the living room and says are you okay, buddy? We wondered where you went.

I ask them to hand me my Tums and I suck on one and say in a chalky voice that I just need to lie down for a while. But I can't get comfortable. Everything is churning and pressing and clenching and aching and I don't know how to calm down. I try to breathe. I sit up. I stand. I lie down again. I lurch to the kitchen and try to pour a glass of water but my hands shake.

Are you sure you're okay? Emma asks.

I nod, but the room is tilting.

I run a bath and lie down as it fills but my body keeps telling me to get up, get UP. And then I get up and there's blood in the water.

EMMA DRIVES US TO THE HOSPITAL. I can't stay in the seat. I crouch in the footwell like a dying animal. I moan and puke the rest of the ice cream onto the floor. Then the car stops and Linh is yelling for someone to help us, they run through the sliding doors and run back out followed by someone with a wheelchair, and I'm rushed inside and into the elevator where my moans howl around me. We speed down the hall and I hunch over my belly and beg the salamander not to die. Then we're in a room and someone is pulling my soaked pants off my legs and trying to help me onto a bed but I want to be under it, I want a small dark cave, these lights are so bright. I hear a nurse ask for my name and how far along I am and Linh's voice answering.

She's early, the nurse says.

Yes early. Too early. Too fast. It's not supposed to happen like this.

Are we going to die? I cry to the nurse, and then pain rips through me and I can't speak.

The nurse brings her face close to mine. Honey, you're not going to die, she says. You're in labour. Too far along to stop now, by the sounds of it.

But where's Agnes? I cry. I can't do this without her. I can't. I can't.

Let's get you up on the bed, the nurse says.

I climb onto the bed and I'm naked but I don't remember how I got that way, and the nurse says try lying down but my body won't. We'll call your doctor, she says, and I say no, I don't want him, I want Agnes, and I scream like I'm being split apart.

I hear Emma on one side of me say call Agnes, can you call her? Linh, call her! I sob that she won't get here in time, she's too far away. And Linh says hang on buddy, keep breathing, and I try to remember how.

The nurse comes and straps something around my belly and the room is filled with beeping.

What's that? I pant.

The baby's heartbeat, the nurse says.

And I say okay okay okay because we're not dead yet. But my body is burning and tearing and I don't know how someone can push a baby out of themselves and survive it.

The nurse tells me to lie down and I say no. She says she needs to check how far along I am and I say no, I need Agnes, it's too fast, it's too soon, she's supposed to be here to catch it.

And then Agnes is in my ear and she says lie down, hen, lie down. Let the nurse help you.

I nod my head and lie down, and the nurse checks and says you're fully dilated but don't start pushing until the doctor gets here, okay?

But the salamander wants out and I want to push and so I push. I push and scream and fuck, this is so fucking hard how can you feel this much pain and not die, oh my god, and Agnes says you can do this Sorcha, bring your baby out, and I'm crushing Linh's hand in my hand and I push like our lives depend on it, and the nurse says okay there's the head, the head is out, and I take a breath and Agnes says tha thu cho làidir, you're so strong, one more good push, and I bear down with all my might and everything rushes out of me in a flood of blood and the nurse lays a small wet creature on my bare chest, and they look up at me.

Hello, I whisper.

We blink at each other and we're not dead, despite it all.

I can tell the salamander is hungry, and I have what they need.

ACKNOWLEDGEMENTS

So much gratitude to Whitney Moran, managing editor of Nimbus Publishing and Vagrant Press, for understanding exactly what I was trying to do, asking such insightful questions, and bringing this story into the world with passion and care.

Thanks to Tate Young, Elly Ryland Beggs, Gavrel Feldman, Katie Wayne, Mary Brown, Joanna Simpson, Sarah Walsh, Jane Gavin-Hebert, and my mum, Kathy Ogryzlo, for reading early drafts of this novel and helping me make it better. Thanks to Lauren Murphy for ensuring I got the law right when I stepped out of my legal wheelhouse. Thanks to River MacAskill for checking that the Scottish parts rang true, and to Màiri Sìne Chaimbeul for reviewing the Gaelic.

I'm beyond grateful to my parents, my sisters, my friends, and my girlfriend for showing up for me with fierce love and solid support when I've needed it most, especially recently. I couldn't have written about such good and steadfast love if you hadn't shown it to me.

Thanks eternally to my kids for existing. I love you so much.